The Dude See Scrolls

Sagas

Volume I

By Nuna Dudeist Monk Berb

(or if you prefer,

Will Fielder)

Table of Contents

Page 1   Title
Page 2   Table of contents
Page 4   Prologue
Page 9   Book I- The Quest Abides
Page 10 Chapter 1
Page 18 Chapter 2
Page 22 Chapter 3
Page 27 Chapter 4
Page 31 Chapter 5
Page 41 Chapter 6
Page 44 Chapter 7
Page 47 Chapter 8
Page 52 Chapter 9
Page 57 Chapter 10
Page 63 Chapter 11
Page 69 Chapter 12
Page 73 Chapter 14
Page 79 Chapter 15
Page 84 Chapter 16
Page 89 Chapter 17

Page 94 Book II-Beyond Dudetopia and Reality
Page 95   Chapter 1
Page 101 Chapter 2
Page 105 Chapter 3
Page 110 Chapter 4
Page 114 Chapter 5
Page 119 Chapter 6
Page 129 Chapter 7
Page 136 Chapter 8
Page 143 Chapter 9
Page 148 Chapter 10
Page 153 Chapter 11
Page 157 Chapter 12
Page 161 Chapter 14
Page 168 Chapter 15

Page 173 Chapter 16
Page 178 Chapter 17
Page 184 Chapter 18
Page 189 Chapter 19
Page 193 Chapter 20
Page 198 Chapter 21
Page 204 Chapter 22
Page 209 Chapter 23
Page 215 Chapter 24
Page 221 Chapter 25
Page 226 Chapter 26
Page 231 Chapter 27
Page 237 Chapter 28
Page 241 Chapter 29

Page 248 Book III

Well that about wraps her all up... Parts Anyway

Page 249 Chapter 1
Page 253 Chapter 2
Page 258 Chapter 3

The End, or is it?

Prologue

'The Absurd may make more sense upon review'

The swirls of darkness absorbed the light. Flashes filling the sky above the tower where only one constant pinpoint of light shot outwards. Ravenous crows fled, fearing the evil within. It was common knowledge that all bones would be picked clean here before they were discarded. The source of that light, was a room filled with five men born into their seats of power, previously held by their ancestors. These men answered to no one, and laughed at those who thought they knew power. Combined they controlled a third of the world's wealth, leaving the Muslims and the Chinese to fight over the rest.

This room, which sat at the top of a tower, the highest in the city, wasn't always occupied. Tonight, however, a full meeting of The Star Chamber Cabal had been called. Rupert Von Klaussen, the media mogul; Robert Klein, the Banking Lord; Sir Richard Evermore, the wealthiest land owner in the world; Francisco Vocelli, the Prince of Venice; and Manuel Juarez Ricardo Juan Lupe Fernandez, The King of the Cartels sat at the star shaped table. The ebony wood had been coated with thirteen coats of lacquer to give it the appearance of having been dipped in glass. In the center, the world's only fully functional, four-dimensional holographic projector, capable of predicting the future within ninety percent accuracy. It rose from its hidden compartment inside the base of the table.

The Gothic-inspired room was shaped in the same star pattern as the table, each triangle decorated to represent the family who held the seat. Above the table, a crystal dome looked out at the stars above with contempt. Five gas-lit lamps ringed the room, burning away, never varying, never flickering, a constant glow.

Each year the chamber shifted, spinning seventy-two degrees. The chair facing magnetic north was the reigning chairperson for the next three hundred and sixty-five days. Rupert Von Klaussen held that position now, this the first day in that role. He had come fully prepared, ready to present his agenda to the other members. It was the seventh time that he had the luxury of having the North Pole at his back since the death of his father, and as always he had a brilliant, professional package put together.

    "Welcome brothers. Again we have reached another milestone. A year of prosperity beyond expectations thanks to Brother Manuel and his effective take-over of Argentina's drug trade. Now that we have all of Central and South America fiscally aligned we can proceed once again by turning our attention towards that troublesome Russian President. As you can see by examining the portfolio in front of you, oil prices have been lowered considerably, thanks in part to our flooding the market with stores from our abundant reserves. Now if this does not rattle the bear's cage, nothing will. It's about time Russia joined the program. I know Yuri Chenkov, (the Russian Mafia boss), would like nothing more than to get a seat added to this table, but until his worth tops a trillion it wouldn't be worth our time. I believe it is better to own a man like that, than to have him eating at your table, no? Well, I know we all agree on that. In addition to poking the bear we have also effectively bankrupted the last of the U.S. Federal Reserve. Many economists are worried about the Chinese calling in their debt, but imagine what they would think if we called in ours?" He allowed a chuckle to float around the room before continuing. "We now dictate the policy decisions being made, no matter which party holds the seat of power." Again he let a ripple of chuckles pass before continuing.

    "So where Brother Manuel left off, I propose we continue forth by allowing the slow legalization of drugs permeate the U.S., so that we can successfully wrestle that last stash of unchecked money hiding amongst the lowly cartels, and triads. This will force the small players to join in our ventures, investing their money with us, in hopes of staving off irrelevancy, but we all know nothing is going to change that inevitable fact." Again another round of laughter. "With legalization comes taxation, creating even more corruption than these libertarians could have imagined. After a couple of years of letting the government control things they'll wish that their vices were illegal again, which brings me to the next point. Prostitution. We are all set to get that ball rolling within months. We've got the right cases coming up in court, with the right judges presiding, and soon enough we will have the Statue of Liberty selling her stuff on Broadway during Macy's Parade! Again the taxation, and government control will leach the last of that money out of the streets."

"And now we can turn our attention now on the Middle East. China can wait, we will need something to do in ten years' time." Laughter. "As for the camel herders, well I can safely say that it's been fun, but it's time to castrate the males before they completely ruin Europe. As much as I love my home, as do you, Sir Richard, and Francisco will agree: it's almost an embarrassment to acknowledge where you are from these days. So what I have in mind is turning the media loose on this whole idea that Saudi Arabia has really been behind the Jihad movement all along, and that they have worked intimately with the Syrians. That should really stoke the fires, and get us some foreign troops back on the ground. We can move towards befriending Iran, but only enough to let them waste their resources bringing the other Sunni states down. Once we have them killing off each other, Israel can partner up with Turkey and complete the overhaul of the region. We all know this is desperately needed to stem the flow of refugees entering Europe. The combined power of those two regional countries, should be enough to bring some form of peace to the land. This will allow Israel to gain upper hand, as everyone else around them will have depleted their armies, funds, and goodwill with the rest of the world. I believe a few bombings here and there should get the whole thing off the ground and running.

"Back here in the U.S., we have a few interesting

ideas, other than the ones mentioned previously. We were toying with the idea of letting an animated film win best picture. Have the Cubs lose in the World Series, and for shits and giggles have a Democratic president come out as openly gay. That should really fuel the fires in the south, knowing their president likes to munch on carpet. This of course will be part of the set up towards the next civil war, the one that has been in the works for some time. Of course, it would not be wise to launch that ship until we finishing cleaning the rats out of Europe. We will need a safe place to establish our new headquarters."

The four dimensional holographic projector fired up, showing the gathered members the unfolding of time, and their well-orchestrated plans. Nothing was left to chance, and their finger print was stamped on everything people in this world considered important. They could zoom in on a production line in that was producing herbicides in West Kentucky, or to the state assembly meeting in Oregon where the legalization of marijuana passed. They zoomed into an Israeli market two days from now where a pro-Palestinian reformer was assassinated in broad day light, with hundreds of onlookers, by an American mercenary posing as a Syrian Islamic Fundamentalist. Scrolling across to China they watched another environmental disaster unfold as torrential rains caused severe flooding on the Yangtze River, erasing a whole city from the map. Lastly they looked in on the Pope in Rome, making decree after decree that threatened to bring the Catholic Church into the twenty-first century. It was an impressive presentation when all was said and done. Then Rupert rolled out his coupe de grace.

Three hundred and twenty-two major news outlets around the world were a day away from a simultaneous link, in which all stories would be doled out from a central hub in Los Angles, California. The makeover was an attempt to invigorate new life into much maligned industry that had watched the governments of the world stand on the sidelines, as hunger, war and global warming threatened to put an end to life as we know it. The new conglomerate had hired Disney's chairman, who had so successfully revamped old movie franchises into modern works of art. His task was to make news hip again. Of course, it was all a ruse. Rupert's empire was just a smoke screen for the Star Chamber's true objectives.

They knew from long years of domination that controlling what the people believed to be happening was the key to complete control, and made it so there was little anyone could do.

Or so they thought.

Book I
The Quest Abides

Chapter 1

'It is scary to put yourself out there, to chase that dream, but if you don't you will never realize it'

It was a quake, but not the earth-rumbling phenomena that occurred along the seams of the vibrant Earth ship. A deep cold had penetrated into the strata, hence forth heaving the upper layer, creating a deep rumbling resonance that traveled exactly at the speed of sound. Those who had never experienced such things before, were caught completely off guard, and a touch frightened. To hear the Earth ship moan in such pain could weaken even the strongest of folk.

Thankfully it was the women, the strong protectors of the realm, who comforted the frightened men, telling them that everything was going to be okay. The Earth ship would be fine, and what had just happened was a natural occurrence. The meteorologists named it an ice quake, the result of a sudden harsh freeze to the surface that had been enjoying an overly warm fall season. The experts agreed that this was normal, the Arctic powers were just flexing their muscles.

No one among the common people had ever heard of such a thing, but many common people had forgotten that such was the way with life on the Earth ship. New shit happens and new shit gets newly named, just like twerking. Prior to Miley Cyrus doing her thang at a televised music award show, we just called it shaking your ass.

Am I wrong?

The descending deep freeze had crept down from the farthest reaches of James Bay in Northern Ontario and had spread across the invisible line into the United States, catching the populace unaware. The Niagara Falls had frozen overnight, one massive sheet of unmoving ice now releasing clouds of ice fog into the air. Homeless people in Buffalo quickly discovered just how fast a person can find shelter when in dire need, and the road crews in Ohio realized that the repairs scheduled on their snow removal vehicles had been scheduled for an inappropriate time.

Oh, the cruel Mother that housed this calamity of people liked to flex her muscles once in a while to remind these ungrateful guests that there were some things you could never be quite prepared for.

The boom from the ice quake could be heard over an eight hundred mile radius, as loud as the strongest thunder clap. Windows in tall apartment buildings in Toronto were rattled by the force of quake; thankfully, though, none broke to expose the people inside to the harsh realities of the world around them. Sensitive car alarms had gone off, some squealing away for hours in parking lots far away from their owners, who were busy toiling away in the caverns of progress that were erected to make a better world.

In a hospital room on the tenth floor of Scarborough General, amid all the alarms and general chaos following the sudden shock of the ice quake's bothersome boom, an old man woke from a month-long coma. As unsettled doctors and nurses and frantic hospital administrators scurried by in the ensuing pandemonium outside his door, the old man's cobalt eyes slowly fluttered open to reveal two points of intense light that scanned the unfamiliar room with the utmost scrutiny. His weakened arms raised up from beneath the blankets with several leads and thin plastic tubes attached, distributing fluid to his organs, making it difficult to get clear of the blanket. It was at this moment, thirty-three seconds exactly after the loud boom, that the old man realized he was able to see out of two eyes. It had been a very long time since he would have been able to claim this feat.

Unable to sit up, the old man gazed at the strange room in which he found himself. He knew that he had been asleep for some time, but had things changed so drastically? Had the future caught up to him after all those years of avoidance? It had been so long since he had the visions showing him the end of his world, and the beginning of this heathen paradise. A groan escaped his lips as he struggled to comprehend everything that was happening.

Minutes passed like hours, and hours seemed like days before the incapacitated man finally had a visitor. After the general commotion settled down after the big boom, a portly woman in a purple two piece uniform with a stethoscope dangling around her neck, entered the room wearing comfortable shoes. As she entered her head was down, not anticipating a wide awake patient, and when she did look up, she took his present condition in stride, without missing a beat.

"Ah, Mr. Olsen! I see that you have decided to return to us." The nurse mentioned as she came close enough for the old man to smell her fragrant perfume. Lilacs and jasmine he guessed.

"Returned yes, but not as you may perceive." He responded as the nurse adjusted some of the leads and tubes attached to his arms, allowing him more free movement. His voice crackled like tinfoil being dragged over sheet metal.

"Oh, that's nice," the nurse replied. "Hopefully feeling better than when you went down! Your vitals look good and you appear to be coherent."

With less grace than a castrated bull, Mr. Olsen raised his arms up in a slow sweeping motion. "The man before you is not any mere mortal, young lady," he intoned. "The man you see before you is none other than Odin, father of the Asgard and seer of visions."

The nurse nodded without even looking at Mr. Olsen. She was writing some things down on a sheet of paper and checking the watch at her wrist. Her pen moved faster than her thoughts, and she had to correct herself twice.

"Oh, is that so! So you are still not feeling quite like yourself then? Hm?" Now she looked at the withered figure, studying the intense blue fires that burned in his eyes.

"Well except for the fact that I now have two working eyes, I haven't felt more like myself in sometime. Centuries perhaps by the look of things." Odin answered.

"Yes, well, um, I'm gonna give you a little shot from my magic stick here to ease your transition back into the here and now, okay?" the nurse said. "Don't worry, you won't feel a thing, I'll just put it right in this tube we have here that has been feeding you while you slept. In about ten minutes you are going to feel better then you have in decades, okay? Yeah, just a minute here."

The purple-clad nurse took out a needle and stuck into the intravenous tube, pushing the plunger in all the way until the magic potion flowed through his veins.

Meanwhile, two time zones west of said hospital, a Toyota hatchback loaded with three dubious characters was racing down the Yellowhead highway ten kilometers west of Edmonton, bound for an unpopulated region in the foothills of the Rockies.

The ensemble huddled together in the red car included an amateur musician, an internet blogger, and a yoga instructor from Winnipeg who enjoyed the scent of lavender mixed with tea tree oil. In the same order their names were, Julius Hawk, Carl Carlson, and Willow Leclerc. All three had received The Call to assemble, and all three had willingly left their homes to embark on an urgent quest of the utmost importance.

Julius Hawk had traveled the farthest, coming all the way from Halifax, Nova Scotia, and the red '98 Camry belonged to him. He was the dreamer, prone to bouts of mania and mischief. By day, he was a bakers assistant and dishwasher at popular local diner. By night, he became Jack Clash, the savior of rock and roll in the digital remix, Hip Hop world. The quest, set in motion from the west, had begun far in the east with two scheduled stops along the way. The first, Montreal, to pick up Carl, the smoke-savvy, often high, writer of the internet smash hit, *One Hit at a Time*, a page dedicated to everything pot related and ways to grow your own without ever arousing suspicion from your neighbors. In his one-bedroom flat above a pizzeria, Carl claimed to have four hundred plants growing, all natural, all without the aid of hydroponics. When he wasn't blogging, he was delivering pizzas and selling pot to a select group of regular clientele. The Supreme with olives and anchovies got you enough food for two meals and enough weed to keep you going for a week if you were conservative in your approach.

Willow Leclerc, a half-Metis/half-Icelandic lass, grew up listening to blues music while spending most of her childhood in between her mother's house and her father's. She had never traveled outside of Winnipeg except for once to go to India after her high school graduation, where she wanted to meet a real-life yogi, experience enlightenment, and become a teacher of the art herself. Unfortunately, India didn't turn out to be such a good idea as every man with hands appeared to have more worldly interests. They tried desperately to grope the light-skinned woman's body and touch her blonde hair. Her yogi, a sex-crazed man who didn't believe in bathing, made continual advances on her that eventually led to a late night escape back to the nearest airport, and back home. Since that experience, which was more disillusioning than enlightening, she never had the desire to travel again. In Winnipeg she lived amongst the artsy-fartsy folk who appreciated living the life of counter culture. Tattoos and piercings, poetry and dissing the man, were all acceptable ways of proving you would never conform.

What had brought them together in that red Camry was answering The Call to a quest set upon them by a mysterious Dudeist Monk that they had mutually met online in a Dudeism Facebook group. This monk, who claimed to roam the wilds of Alberta tending sheep at an undisclosed location of course, had cryptically assured them and the rest of the online group that he was in possession of the fabled *Dude See Scrolls*, and that he was in need of three brave souls to go out into the world and find the author of the scrolls. Apparently hints of new revelations were hidden within the coded texts, and only the original writer knew the code to unlock the secrets. These secrets were supposedly game changers, and he had provided enough evidence to those who were well connected within the Dudeism circles to support the call for such a quest.

The slowest growing religion in the world was attracting all kinds of 'slackers' and relaxed folk, who were just looking for others whom they could relate to, and share their beliefs with, without all the trappings of conventional religions. It was all about taking it easy, going with the flow, and not being a dick.

The online community held a fundraiser, raised a modest amount of money, and selected three willing participants from two hundred and twenty volunteers across Canada. No one with a family, or any other religious affiliations, or with a criminal record preventing them from the crossing of national borders, was to be considered. These preconditions narrowed the number down to thirty five, of which the names were drawn from a bowling ball case, live via internet on the April the fourth, 4:20 pm. mountain standard time in the year of our Dude, two thousand sixteen. Strangers in reality but familiar in the virtual world, the three had packed lightly, had sworn oaths to uphold the standards of Dudeism, and abide as best as possible. Sixteen hours from Winnipeg and the vibe still remained positive amongst the chosen.

"Do you think he really lives in cave?" Julius asked. "I mean I have heard that there is a small monastery somewhere out in the foothills, but I also heard that he lives in a cave and only visits the monastery to make sure the acolytes are abiding."

After five days of driving he was beginning to get that crazy gleam in his eye that came from monotonous repetition.

"I don't know, dude," Carl replied, passing a newly lit joint to the driver. "What do you think, babe?" He asked Willow.

Willow sat in the back seat. She had insisted upon

it. Not comfortable with traveling—especially with stranger, and even more especially with two strange bros—she remained in her zazen pose, legs crossed, and eyes closed as the brown grasslands passed by on either side.

"First of all, I am not your babe," she said, as if imparting the eternal wisdom of the ages to them. "I am to be addressed by my name. Not by sweetheart, toots, honey, sugar, and certainly not babe. Your chances of scoring with me are zero, and the driver has a three percent chance. He only has that because he hasn't stared at my tits yet. So if you wish to include me in your conversation, please do so in the specified manner that I clearly outlined in my email to you both, otherwise I am going to tell this monk we're en route to meet, that you are both totally unacceptable as traveling companions."

There was an awkward moment of silence as Julius looked at Carl, with Carl looking back at Julius. Nodding, Julius passed the joint in between the opening of the two front seats. "A peace offering, then." Opening her eyes, Willow relented when she saw the joint's inviting warm glow and smelled the sweet fragrance of its incense-like smoke. She accepted the offering and took a long haul off of it.

"Now that we have cleared the sexual tension from the car, what do you think about the cave theory Willow?" Carl asked receiving the joint back and inhaling.

"A cave? Are you serious?" Willow responded. "He started that rumor to make himself sound more mystical. I'd be surprised if we didn't find him holed in a mobile home, completely off the grid except for a telephone line and internet connection. No one lives in a cave anymore."

"I don't know about that," Carl noted as he continued to pass around the sacred offering. "There is this tribe in Borneo, or somewhere like that, and they are still all primitive and shit. They even believe white people are gods."

"Where did you here that? On the internet?" Willow asked. They had picked her up in the middle of the night, so she had slept the better part of the journey so far. As it stood, she was having a hard time finding a way to warm up to these two strangers, even with the relaxed mood the week put her in. Guys in general were usually so preoccupied with sex that she had found little time to engage them, but these two had gotten her message and were doing their best to make her feel at ease. She wanted to feel that way, but just didn't know how.

Chapter 2

'When you embrace the Dude in you, the amount of fucks given decreases dramatically in the first minute of transformation.'

Beneath the suburban haze of a lost generation, another ripple of the past flicked its finger on the ear lobe of one Tyson O'Malley, the largest Irishman to roam the streets of Boston in the modern era. He winced in pain, and rubbed the lobe while looking around to see who had the balls to test him. His fists automatically clenched, chest puffed and his feet assumed their familiar, balanced stance, though looking around the street he found it was completely empty. Shrugging it off, he turned the corner, opened the door to his flat and climbed into bed.

Screams filled the night, wisps of smoke, haze and fire surrounded the large Irishman on a field close to some foreign shore line. He turned in the chaos, again finding himself alone and disturbed. At his feet was a great war hammer, runes covering the handle and head. Above him a hole parted in the thick gray smoke allowing a beam of light to descend, encompassing the brute. A dream, he suddenly realized, not a familiar one, but a dream nonetheless.

"If only that was true," boomed a voice from above the clouds.

Looking up into the light, Tyson raised his hand to shield himself from the unbearable brightness.

"I am in need of you." The voice boomed again like thunder cracking the sky.

Cowering for the first time since he was a whelp in grade school, the large man tried desperately to awaken. Something was terribly wrong with this dream. That feeling that he was no longer in control, was flooding over, just like when the bullies growing up waited around the corner from his house to beat on the boy who had been separated from his friends.

"It is time now, do not resist." The voice announced.

"Time for what?" Tyson whimpered, his underwear bunched up in knots.

"Time to go find my father, of course, and right the wrongs that have befallen me." The voice replied. There was a strong vein of steel running through the words that could not be denied.

The light surrounding Tyson grew brighter, and with it came a fierce gust of wind pushing the giant man down. Again, he raised a hand to shield his face, but it did little, and again the voice boomed.

"Do not resist! The fates have determined your destiny mortal."

When Tyson awoke, he was no longer himself. He had been supplanted by another soul, a much older, more chaotic sort of soul that came marching down the hall as if followed by a herd of buffalo. Crashing, and banging, chasing away the consciousness known as Tyson O'Malley, and now in its place resided Thor of Asgard!

The God of Thunder and other such noisy things.

The mightiest of warriors, and most feared combatant in the seven realms.

Stretching his mighty arms, Thor rose from the bed to gaze upon the world he thought he would never see again. Instruments of the smallest sizes were strewn about the top of wooden chest of drawers. Thin clothing, the likes of which would never keep a grown man warm on the sea, lay about in piles on the floor. A small, strange looking lizard lay contained in a magical glowing cube, staring at him, flicking its tongue as it lounged on a rock near the edge of a small pool, beneath an unnatural light.

"Well you are the smallest dragon I have ever seen," Thor mused. "Pathetic, really. Back in my time, long before the breaking of the world, I used to turn your hides into shields for my most trusted of friends. Your teeth I used as daggers, and your spine decorated the beverage halls where tales were sung."

Thor watched the lizard's tiny flicking tongue.

"Even an infant could slay you, though," he said. "Or is this some kind of magical box, holding a spell over you, keeping you in such a small, pathetic state? If I freed you would you grow into some fearsome creature that I would be forced to hunt down? Do not fear, I would let you roam for a little while though. Terrorize the citizens long enough for them to call out my name. Then after I have had my fill of drink, I would call upon my trusty war hammer and hunt you down of course. Slay you, and milk the fire from your veins to heat up my supper. What do you think of that dragon?"

The lizard flicked its tongue again.

"Okay then, it shall be." Thor raised his hand and brought it crashing sown upon the magic box shattering the aquarium into thousands of pieces, many of which imbedded themselves in his hand. As the blood began to seep out of the many gashes, the little lizard slunk away from the wreckage, flicking its tongue, disappearing under a heap of clothes.

"Gods be damned." Thor yelled in pain as he examined his wounds. "What kind of fell magic is this?" He reached down in the pile of clothing, and grabbed a Red Sox t-shirt, which became a temporary bandage. He cursed and staggered about, confused by the dwelling and the things it contained. He tied the t-shirt tight to sop up the blood and dressed himself in the strange clothing.

Everything in this strange abode was made of the weakest materials the god had ever encountered. The door to the bedroom went crashing into the wall, creating a hole in the drywall as he flung it open, underestimating its weight. The handrail on the stairway leading to the ground floor came off the wall in his hand. In disgust he smashed it against the stairs where it snapped into two pieces.

Where in the Seven Hells had he awoken?

Outside of the strange house, the world was even stranger. Horses had been replaced with metal machines that emitted a foul odor into the humid air. Houses were crammed together for as far as the eye could see, and the trees that had survived the Ragnarok cried out in mercy as their roots battled desperately beneath the hardened surface that covered the Earth. Odin had warned him that the worlds would change, that their way of life would someday be gone, and that the weak would rise above the strong. He could not have imagined it, and yet here it was.

Now, free from Limbo, Thor knew that in time he would have his vengeance on those who had cast him out. First though, he had to find out if he was the only one of his kind who was freed from that infernal place. He walked past the metal sleeping insects, the glow of hanging lights, and breathed in the foul tasting air.

"By the gods," Thor moaned. He looked at some of the people walking the streets. Humans, of all shapes and color.

So Earth it was.

He needed a drink.

Chapter 3

'If I bite my tongue, it is to spare me the grief of explanation.'

  The palaces of men can be erected from the most fragile of materials. Paper, woven fabric, and even cardboard could be arranged in such a way to defy those elements that would eventually seek out to destroy such a lavish abode. Under bridges where these abode thought themselves safe, wind gusts swirled and pulled violently, yet through the sheer force of will, these seemingly flimsy structures would not crumble.
  The destitute huddled around fires that burned through the night, their tales the only entertainment. Conversation, a lost art throughout the world, flourished here, where one could learn just about anything one needed too. Here failure was a badge worn humbly, for there was no shame amongst the destitute. This was no place of pity. This was the shanty town called Reality, USA. The sign marking the entrance into the hamlet had been painted using eleven different colors, drawn forth from cans donated by the street artist named Raver. His works were all over, on the walls lining the freeway into Seattle, on the three separate schools, in three separate districts. Even his mural of the Seahawks feasting on the carcass of a Bronco, which was painted on the side of a public works building just down the alley from City Hall, was revered by many. His pictures had captured the heartbeat of the underground society. The place where the forgotten roamed. So good was his work that plans by the municipal government to cover up these murals with standard coats of conformity were met with protests and violence.
  The pictures stayed.
  Reality was considered by some to be the safest place to walk these days. The police never ventured down

below the bridge unless someone was murdered, and usually the only time someone was murdered below the bridge was when they were fleeing from the police. Here the homeowners protected themselves and their possessions with feverish passion, for this was all they had. There was nowhere else for them to go. Everyone looked out for their neighbor and their neighbor's belongings, and anyone caught stealing or disturbing the peace excessively was cast out of Reality, forced to roam back above the bridge, into the lands where they were unwanted.

Gerald was quite comfortably asleep, night or day. Time was irrelevant to the man who followed no line up. Even its conceptual existence wasn't worth pondering over. Watches were the most useless thing man had invented, in Gerald's opinion, right beside the eight-hour work day. His home was one of the nicer in Reality, constructed from two, not just one, large packing boxes that had been previously used to protect new home furnaces during shipping. A dude/plumber/heating expert had saved them both for Gerald, knowing just how much the man would appreciate them. Fully intact, without any exterior damage, they replaced the three banana, two bread, and one Maytag washing machine boxes. The former had served their purpose well, but were made from an inferior cardboard and were in the second stage of deterioration. They would not last much longer in the moist Seattle environment.

The dude/plumber/heating expert knew exactly who Gerald was. He was well aware of his former title, and the contributions he had made to the rest of mankind. Helping Gerald out was the least he could do for the network.

"Well those bastards are up to it again," Left-Handed Larry announced sitting down in front of the humble abode.

"No riddles, dude," Gerald moaned from his bed. "You know how I fucking hate riddles, man. Just get to the point or move along."

"The police man. They just busted up a bunch of people for protesting this whole GMO thing. Heads were cracked, blood was spilled. Total aggression, Mad Man.

Total fucking aggression." Left-Handed Larry lit a smoke butt, one that someone had thrown away even though there were still four five good pulls left in it.

Rolling over and opening his window flap, Gerald threw a brand new cigarette at the war vet. "Some asshole gave this to me yesterday thinking because I'm a street guy, that I was probably a smoker. Fucking shitheads everywhere these days, man." Sitting up, he adjusted his poncho and pulled on his rubber boots before continuing.

"So these idiots will never learn, eh! Walk right down the middle of the road with bulls eyes painted on their goddamned foreheads, crying for change. No wonder the police let them have it. Stupid fuckers will never learn that you can't beat the game by playing off the board. You got to get some pieces on there first, and then you may have a chance. But when you walk up to these serious players yelling, and hollering at how bad they are, of course they are going to turn their goons on you. Too many assholes have ruined protesting by burning shit and looting. Now the police just wait for the chance to try out their new toys."

Left-Handed Larry looked at the whole cigarette that lay only inches away from him with love in his eyes. Of course he would finish the butt he was working on now, and then when his hand was free, he would put that baby in his special tin he carried in his coat pocket to protect the precious.

"So you are okay with this GMO shit then, Mad Man? I hear that they cause cancer." Larry stated as he finished his cigarette.

"GMO, Jesus Larry. Much bigger problems in the world, dude. Hell, farmers have been modifying crops since day fucking one when they left the goddamn jungle and decided to plant crops. Now scientists do it without the fear of having to go hungry because some horrendous failure. Shit, nectarines wouldn't even exist if it wasn't for modifying the genetics of grown food."

Larry smiled. His big pearly whites shining in the morning gloom of Seattle's constant cloud cover.

"I love nectarines."

"Of course you do." Gerald responded, pulling his thermos out and pouring himself a lukewarm cup of coffee. "They are tasty treats and I don't believe for a second this ridiculous crap about cancer. Everyone knows it's in the goddamned water supply. Jesus mother of Mary, they add all kinds of toxic substances to it, dude, and they have us believing it's for the best. Guess what is the most important thing on this planet? That's right, water. We should be more careful about the people we elect who back these crazy policies. Honestly, someone who gives a shit about the goddamned environment."

"Aren't you Canadian, dude?" Larry asked, safely securing the precious away in his tin, and then into his shirt pocket.

"Even Canadians elect dumb schmucks too," Gerald observed. "In fact, we keep them in power indefinitely if they keep up the charade long enough. There is this asshole in power now, he has turned us from one of the most peaceful countries in the world into another fear monger state. Did you know Canada used to be number one in the world when it came to shipping peace keepers overseas? We are down in the teens now. Hell, we will soon be the fifty-first state if this keeps up."

With his hand free, Larry helped himself to the coffee, pouring some into an empty jam jar he cherished. It was square one, with a round top which he thought explained life better than most philosophy books. There was no need to ask when it came to grabbing some java, in fact it just made the Mad Hermit angry when you did.

"So is that why you don't go home?" Larry asked.

Turning with that gaze that could penetrate rock, hair disheveled, sticking out here and there like the Mad Hermit, Gerald the Herald smiled.

"I would, dude, you know return to my beloved Salt Spring Island, but that would be too predictable. No, I will remain here in Reality where I can be invisible. The future is full of shady characters and turbulent upheavals. Any day now I fear we will be caught in the middle of a real shit storm and I didn't bring an umbrella. My best bet is to stay put with you, my friend. Here we can ride out the hurricane until the need becomes too great and we are forced into action."

Chapter 4

'Keep your head in check by eliminating the pawns obstructing your view.'

Pride comes from deep within the fanned flames, dropped on to the anvil and pounded into shape. Tempered in rain water, then reheated again and again. This process continues on until at one point, its owner polishes it to an immaculate sheen, where a clear reflection can been viewed. With this, the owner can then move out and test the strength of said pride against the skepticism of mankind. Parading its luster and sheer exuberance for all to see. Others, would claim, though, that if you are wise you keep it sheathed and well oiled.

Odin had found that this new body and its dependencies on others almost unbearable. A being who could see into the future, knew where stars aligned, gave birth to the mightiest heroes in the seven realms, now needed someone to change his diaper. True it wouldn't last forever—already some of his former strength had returned—feeding into these aged limbs that had been inactive for some time. Soon his indestructible will would force them to carry his sorry ass out of this sterile hell.

"Do you feel any stronger today, Mr. Olsen?" The purple-clad nurse asked. One week of the same bloody questions and same intolerant attitude.

"Of course I do!" He exclaimed. "I am sitting up on my own now, am I not? Soon I will be strong enough to take you to bed and stop that blathering mouth of yours for a couple of minutes."

This kind of comment often made the nurse chuckle, which infuriated Odin even more. In his day women knew their place, especially in the presence of a god. This mortal woman would soon understand that some things will never change.

"Well, it's been a while since I've had a nice date, you know," she said. "Perhaps if you clean up that foul potty mouth I will overlook the fact that you are twice my age and probably lacking the ability to raise the roof."

Modern humans spoke without meaning, Odin concluded. He could not tell if he was being insulted, mocked, or both. Instead, he closed his eyes and sought to regain more of his mental strength. Images had begun flashing through his mind in the last few days. Pictures of strangers with familiar souls locked in them. His children, he concluded. Some were still out there. Not all had been abandoned to the abyss.

"When will I be able to leave this infernal place?" Odin demanded

"Oh, they are coming to pick you up this afternoon and take you back to the home," the nurse answered as she pulled the leads off of his body and removed the hoses that had been feeding him from his arms. "I will be sad to see you go, but now all you need is some rest, and then you will be back on your feet."

Home. Soon he would be able to get out into the world and find his children. Some were starting to awake, he could feel their unease. Without his guidance, this world would surely be in for some trouble.

Two men in uniforms showed up later that day to take Odin home. They helped him into a wheel chair against his wishes, and then wheeled him into the back of an ambulance. Inside the back of the vehicle the elder god watched the strange world pass by through the rear window, toward which he was facing.

"It never looks exactly as you dream it," he announced to no one in particular, though the EMT riding with him felt obliged to answer.

"What exactly is that, Mr. Olsen?"

"The World. Even the sky has a different hue to it. It is less blue, and the air has a haze to it making it appear as if it is shrouded in some kind of secrecy." Odin commented.

"Yeah, I guess you were out for a while. Being in a

coma for a month would definitely change your perspective I imagine." The EMT was scribbling notes on to a tablet he held in his hand. He had taken the old man's pulse and temperature.

"A month would be easy to adjust to, fool," Odin growled. "Imagine two thousand years, and then you might understand what it is I am saying. Are all humans as dense as you so called health care people, because if you are then I might just want to go back to sleep?" Odin's statement prompted more notes to be written on the tablet. He wondered if the fool even realized that if it wasn't for him, he would never had this opportunity to exist. Frost Giants would be the ones cultivating the riches of this world, sowing their evil seeds. Wolves the size of huts would be stalking the Great Plains and dragons would rule the skies. It seemed that all had been forgotten, but that would soon change.

Home was the Sunnyside Grove apartment complex on the corner of Markham and Finch. The retirement facility had a large U-shaped driveway that allowed the ambulance to pull up alongside the front doors. The driver hopped out, opened the back door, and together the two men lowered Odin down on to the sidewalk.

"Well, Mr. Olsen, are you glad to be home?" The EMT who had been riding in the back asked.

"Home? What is this place? It is crawling with invalids and cowards! What ever happened to dying a good death? Look at these people," His hands made grand gestures at the retired folk who were sitting on benches outside, others were gathered around the front entrance gossiping. Two were trying hard to hide behind a brick column as they puffed away on a cigarette. "This is no place for the father of the Asgard. Is this some kind of trick? Are you agents of Loki? Have you dealt with the master of shadows and found some hole in which to hide me? Speak up, worms, before I call down a lightning bolt to send you off to limbo where you belong!"

The two medics looked at each other, shaking their heads. A coma could do strange things to the inner workings of the brain. Go in one side, fine, come out the other completely turned around. Neither of the two were doctors, though, and they could only assume that the old fellow was just having himself a moment.

The arrival of the ambulance created quite the stir. Many of the guests who were lingering around the outside of the facility first assumed that one of their own had probably passed away. It happened more frequently than not, since the palliative care wing was opened. When they realized that the transport was bringing someone back, an air of disappointment became palatable. For so many, the transition to the next phase of life was a welcome idea. This zoo-like atmosphere really cramped one's style.

Rolling past the withered eyes and wrinkled smiles, Odin knew that the people of this age had no respect for their elders and abandoned them at the first chance they could. What could turn a world so upside down that it would despise wisdom so?

"Listen, take me somewhere else," Odin pleaded to his two escorts. "Anywhere! This place smells of death. The stench is unbearable."

This wasn't the EMT's first rodeo and they both knew it was better to just remain silent and complete their duty. Inside a little part of them died hearing the agony and despair in the voice of another unwilling participant. Becoming hardened to the situation was necessary if one wanted to continue doing good. In order to do good though, they had to be part of a little bad.

"Survived did ya!" An elderly man dressed in a tweed suit called out from behind the brick pillar, his attempt to hide the cigarette failing miserably.

"Of course you fool. This soul is immortal!" Odin hollered back in anger.

"Too bad." The fellow replied once more.

Chapter 5

'Unexpected is to be expected.'

  The rolling hills were lined with tall jack pine trees that flowed like an endless sea, abruptly ending where the earth had been broken. Jagged peaks that reached high in the sky, in defiance of all life, rose forth into the places where nothing would grow. Only ice found comfort up there. This land leading up to the great divide was the land of wealth. Black gold lay submerged below the surface, and beside that, large pockets of natural gas. This was the land of fortune. The promised land foretold by the capitalists of old, and as liberal people screamed for Eco-friendly alternatives, the world still ran on oil.
  Hard packed dirt roads zig-zagged through the undulating land as man reaped both what was on top and underneath. Logging trucks made the road even smaller for the Toyota, as the party of three were hopeful that they would arrive at their destination sooner than later. Here they were strangers, frowned at by the passing vehicles carrying men and women who could spot bleeding hearts from a mile away. Taking their time, the small car dodged pickup trucks and water hauling trucks alike, looking for a specific marker. A side road appeared off of the main trunk and nailed to a tree was the sign they were looking for, a symbol of great importance. The symbol of Dudeism to be precise, peeking out cautiously behind a low lying bough. The Toyota veered off happily.
  This narrow road was partially overgrown with wild, untamed grasses. It dipped down into a small valley then rose again over another ridge where the impenetrable wall of trees grew sparse, opening up the world that lay

beyond. Mountains appeared in the distant horizon, and before them a large meadow covered with tall grasses bordering a turquoise colored lake, so deep in color it defied imagination. Beside the lake, a small stone building surrounded by a crude wooden fence fought against the passage of time. Inside the fenced area sheep, and a few goats roamed happily eating their fill of indigenous plant life.

"Jesus, he wasn't lying. He really does tend a herd," Julius announced. "Gods be damned. People are going to shit when I post pictures of the monastery! All this time dudes have just assumed he was making everything up."

"You know what this means then? If he wasn't making this up then he probably is telling the truth about the scrolls." Carl replied, reaching for his smart phone.

"I don't think you should post anything without asking the Dudeist Monk first. He could have easily dispelled all the guessing with photos of his own, but for reasons unknown to us, he has kept it mysterious and open to interpretation. Very monkish of him." Willow explained.

The road ended at the top of the meadow and the three exited the car and continued down on foot. The grass was long in some areas, shorter in patches here and there, where it was obvious the sheep and the goats had been busy. As they neared the stone structure it became quite clear that the building had been there a long, long time. Just guessing, Julius imagined that it was well over a hundred years old. He asked his traveling his companions aloud what they thought, when an answer came on the wind.

"Well the natives tell me that it's at least eight hundred years old, or that is as far back as they can recall. Sometimes you lose track of time when you don't keep written records. That's just the way it goes I guess."

The source of the voice on the wind was a man who appeared out of the tall grass. He had been lying on the ground looking at the clouds drift by when the trio had arrived, waiting until they were almost upon him before announcing his presence.

"Whoa, dude. You scared the shit out of me." Carl

said bending over to pick up his supply case. Inside was a half a pound of weed, enough rolling papers to cover the side of a house, and a small, but very sharp pair of scissors.

"Sorry about that." The man apologized, He moved closer with his left hand extended. His brown bathrobe parted the grass before him, sparing his bare legs from being scratched. In his right hand he held a staff, carved intricately with the word ABIDE, standing out amongst the vines that wound their way to the top. He used it to support what appeared to be a bum knee.

"You must be Nuna!" Julius said grabbing the out stretched hand and shaking it with great enthusiasm. "Dude, we've been wondering about you. The stories, the guessing and now to see that it's all true, well, it's beautiful man!"

"Well I'm glad that my first impression has lived up to your expectation Julius. I've been contemplating posting pictures, you know, letting the idea roll around in the noggin, though I am quite fond of leaving things to the imagination. It's kind of cool being mysterious as well," the Dudeist Monk confessed.

Willow reached into her pocket and pulled out a small, red stone statue of a laughing Buddha. The chubby Chinese Buddha who constantly traveled.

"I come baring a gift. I hope you will like it." She handed over the present. A smile almost emerged on her face as she did, but she was not ready to go that far yet. She was very committed to her seriousness.

"I love it. It will look great beside my miniature obelisk," Nuna said, a wide smile brightening his face. "I use it to channel good vibes while I am working on my computer. This little dude can help carry them on the winds as he wanders." He placed the statue into one of the robes pockets.

"This place is really remote and hard to find. Everyone else driving these parts looked at us funny." Carl pointed out.

Nuna laughed. It was a free from constraint laugh that made people feel at ease. "Yes, this is where the serious come to make their money. They fear the alternatives to their way of life, and this makes them distrustful and generally unhappy."

"It's a shame what they are doing to the earth," Willow spat out. She was one of those who just assumed that it was evil intent driving such people.

"It is, but it feeds the monkey," Nuna replied. "Most of them just want to provide for their families and have a comfortable life. Where there is demand, these people go, as people have since the dawn of civilization." He paused as a gentle breeze moved the tall grass and his hair with a whisper. "I think if you just realize that they are only doing what the world is asking of them then you would learn to cut them some slack." Nuna concluded.

"Yeah. We are pretty dependent on oil," Carl added. "From plastics to lubricants to pharmaceutical needs. It's going to take some time to ween ourselves off of it."

"We just need to spend more money and time making it more environmentally friendly. Pump money into technologies that will clean up the mess as fast as its made," Julius chimed in, feeling left out of the conversation.

After a thoughtful pause, Nuna motioned his ABIDE staff in a certain direction and said: "So, dudes, let's go down to the monastery and have ourselves a Caucasian. What do you say? I imagine after that long drive you are in need of a long unwind."

The initial sense of wonder soon tempered itself as the four sat in the round common room, sipping on a White Russians and revisiting past conversations they all have had on the various Dudeist web sites. They talked about their favorite dudes who posted on the walls, and gulped down their offerings. The stone walls created echoes that carried their voices, allowing them to speak in soft tones. The wooden benches in which they sat had been hand hewn from local trees and were much more comfortable then they appeared. Wall sconces held large candles which heat and lit up the space.

"So just what is this place exactly?" Willow asked.

She couldn't care less about the small talk; ever the seeker even after her less than spiritual experience in India, she was more interested in learning as much as she could from the monk. This entire journey still seemed surreal. It was hard for her to actually believe that she had stepped so far out of her comfort zone. She really wanted to question why she had, but came back to the now when Nuna moved.

Scratching his beard, Nuna got up from his seat, walked over to the fireplace and brought back a flat stone, no bigger than his palm, and laid it on the coffee table in front of the guests. On it was carved a symbol, unrecognizable to any of the three.

"It's Gaelic, and apparently it's a land claim stone," he explained. "The Cree who own this land gave it to me when I first made my pitch, explaining what I intended to do here. In exchange for allowing me to live here, I trade wool and meat with them. Their Medicine Woman, a great lady with the wildest imagination, explained that the land wasn't theirs really to begin with, but had been given to these European settlers around 800 years ago. Welshmen, if you can imagine that. Well, these settlers became quite friendly with the locals, friendly enough that the natives have preserved this site ever since the original settlers died from sickness. The Shaman, from back then, convinced his people that this land was cursed, because of the strange sickness that befell only the white man. At the same time they proclaimed it sacred, because these people had brought the gift of mutual love with them. Since then it has been kind of a museum for their people, until I came along."

"Welsh settlers, 800 hundred years ago! That doesn't make any sense." Carl said voicing his skepticism. He finished rolling a joint and handed it to Nuna. "If you would do the honors, wise one."

Receiving the gift with a gracious thank you, the monk lit the sacred herb and took a long drag before handing it off, watching as it got passed around the circle.

"Don't be so quick to believe the history, you know," said the monk. "Lots of the natives in these parts have tales of white devils roaming the lands long before Columbus and his lot of goons showed up. Take the Viking site in Newfoundland dated a thousand years old. There are many tales, many artifacts, and many good reasons to believe just the opposite. Theories of copper mining in northern Michigan by the Phoenicians, of the lost tribe of Israel in South America, and the Welsh down around the Mississippi. In fact, I am quite sure that Columbus knew exactly what he was going to find when he set out, but lied so that his Spanish backers would feel good about the trip. China, India, were proven riches. Investments worth making. North America was an unproven resource, populated with savages who drank blood and worshiped pagan gods. Not that the Chinese and Indians didn't do that as well, but at least they had a form of society some dark age Christian king could wrap his brain around. North American natives were a complete mystery."

It took a minute for that to sink in. History was always a fickle thing, especially among the conspiracy theory generation of the now. People had a hard time believing anything, except that which was contrary to popular belief. New theories sometimes had a better chance of gaining a foothold on the internet web sites, than the written histories taught in schools.

"Wow, this place looks pretty good for being over 800 years old, then," Julius Hawk announced in between coughing fits. His lungs had taken a beating since picking up Carl the Chronic.

"Well, it did take us a while to fix the place up," Nuna admitted. "Like I said though, the tribal band in this region still possess that same friendly streak that was present when the Welsh settlers came. They had maintained it, keeping it from falling into disrepair. The last thing they wanted to do was anger the spirits.

"It took me a while to win over their favor, though. With a little bit of bartering, you can build strong ties with people. Both I and the natives have a strong belief in preserving the land, and loving the creatures that inhabit it. From that our relationship has prospered and we have adapted from each other. The funny thing is that they really have developed a taste for lamb and goat.

"So now that you know a little more about this place, let me tell you why exactly I have gathered you here," Nuna said, taking a toke of the joint and passing it on. "To begin with, I was entrusted with the *Dude See Scrolls* for some time now, back before the snows fell in the mountain passes, by a man who had purposely sought me out. His name was Gerald, Gerald the Herald to be precise, but as of late he has decided that the handle the Mad Hermit suits him better. Why, you ask? Well, he believes that anyone crazy enough to speak the truth in a world so hell bent on avoiding it, must be mad. Can't say that I disagree with him there. The Hermit aspect is more in reference to being alone on the island of truth, rather than being physically separated from society. He is, and always has been, immersed amongst the people.

"In his writing there are many observations about humans, and this whole experiment that we are part of. These are the lines which I post everyday on the websites. In addition to these little tidbits, there also other aspects of the scrolls which require much more of my time to translate into acceptable English phrasing. Coded passages which deal with predictions of the future. Now I have only managed to piece together a few which have come true so far. Signs that speak of a great change heading our way. Knowing what to look for has got me frantically trying to puzzle out the solutions to the problems we will face. I assume that knowing what will happen will help to avoid unpleasantries, though for reasons unknown the hermit changed his coding method. I have been stumped, but that is not saying much when you consider I am not the best puzzle-solver out there. So with time constraints and such, I am quite convinced that this piece needs to be translated as soon as possible. I will read you what I have here:

'And the elder spirits shall awaken with the renewal of faith.
The powers that once shaped the land will walk amongst us again.

The Great Empire will eat itself as cities begin to burn.
You will know it is upon you when the earth shakes
from the scorn of the cold shoulder.'

"And that's where the code used to keep the messages secret, changes," Nuna continued. "Like I said, I'm no expert at these sort of things and as such I am at an impasse.

"By the way this is great weed!" The monk just had to point out before going on. "But getting back to my reasoning, so far everything Gerald the Herald has said has been riddled with the truth. So much so that even I, the usual skeptic, have become totally convinced that he has had visions of the future and hid them in these scrolls. Paganism is on the rise, old religions are more popular than ever since this current Pope has basically said the Catholic Church has not always been right about all things. It's as if the Pontiff's admittance has given the green light to those who might have been on the fence. When you start to think about how momentous such a statement is, you have to start wondering what is just over yonder.

"One last thing of note, is that protests and rioting in American cities has been on a steady rise in the past year. I've gone through all the data and they are on the rise by a whopping forty percent. From the right, left, center, and off the political spectrum, people are up in arms about almost everything! It's as if they had just woken up to see what the world has slowly become and they are unhappy about it. If it continues at this rate, you are going to see a lot of shit hitting the fan."

There was a collective moment of silence as the three guests pondered what the monk had to say in the bluish haze of the smoky room. As pleasant as the buzz they shared may have been, doubtful stirrings among the three travelers about the purpose of their quest had begun to harsh their mellow somewhat. Surely nothing short of bad acid trip would bring on such belief in some theory so convoluted. There was nothing about the monk that screamed madness. His faculties seemed fully intact. The sudden realization that they had crossed the country on such a flimsy premise to begin with, without truly questioning the reasoning behind it, lent more credence to the words.

"This is why you are here," Nuna said, sensing the doubt among the three but savoring the dudely effects of the weed. "This is why the Dude network has had a fund raiser to get this off the ground, staked on my reputation and my beliefs. Trust when I say I know how sketchy this all seems, but if you had met the Herald, like I have, you would know that there is something to all of this. I know where to find Gerald and I need you to bring him here to help me figure this out. My gut tells me that this is super, duper important."

"Why wouldn't you have gone to find him yourself, if it is so important?" Carl asked. "Maybe brought the scrolls along with you. It would make a lot more sense than having three strangers drive across the second largest country in the world, convince them of something highly unbelievable, and possibly let the fate of our world rest on untested resolve."

Nuna laughed. He was higher than he had been in some time, which was saying a lot.

"I can't leave the herd, dude," Nuna explained. "I can't leave my family who depend on me, all on a hunch. What I can do is help organize, and plan, and make the thing happen. The reason you were even eligible for this quest was the very fact that none of you really have strings holding you back. You can pick up and go. You can take a little faith, a little positive energy, and stretch it a lot further then one who has responsibilities to others."

The monk gazed at his three new proteges with a reassuring smile.

"You are the beginnings of a new order of dudes," he said, suddenly feeling either really high or divinely inspired or both. "Ones willing to do what might just seem crazy to others in the pursuit of helping the world maintain. I wouldn't ask anyone to do this without fully believing in the cause, and the possibility of success. Think of it as an unexpected adventure. A chance to live without following the norm. A chance to be righteous."

Chapter 6

'The closer you get, the farther it seems.'

Unlike those who experience the more laid-back vibe in the heartland of America, a store clerk working at a convenience store in a Boston suburb does not have the patience to deal with indecisive, or very high customers who prolong the all-important smoke break. This particular customer, clad in communist Soviet-era clothing, kept wandering in circles looking at several items but not choosing any.

"Hey buddy, you gonna buy something?" The clerk asked. His thick Bostonian accent poured out like pea soup onto a fresh tea biscuit.

The patient patron looked up, pushing his furry hat to the back of his head. He reached out slowly for a Mars bar while looking at the clerk, his blood shot eyes never leaving him. In a Russian accent he replied.

"Americans always in a hurry, dude. Why not chill. There is time." He pushed back the flaps of his long wool pea coat and reached into his standard army ware pants, retrieving a leather wallet that was attached to a chain, hooked into a belt loop.

"Look buddy, I ain't in no hurry but at the same time I want to close the store before the sunrises, okay?" the clerk snapped. "So make up your frickin' mind and be done with it."

"No worries, cowboy. I'm a shoot straighter. No problem. I pay, you see then I go and find beautiful American woman to teach me about this thing you call twerking."

The clerk couldn't help himself but had to laugh. All his tension evaporated like hot water on a sub-zero day, dissipating into stream as soon as it hit the air.

"Well I'll tell you what, buddy," the he laughed.

"Dressed like that and as high as you are, you'll be lucky to find a girl who will give you the time of day."

"No need for that, good friend, I have watch." To which the Russian showed the clerk the largest wrist watch the man had ever seen. Soviet in make, built like a tank, it was guaranteed to survive a nuclear blast, because, you know how important it is to know the time if you manage to survive.

"Well, good luck with that buddy." The clerk rang in the Mars bar and gave the customer his change. Walking as slowly as he did coming in, the Russian left, opening the chocolate bar along the way, and then taking a healthy bite out of it. As he was passing through the front door a large man who was muttering to himself pushed past rudely.

"Excuse me," the Russian apologized even though it was he who should have been shown such courtesy.

"Humph." The brutish man replied. He marched right up to the counter where the clerk looked very uncomfortable by the new arrival.

"Oh jeez, not tonight, Tyson," the clerk called out. "You know the deal, once a week, no more, man. Otherwise I'm going to get fired." The clerk called out. He had almost made it out from behind the counter. His smoke break would never come at this rate. When the big man didn't acknowledge him right away he became more uncomfortable.

"Listen, mortal!" the hulking figure thundered. "I care not about this Tyson fellow. I am looking for ale. A strumpet across the street told me this the place where I would find it."

As the Russian attempted to clear the entrance again, his coat hooked on the door, stopping him in his tracks. There was no impending need to hurry, this delay allowed him to overhear the conversation that was unfolding.

"Jesus fucking Christ, Tyson!" the clerk muttered. "What the hell are you on tonight? That smack will kill you, man."

The large man drew up to the clerk, inches from

him, face to face and studied the smaller man, who was now showing signs of fear. It was in the eyes, a steady flicker of the upper eye lids, the smell of sweat glands going into over drive. He knew fear better then fear knew itself.

"Ale, now!" the giant commanded.

Shaking, the clerk pointed towards the glass refrigerator door where a wide selection of the finest brews New England had to offer awaited him. He eyed the weaselly clerk as he moved towards the prize. Still standing in the door way the Russian looked on curiously. Perhaps it was the drugs making this more interesting then it probably was, but for him it was the most entertainment he had come across this night.

This world was as crazy as some of the others Thor had visited in his many years of traveling. The need to package everything was beyond his comprehension, and the bottles that they put the ale into were so pathetically small that a man would need cases of them to achieve any form of a buzz. He grabbed a twenty-four Samuel Adams, for no reason other than it was the first in sight.

"That's going be twenty-six dollars, Tyson," the clerk announced, nervously retreating to the safety behind the counter once again.

"That name you keep calling me is becoming annoying," Thor grumbled. "One more time you little wretch and I will send you to Valhalla to be a servant boy!"

It was at this point in which the Russian decided to get involved. He moved up to the counter threw down the money and nodded at Thor.

"It's okay! It is only money," the Russian told Thor.

Containing his anger by the thinnest of thread, Thor turned and left the store with the Russian following behind. Outside, the big man turned to the walking museum.

"Do you drink ale and think of glory?" Thor asked.

"Does Moscow have whores?" came the Russian's philosophical reply.

Chapter 7

'Your partner in crime should be chosen wisely to maximize enjoyment.'

    Delroy LoneTree was walking along the edge of the river his people called "The Little River," looking to find some snake grass to take back to the medicine woman. She had been pestering him for days with her demands, and now was threatening to have him round up the stray dogs that roamed the reservation. Half of them were nasty buggers that would nip you just for the hell of it. It was these little demands that made Delroy want to leave the wilds, and his people, and to go forth to live like the white man lived. Life on this particular rez was not his cup of pine needle tea. The few times he had ventured off the reservation and into the hectic world he felt more alive than he had ever felt walking alone in nature with the Great Spirit watching over him.

    "Oh Great Spirit," he prayed. "Why do I have to be trapped by these people to whom you have set upon me? They are watching the world pass by without ever taking part. They cling to the past like I cling to my porno stash. Where are the great warriors who roamed the plains? Where is the medicine wheel that turned our souls into fearless eagles? Why must we live in the past?"

    There was no answer. The Great Spirit never answered anymore. The Medicine Woman had told him that she talked with it all the time, but the Great Spirit never listened to anything he said. Perhaps he should hide in the Medicine Woman's house and wait until she summoned the Great Spirit. He was feeling at this point that he needed some proof that there was a great force out there guiding his people.

"When you do make yourself known to me, will you do me a favor and tell the Medicine Woman to relax a little?" Delroy ruminated. "There is only so much one man can take before he just starts blocking out everything she says."

Down on the bank, by a bend in the river, there was a glass bottle, the size of a large pickle jar, nestled in between a rock and branch. Delroy jumped into the shallow water and walked over to see if there was anything in it. He was hoping that it might contain some fire water, for the reservation had a strict ban on spirits to preserve the peace. As he neared the bottle he could see that a piece of paper had been taped to the face, and at one time there had been some writing on it, but the water had effectively washed away whatever had been written there. On closer inspection the jar appeared empty, which left Delroy feeling dismayed.

"Oh, Great Spirit, you are cruel," he said. "You give me an empty jar when I could have really used a drink!" Delroy decided that the bottle would suffice for carrying any snake grass that he would find, so he picked it up, climbed back up the bank and made his way towards a field ahead where he could complete his quest.

When he reached the clearing where he knew he would find plenty of snake grass, a band of clouds rose over the jagged tree line to the west. Dark, looming thunderheads were being carried quickly along by a strong wind that was blowing the grass sideways. Not wasting any time, Delroy began to pick the blades. With a handful, he grabbed the jar and began to twist the lid off. As he turned it, it felt to him as if the bottle was starting to shake, as if something was inside stirring, hoping to be released.

"Must be the wind, or maybe a trapped Genii!" Delroy called out to the Great Spirit. He really hoped it was a Genii, but knew that it was probably just his imagination.

The first drops of rain began to fall. Golf ball sized drops that made a thunk sound as they landed, falling all around the young native man as he opened the jar. The lid came off with a whoosh, and Delroy looked right into the jar to see if a Genii was appearing, but there was no Genii.

Instead an invisible force slapped him across the face and sent him reeling. The snake grass fell from his hands and the jar landed on the ground smashing into many pieces. Shaking his head, Delroy suddenly felt depressed, even more down than he had felt the time the Medicine Woman had made him explain why he had been leaving dog turds on her front step.

With the rain now pounding, Delroy regained his poise and looked down the remains of the jar. The paper that had been taped to the face lay on the ground in front of him now. On its back side, where it had been sealed against the glass with a layer of tape words were visible that he had not noticed before.

NEGATIVE VIBE JAR

"What the hell."

Delroy felt the despair take hold. It was as if some evil spirit had crawled under his skin and laid parasitic eggs. The deluge soaked the man who stared at the smashed vessel, wondering if he should clean it up. Carefully he picked the pieces up, poked himself a few times drawing blood, then carried the shards back to the river. Here he moved a bunch of rocks, dug down into the moist soil underneath and buried the broken glass. He then piled rocks on top of the site, dropping one of the bigger ones on his toe.

Dancing and cursing in the rain, Delroy flung his arms wide, before finally saying fuck it, and headed back home.

Chapter 8

'You must become immune to the pestering, mundane, and endless chatter to find the peace you deserve.'

"Behold the staff of the Wandering Abider," Nuna the Dudeist Monk announced to his three young cohorts. "This once belonged to the Mad Hermit, Gerald the Herald, and was given to me when I took possession of the *Dude See Scrolls*. As the first three indoctrinated into the Order of the Righteous Dude, I pass this staff into your possession so that when you do find the Mad Hermit, he will know that I sent you. The future is upon us, and the spirits of old have returned from their sleep. We must decipher the remaining scrolls in order that we stick to our prime directive, which is to keep balance, balanced. The signs are everywhere, and soon the Dudaclypse will change the very world we know. Go forth and abide."

Nuna handed over the staff which measured four feet in length. On the top of was the Dudeism symbol carved into the weathered wood. Below that the word ABIDE was carved vertically along the shaft just below the grooved hand hold. Beneath that what looked to be branches and leaves wrapped around the bottom two thirds. Willow took it and held it high above her head.

"We will find him, Nuna," she promised. "The Order of the Righteous Dude has its first quest and we will succeed. No Nihilists, nor bureaucrat shall deter us."

"No bad vibes will hold us back!" Julius chimed in.

"And I've got the weed of insight, along with the bong of endless bowls," Carl added as all three faced the monk and his home one last time.

Their initial doubts had been allayed somewhat during their time with Nuna. His sincere words, his relaxed presence, and the sacred elixir of White Russians combined with Carl's potent weed had forged a bond among the three, uniting them in an unspoken spirit of just taking it easy.

"So shall they be known throughout time as the most relaxed heroes of this generation," Nuna declared. "Abide and know that I am only a text away."

Armed with everything they needed, the trio piled back into the Toyota and began the drive down the logging road. They would head due south, once they reached a proper road, cross the border into the United Snakes of America, and then angle west to Seattle. There, living anonymously among the people was the one man who could help decipher the scrolls and lead them through this uncertain future. Unrest was beginning to build across the lands. People were taking to the streets to voice their opinions, and dark tidings were afoot and at hand.

"That dude was really living the life, wasn't he?" Julius asked as he navigated the Camry around the lane's ruts and potholes.

Willow was sitting in the back again, holding the staff and studying each carved notch as if the secrets of the world were contained within.

"The dude is the real deal," she agreed.

"What I find fascinating," Carl noted, "is that he lives in this medieval building, with candle sconces, wood fire for heat, a cistern, and then in that small hidden room in the back, he has his computer with all the modern gadgets, recording equipment, and solar panels neatly placed on that thatch roof to power it all."

"Yeah, the dude can write, but he isn't much of a singer," Julius pointed out to which they all heartily agreed. They had listened to the monk perform three original tunes late last night when the drink and smoke had taken full affect. His day time job was in no jeopardy of being supplanted.

Nearing the Crow's Nest Pass, the Toyota chugged along as the Order neared the end of the Cowboy Trail. Soon they would cross over into British Columbia briefly, and then dip down into Washington State where the call of the quest would take them. They had been cruising on this incredible vibe, even Willow had tried her best to be social, her shell softening slightly. The boys could engage her more openly, though it still felt as if she was an epic novel, like *Anna Karina*—deep and interesting, but also complex and somewhat difficult to comprehend. At their feet lay the evidence of their travels, empty bags of potato chips, crumbs and empty bottles that once contained water, rolling back and forth. The Rockies had flanked them to their right during their entire journey south, tall jagged peaks of broken earth. Tree lines ended abruptly to expose the rock like teeth.

"They are impressive."

Carl agreed with Julius. They were indeed impressive. The world had broken here, and it was somewhat comforting knowing that in the maw they would find the answers. They were the Egyptian Plover, looking for that little bit of nutrition that would keep them alive. Fear was meant to be conquered, especially blind fear. Walk into that moment of discomfort, and let go of hesitation. Willow could feel the forces that Nuna had spoken of, awakening as the great Vibe reverberated against the stone wall.

"Shit, I better not straighten up, or else I will realize just how crazy this whole quest thingy really is," Carl said. The old doubts were stirring again as the take-it-easy vibe they had shared in the haze of Nuna's monastery began to fade as they rode on toward their destiny. Or was it really only just their destination? There is a difference.

"Any sane person would just look at us and laugh, and then return to the real world," Carl said.

Julius laughed at the proclamation, and it was Willow who asked the question any sane person would ask.

"Well, why are you doing it, then?"

"What else am I going to do?" Carl responded, looking through his reflection on the car window at the scenery passing by. "Honestly, I make money whether at home or on the road, and this shit is crazy enough, that when retold, people will have to believe."

"So you are not really dedicated to the cause, then."

"Look, Willow," Carl sighed. "I know you've got

this 'I'm a woman, I don't need a man thing' going on, so of course you are going to look for any crack in my armor, but truth be told, no. It is craziness, but it's the kind of craziness that goes real well with a buzz. Sure there are forces at work, I sense something happening, but finding a homeless dude who can predict the future just seems a little too much. But hey, what else do I have to do?"

Julius, being the consummate science fiction nerd, could not let this opening pass without a quote.

"I find your lack of faith…disturbing," he recited in a deep booming voice.

"Both of you two testosterone-laced burnouts have some serious questions to answer to yourselves," Willow the seeker scolded. "Can you not see that this is more than just a quest to find a person? This is a quest to discover who we really are. A chance to see how we will react when confronted with something that cannot possibly explained without experiencing. That is why I am here. It might be batshit crazy but good people believe things are happening, and we have been chosen, so you better buck up and prepare to open your mind.

"And no, Carl, I am not anti-men," she continued. "I am a strong woman, something that you have probably never encountered before."

"Yeah, well okay, but that's just like your opinion man," Carl shrugged, quoting a favorite Dudeist saying. "I mean, you act like all tough and such, but honestly I can't figure out why you would agree to this whole proposition. I mean, Julius is obviously a free spirit who will follow a butterfly off a cliff." To which Julius nodded in agreement with the biggest shit eating grin he could muster. "But you, you are all loner like, and introverted. Hardly the adventurer type."

Willow remained silent, she wanted to rebuke Carl's observations, but he had come too close to the truth and she didn't trust herself to answer. Instead she studied the staff again, hoping the topic would change as quickly as the joint changed hands.

"Well? I mean we are like an Order and we have to

trust each other, and if Barney of The Purple has taught me anything, it is that we develop trust through sharing." Carl pointed out.

"If you really have to know, then I guess the reason why I wanted to do this was in hopes of finding love," Willow lied. It would throw the two boys for a loop, giving her back her peace and quiet. Hopefully.

Both dudes were slightly stunned by the answer. They had indeed expected some feminist statement of defiance, not one so simple and sensitive. It effectively changed the subject as both secretly hoped that with enough time together, one of them would be the one who won her affections.

Turning on to the highway that led through the Crow's Nest Pass, Julius pulled the car over to the side of the road as he noticed a Native American man hitch-hiking, heading in their direction with dark clouds beginning to loom over head.

"I hate to say it," Julius said. "But we got to give this guy a ride. The sky is going to open up at any minute, and besides, it might be the love of your life, Willow." He really hoped it wasn't the love of her life, though. Willow raised the staff of the Wandering Abider and gave the long hair, rock star wanna be a knock on the head. He let out a little yelp, and made a note to keep his sarcastic mouth under a tighter rein when she held that staff.

Delroy ran quickly towards the Toyota, he had almost dried out from the last down pour, and wasn't looking forward to being caught in the Great Spirit's wrath again.

"Where you heading, dude?" Carl asked with his head hanging out of the passenger window.

"Anywhere but here, doode," the young man replied.

"Well, shit. Hop in. Don't mind Willow, she's a feminist, and maybe even a lesbian." Carl joked, which earned him a crack across his noggin from the aged wooden staff.

Chapter 9

'Never underestimate how much you do not want to do something.'

The Sunnyside Grove retirement home was rocking on a Thursday night.

It was fifteen minutes past six pm., and the turnout for pub night was better than the director could have hoped for. At least one in three of the residents had stuck around after dinner to listen the Down Town Players, and drink some of lovely punch the woman's auxiliary had made, alcohol-free of course. Many of the residents were on medications that would have adverse effects if mixed with a proper beverage. Singing along was encouraged, and those who knew the words did so with as much vigor as their aged vocal chords would allow.

As the accordion rowed the boat, while Odin tried desperately to wheel as far away from the gathering as he could. The so called, "Pub" night was the most painful experience that the immortal had ever endured. He had tried desperately to get an orderlies attention to help him to his room, but the cruel bastards seem think that this was for the best. For the best! Having his eye plucked out by a raven was more enjoyable then listening to this rabble destroy music once and for all. When the day came that he regained his strength, he would banish all accordions off of this world, down to the seven hells where they belonged.

"Mr. Olsen! So happy to see that you are mingling. We were getting worried about you." Cathy Lessard, the Grove's administrator said as she was locking up her office. Odin wheeled his way past her though, towards the elevator.

"Mingling! I am most certainly not mingling with this rabble. I've been trying to get one of your stooges to take me to my room but those ignorant fools seem to think that this form of torture is somehow therapeutic! If I could cut my ears off, I would." He cursed just as the band jumped into roll out the barrel and everyone, including the attendants joined in.

"Well, I'm sorry you feel that way, Mr. Olsen," Cathy said. "But the residents look forward to pub night. Once a month we bring in the finest talent we can to give them a sense of community, to give them some memories, and revive their long-ago memories. At this stage in your life it's all we can do to stave off the depression."

"Perhaps if you had ale and wenches, one might be able to bare the caterwauling," Odin groused. "Your false advertising has left me wanting to run you over with this chair, if only I could muster enough speed."

"Now, now, sir, there is no need to make idle threats," Cathy tut-tutted like a school teacher with a difficult child. "I can easily have you put back on a special diet and have your television time revoked. Unlike the other guests here, you don't have family visiting you. In fact, do you even have a family, sir?"

Odin's rage threatened to dislodge him from his wheel chair. His hands gripped the metal frame on either side as he made an effort to pull a lightning bolt down from the sky and end this wretched being's life, but still the sky did not answer him.

"Be gone woman before I lose my temper." Odin spat as he rolled towards the elevator. He was hoping that he would be able to figure out how to use the contraption. Arrows were easy, figuring out the number system was a little trickier.

"I'll help you." A quiet male voice announced.

Odin turned his head to see a young man, dressed like he had just survived a battle with a flock of raven. His clothes were torn in what appeared to be sequential patterns, piercings in his nose, ears and cheeks. A red bandana was tied across his forehead and his silver dyed hair was tied back in a long pony tail that reached down to his buttocks.

"What the in the seven hells happened to you, boy?"

The teen chuckled. His eyes had been tinted green and his teeth were capped with silver plates. In his hand he carried bouquet of black roses.

"Well, have it your way, old man," the young stranger shrugged. "I'll take the stairs." He moved to leave the elevator but Odin reached out and hooked a finger in a ripped sleeve.

"It doesn't matter. I need to get up to the seventh floor," Odin blurted out. "I'm having a hard time figuring out this numbering system." He swallowed his spit as he spoke the next line. "I would be grateful."

The teen reached over and pressed the correct button. A sly smirk crept up to a stud that ended in a green stone in his cheek. "Coincidence or not. I am also going to the same floor."

The ride up was quiet as both passengers studied each other. This was a strange world, the children even stranger then the adults. They purposely fought against conformity, not wanting to be like their parents. Fighting everything they stood for. Open rebellion such as this would have been squashed immediately in Asgard. Even his beloved Viking tribes had exhibited respect for their elders. In this age the elders were just a nuisance that cost the youth money to keep.

"You are rebelling against those who lead, I assume." Slowly Odin's powers of perception were crawling back. His visions of the future, the ones he had long ago were starting to fall into a semblance of order allowing him to ascertain more understanding of these people. Now, if only his physical strength would return.

"There are no leaders amongst us, old man. Haven't you heard? It's every man for himself. The American way has permeated the entire fabric. We all sleep under the same blanket. The lines of have blurred and the shadows consume hope."

"The shadow cannot hide the truth forever," Odin replied. A strange and disturbing darkness surrounded this young man.

"Perhaps. The light can also hide things," the

ominous youth said with an odd lilt in his voice. "The righteous can stand with it, at their backs, but even they twist the truth and bury it when need be. They just say it is for the better good, when it comes time to justify themselves. If you are looking for truth in this world, old man, it is better to study the past, and see that it has never been considered a goal of man."

"Your words are familiar. Your tone even more so," Odin said with insight. "How long have you been awake, Loki? It seems that you have a firm understanding of the present."

"Oh, I do, Odin," Loki grinned. "I've been around a lot longer than I care to admit. There are times when I would have loved to enjoy the slumber that you and your kin enjoyed, but then that would not have really suited me well. It would have been hard for me to lie still for so long."

"So tell me, what mischief have you've been up to?" Odin asked. "Looking like that I can't imagine many would take you seriously."

They rode up the elevator together and went back to Odin's room. Once inside, Loki dropped his illusion and retained the old form that the father of the gods remembered so well. He rolled Odin's chair over by the window and took a seat in the reclining chair allowing himself to float back into a very comfortable position. There was tension amongst the two, but there had always been. A complicated history could do that.

"So tell me how badly you want out of here." Loki offered.

"Knowing you, I would be better off making a deal with the Christian Devil," Odin grumbled. "At least his word is good."

"Now, now Odin. I have had a lot of time to myself and in that time I have changed. I have been stuck down here on this world, walking amongst the mortals trying to make sense of my own existence. The mirror," He accentuated the statement by putting his hand in front of his face, "has never been closer, and I have come to a few conclusions. One, is that mortals are boring when left to their own devices. Sure they war and create their own mischief, but it's not the well-thought-out mischief that I can appreciate. These petty squabbles have not led to any glory and even those who do show promise have no way of reaching Valhalla, where their deeds might be appreciated. Sure I've made some moves, had a part in some of the bigger moments of the past century, but honestly without having anyone to share them with I have become quite depressed."

"Depressed. What do you take me for? A fool?" Odin wanted to know, a scowl darkening his face. "You cannot feel, Loki; that is your special gift. It is what has kept you from falling into this dreadful sleep that consumed your kin."

"Well, there is some truth to that, Odin," the trickster replied. "I'd call you 'father' but it's better we not go down memory lane now that we are on the brink of renewal. This sleep that you all fell into was, I'm sorry to say, kind of my fault. I convinced your followers that you, and the rest of your merry band were mythical beings, and that this Christian god was the only true god to turn to. It was this sudden lack of faith that stripped you and all of our kin of your power. A god needs faith to be a god, and without those who carry it for him, or her, there is no divine essence. My mistake was thinking that you would just be banned from this world, leaving me to finally have the fun I deserve. Little did I know at the time that your fragile minds would not be able to comprehend such loss, putting you into this catatonic state of despair. I watched your souls floating about in the ether, then onto limbo, dormant, unable to accept the fact that these mortals no longer believed in you. You were like rape victims in denial."

With immense effort, Odin rose from his seat, trembling. The anger that had infused his muscles gave him the strength that had been lacking. Even his mind began to clear.

"I am going to kill you once and for all, Loki."

Chapter 10

'When you find the one, hold on tight for it will be a wild ride.'

The water laps on the shore, slowly grinding the rocks that occupy the sea side vista. Over time they wear down, for nothing can resist entropy. All that remains, grains of sand, the only evidence of the stone had once existed. At peace now, the energy that eroded away form, released the energy of cohesion, back into the wild again.

A paradise to some, this new world, a land that had been rediscovered many times over the centuries by many different cultures, was now a melting pot of cultures. It was just down the road from this particular place, where this particular rock was eroding, that the pilgrims landed for the first time. Outcasts from their ancestral home, looking for a place to live, free from persecution. With them they would bring freedom, modern European civilized society, and pesky little bugs that the natives would be unable to defend themselves against. They would take without asking, spread out like a blanket at a picnic, and transform the land from its raw unproductive state, into something more productive. They would turn from the persecuted to those that laid down judgment.

The Russian and Thor were sitting by the sea, high on a bluff, the city in behind them. Trains rumbled on by on in the distance, carrying cargo shipped in from the sea. These goods were destined for other civilized parts of the country. The case of beer that the Russian had paid for had a serious dent in it now, and still only five words had passed between the two.

"Would you like another?" Thor asked.

"Da."

Both men had stared at the ocean's vast expanse for a long time. Neither had watched waves lapping against the shore in a long time. One by choice, the other due to circumstances beyond his control. A warmer breeze was pulling the seafaring birds farther north as winter receded back into its corner for another six to seven months. On the horizon, large container ships moved slowly against the current taking things people needed, to places where people needed them taken.

"This world has changed drastically," Thor admitted.

The Russian snapped out of his trance and acknowledged the statement.

"When the wall fell, everything changed."

"Walls fall. Men die. Battles will be fought. This is the way it has always been. This was always part of my purpose to be amongst you," Thor confessed. His rage had abated with the consumption of alcohol, making him much more relaxed. It wasn't right to be thrust back into the world sober. Especially a world so foreign.

"Many men in Russia speak like you," the Russian said. "Many do not understand how to get by in this world when people fly white flags before the fighting even begins. I myself, have no problem sitting back and relaxing. At first it was hard for me, but then I met people on the computer who spoke about the Dude, and how he could look at the world and just say fuck it. For me, this works. Fuck it."

"Who is this man, the Dude? Some kind of coward?"

"No, not a coward. He stands up for himself when compelled to, but he knows the world has its own agenda that it doesn't need his involvement. He likes to enjoy his beverage, remain calm, and abide the tide. I like this. I don't care much for what other people think. I like my belongings, like my time alone, and I like punk rock."

"Well, men fight!" Thor asserted, hitting his massive chest hard with his solid fist. "That is how you save your seat at the table in the grand hall in Valhalla. Those that do not, serve the mead."

"So you really believe you are the Viking god?" The

Russian asked. The answer he got in return was unexpected as the solid fist left Thor's chest and connected with his chin, lifting all two hundred and thirty pounds of the Russian up into the air, and planting him on his back in the wild grasses.

"Well, you are strong." The Russian admitted as he rubbed his chin. He sat up and returned to his perch as if nothing had happened.

"And your chin is tough Russian. Most mortals would have died from such a blow." Thor almost regretted the action. He knew that the disappearance of his brothers and sisters from this world would have left a lot of tough questions to be answered. Who knows what these beings believed in now.

"So, you don't like that question. That is okay. I am, how you say, used to this kind of comradery. We should drink."

The square-jawed, square-headed man impressed Thor, though he would never let the mortal know. He had taken a punch—mind you, he was still lacking his godly powers—and shook it off as it were nothing. Perhaps these Russians were the people he should seek out. Americans so far had proven to be very nosy, flippant with their tongues, and full of useless knowledge. In the past three hours he learned more of this modern world from the Russian than he had from that magic box called a television. He would keep him along as his follower, test his merit, and see if he could shake this nonsense the Dude had implanted in his head.

Taking it easy was no way to find glory.

"So people choose weak, oil-skinned vermin to lead them?" This whole democracy thing was back again. Thor had really hoped that this idea of picking a good and just leader by common consensus would have died with the Greeks a long time ago. Even the Romans had found the need to usurp the practice from time to time. "They pick these people based on their words and their looks! Not on their deeds! This place is almost too much for me to imagine, Russian. Surely someone with strength would have conquered it by now."

"The world is connected now in ways you could never imagine now," the Russian began. "Today a man can send a message to another man, half way around the world and he will receive it almost instantly. People unite in groups, with common interest, without ever having to meet in person. The need to be physically strong is no longer necessary if you know how to say the right words, and have people believe them. This causes great problems for rulers who rely on strength."

The Russian found himself buying into the man's claim of being an ancient being. It was obvious to him that the belief ran deep, and as far as he was concerned, that was enough. He had seen what can happen when belief fails as it had in his Mother Russia. He understood the level of commitment to an idea that Thor had, and continued to play along as if he we talking to someone who had been asleep for the past two thousand years.

"Now when someone of power rises, they become great spectacles under scrutiny," the Russian continued. "For the most part they are just figureheads. The real men of power these days have more money than they know what to do with, buying and selling countries like you or I buy mead. They have the people believing that they possess real freedom, choosing their own leaders, but in fact these men who hide in the dark have the say. Strength is no longer the measure, wealth is now. If you are looking for enemies, Thor, then look where no others do. That is where the evil has fled to. It festers like a boil, and you cannot reach it because it is in that one place on your back where your arms will not reach."

There was a twinge on Thor's face every time the Russian spoke his name. The god stood up and raised his hand. A small spark reached out of the air and touched his index finger. His vision improved minutely allowing him to see lettering on the side of the ship that was steaming its way towards the harbor. A smile split his face in half. He patted the Russian on the back.

"Before we conquer this capitalist evil, we need to

gather some followers." Thor pronounced. Faith would restore him to his prior glory.

"Well, there is a couple of dudes in my network who are into Vikings," the Russian offered after a moment. "I could send them a message and we could drive out in Yugo. You can tell them your tale and perhaps they will follow you." The Yugo: pride of the Russian automobile industry from the time of communism. The small rusted hatch back had over three hundred thousand miles on it, and it still kept running. They had driven down to the shoreline in it, both men having to contort to fit into its small passenger compartment.

"May?" Thor raged. "Oh, they will follow me if they are truly the descendants of the ancient bloodlines. They will see me and bend their knees, their faith restoring my power. I will then call upon Mjolnor and rid the Earth of this evil. I do not fear to tread into the shadows, and there is no place my arm cannot reach."

How do you convince people of something so unbelievable, especially when you are just an icon on a computer screen to them? A name that occasionally posts, and comments on posts.

The Russian sat staring at the Facebook group page for the Superdudes knowing that there were two diehard Viking enthusiasts on there who would shit themselves to know that Thor was actually here, on Earth, now. Everything they posted was Viking related. Would they be open to this idea? Was their commitment to the subject that strong, or was it just a thing? A way to make themselves a little different from the rest of the throng. Even the politburo would have a hard time spinning this one.

Thor was anxious, sitting in the corner of the small apartment playing with a World War Two bayonet and singing songs that the Russian had never heard before. Why exactly was he helping him, and why was he willing to believe such a crazy story? There must have been a spell of compulsion placed upon his mind, he assumed. A pagan god's influence that couldn't be denied.

There was a way, nothing was impossible, except explaining why an AK-47 was a vastly superior machine gun over the American made M-16, to an American. In one sense their pride in country and state was almost admirable, except it lead them down many dark alleys of delusion. In truth, the Russian knew that all superpowers, even his beloved home, were flawed beyond reason in a world where information on anything was at your fingertips.

"Tell me, Thor, of something only a scholar of Viking lore would know," he asked the god. "I need something to catch the attention of our fish."

"Well how about,..." Thor began and the Russian typed.

Chapter 11

'Do not sit on the fence unless it has a ledge.'

"In the twilight the songs we sing will not be of who's got who and who's got what. The songs will be about love and tenderness. This is our song we sing and when we sing it, we sing it with conviction. Those who sing about what they have, and what they want, have no conviction. They see the world as an oyster, and they only care about the pearl. They have no clue that the meat will provide sustenance. The shells will purify the waters. Their concept of the world is one for the taking, where as our concept is that the world is ours for giving. Share with your brother. Share with your sister. Find some respect for yourself before you condemn those who have found it for themselves.

"I often wonder why you people do these things you do every day. Your heads down cast. Your blinders up and you hearts sealed off behind walls of granite. Have you not the time to see that the world has been waiting for you to wake up and to speak out? Do you not see that because of our own self-imposed segregation we have let the wounds fester? Or fathers and grandfathers fought against tyranny, with the hope of building a better world for all mankind, yet he we are picking and choosing which evils to punish. Which virtues to cherish. What would those who sacrificed themselves in those great wars say now, seeing us allow this preposterous farce run its course? I say we join together and start filling the sand bags before the flood wipes out our homes! I say we lift ourselves up and look at our duty to the future generations to come! No more hiding! No more hiding! No more waiting! No more waiting! No more pretending! No more pretending! No more!"

Left-Handed Larry handed Gerald his flask of

whiskey. It wasn't a great whiskey by any means, but it would take the edge off, and help ward away the dampness that Seattle endured in the spring.

"What do you think of this guy's speech?"

Gerald looked at the man in tattered clothes, standing on a milk crate in front of six teenagers; the only people to stay past the first paragraph.

"The truth is hard to sell, Larry," Gerald observed, taking a swig from the flask. "Sometimes it's better to hide it under the bologna. Most people don't have a taste for bologna, and if they make it past that mystery meat then they will enjoy what is underneath much more."

"Yeah, I hear what you are saying, brother. The truth is like free milkshakes. After a while you become lactose intolerant."

As the two homeless men walked along the avenue, they kept their eyes scanning the streets for anything discarded that might prove useful. Trash days were shopping days to the folk who lived under the bridge. People who were more financially inclined tend to throw away all kinds of useful stuff.

"You like to talk the talk, Mad Man. Why not do what that dude is doing, but put a hat out? If nothing else you might get enough cash together so we can buy some decent whiskey. I mean this stuff is okay, but once in a while a brother likes to enjoy his drink." Left-Handed Larry was a suggestion man. His days of action were long over, but the suggestions never ended.

"I have done my talking, dude," Gerald said. "I wrote it down, and left it for others to discuss. Now I am free to exist without the burden of worry. I am the rock that sits in the middle of the river watching the water flow by. It matters not if it was to stop, or to continue on. Once you have had a glimpse of the future you'd rather sit the next one out."

As far as trash days go, this one did not offer great pickings. The pair walked along in their usual loop, through a middle-class neighborhood where people generally dispensed with anything that didn't work without some assistance. Eventually they returned to their neck of the woods, walked down a grassy slope and headed back along the waterway towards Reality, where a crowd had gather at the front gates. The man who they had passed earlier, the one speaking about the truths of the world, was there followed by the six teenagers who looked grubbier than before. It looked as if they had rolled around in the dirt before attempting to gain entrance into the homeless habitat.

"Oh Jesus, save us, Larry," Gerald moaned. "If this fool gets in, the town will get its mind full of silly ideas."

They hurried their steps and reached the gates where Fat Bart and Peg Leg Tony were eagerly accepting cigarettes from the teens who were giving them out freely. Left-Handed Larry's eyes lit up at that sight.

"Resist temptation friends!" Gerald warned as loudly as he could. "These kids are not what they seem. Look at those shoes. Brand new, and the clothes might be dirty but they are designer label apparel. I believe we have ourselves a case of Pootles threatening to infest our home."

"Pootles?" Larry asked.

"Rich kids who act like they are poor kids, Larry," Gerald explained. "Bottom feeders who wouldn't know how to abide if it hit them straight in the head. They roam the streets all day, skipping school and buying homeless friends with cigarettes they claim they begged for, except the money really came from daddy's wallet when he was busy getting showered. These are the worst types, Larry, they rank right up there with Taoism Elitists."

"Bart! Don't take those!" Gerald yelled as they closed the gap. The two behemoths who worked the gate were just about ready to let the congregation in when he spotted the two residents coming up fast and waving their hands.

"One second fellows." Bart announced to the Pootles and their tattered leader.

"What's up, Mad Man?" he asked Gerald. "These righteous dudes were just about to join us for some entertainment in the square. They even brought cigarettes."

Bart lifted his hand that held six Camels.

"Don't let them in Bart," Gerald urged. "Can't you tell these kids are Pootles. For Christ's sake, check out their shoes." Gerald pointed out.

Both giants looked down at the feet of the teenagers. Sure enough they were wearing new sneakers. The man in tattered clothing though was wearing a pair of rubber boots that had seen better days.

The leader of the Pootles, a tanned boy with bright blue eyes and a pair of red Nikes, turned to confront Gerald. The others sort of cowered behind him while the speaker with the milk crate stood off to the side and watched as the confrontation begin to take shape.

"Shoes?" the leader began with. "We got the shoes from the shelter this weekend. Everybody did. Somebody donated a whole bunch of them."

"Ah yes, the shelter story," Gerald said. "Funny, only Pootles ever claim to have reaped such rewards from donations. Most of us get used clothing, left-over food, and occasionally refreshed bedding, but brand new, two hundred-dollar sneakers? You must be hitting the shelters up in the swanky part of town, eh!" The youth was a good six inches taller than Gerald, who was rather short for a short man.

"What's you problem man?"

"What's my problem, man?" Gerald moved in closer. "My problem is that you little twats are going to hang out, pretend like you know the streets, then when we are getting ready to fight for warmth all night you'll shuffle away to your 'shelter' back up in the hills and drink liquor from your parents' cabinets while watching *Big Brother* on your 60' flat screen television, posting selfies with homeless people online. Your ignorant friends online will then make comments like; 'How it must be so cool to be homeless and free from the tyranny of parents', while they watch *Big Brother* on their televisions in their bedrooms. You'll all have this circle jerk where you throw your hands up in the air and declare that life ain't fair. Then tomorrow when your parents think you are going off to school, you'll steal some more money out of their pockets, hop on the train, come downtown, get changed into your 'street clothes', and look for some more models to pose with you for your Facebook profile."

"Well, that's just like bullshit, man," the boy claimed. A futile attempt to refute the Mad Hermits evaluation.

"Look Mad Man, we are going to let them in and hang, man," Bart declared, moving off to one side. 'They know not to cause any shit and hey, they brought cigarettes. Maybe everybody needs to spend a little time in Reality." Gerald raised his hands in protest as the kids snickered, walking past.

The speaker from earlier in the day was the last to go, but he paused beside Gerald and Left-Handed Larry. His eyes burned with crazy devotion, his beliefs could be detected from across the sound, and his hair had taken on a life of its own.

"So this is where you hide?" the street preacher asked. "I noticed you walk past earlier today. Did the words I speak not ring of the truth, dude?"

Taken aback, the hermit made a double take assessment of the stranger. A vibe emanated from him when up close. He was hiding something, it sat in the corner of his left eye, a small little tell that most would have missed.

"Do you know me?" Gerald asked, curious to the answer.

"No, but I know what you once possessed," was the stranger's answer. "It has been traveling around, jumping from those who could fully understand, to those that just went insane from such a gift. It never lingers long though, unless you know how to trap it. I once held it for a brief glimpse, and when I did I thought of you."

Thoroughly puzzled by this turn of events, Gerald waved Larry on, telling him that he would see him later. Off to the side, and away from the twin behemoths guarding the gate, Gerald pursued the matter further.

"What is it that I once possessed, dear fellow, that you once possessed as well?"

"Why, Odin's gift of course. The ability to see the future."

Chapter 12

'When you await for approval and reassurance, you may find the line long and spiteful.'

A whole section of the pass had come sliding down the mountain in the middle of the night a long time ago, when living was simpler, or at least when there were less things to distract you from life. In fact, it wasn't simpler at all. People endured many more hardships. They had poor diets, homes that were harder to heat, and jobs that didn't pay nearly as well. The turn of the nineteenth century into the twentieth was less then enviable for those living way out on the frontier. Mining towns were filled with people who soon discovered that there were not many harder ways to make a living.

Here, just inside the entrance of the Crow's Nest Pass, in the middle of the night, a town awoke to a scene out of a Hollywood blockbuster disaster movie. 82 million tons of rock let go off the side of Turtle Mountain, down onto the town of Frank. Ninety lives ended just like that. No warning, no chance of escape. The red Toyota Camry cruised past the scene over a hundred and twenty years later, three of the four passengers staring in awe at the house-sized boulder field.

"Many spirits haunt this valley," Delroy commented. "Sleeping here is like sleeping on a sidewalk in Calgary. All night people are passing you by, making a ruckus."

"I've never seen anything like this!" Julius proclaimed. He had slowed the car considerably, aggravating the long line of pickup trucks behind him who had nowhere to pass the small car. "Can you imagine seeing something like that?"

"That's just it. No one saw it until it was crushing them under. It was the Mother exacting her revenge on the people for digging too deep into her skin. The Medicine Woman says that we are in for one hell of a ride soon because of all the bad things people are doing to their Mother. They continue to poke at the sleeping bear, not knowing that the bear can run much faster than them."

"Delroy, where exactly is your home?" Carl asked. This native was acting too native for his liking. In fact the more he toked, the more he slipped into some kind of role.

"Oh, my home is close to Calgary, in the foothills. My people have lived there for centuries," Delroy replied.

"And you know we are heading away from there right?" Carl wanted to clarify.

"Oh yes, I know. The Medicine Woman has sent me out on a quest to find a man in Seattle. Apparently he is the only one who can rid me of the evil that has befallen my spirit."

The car swerved slightly as all three members of the Order of the Righteous Dude turned to look at the hitchhiker. Unnerved, Julius pulled the car over on to the shoulder at Willow's request and Carl remained fixated upon the face of the hitchhiker.

"Exactly what kind of evil are we talking about?" Carl asked.

Delroy glanced around at the three white faces focused on him.

"Well, I was walking in the woods when I found a jar beside a river," he said, brushing his long black hair back over his ears. "I opened up the jar and suddenly strange things started to happen. Rain came from nowhere. A group of angry squirrels chased me from the forest, and when I made it back to my truck, the wheels were flat, all four. I walked forty miles to get home, through the rain, and along the way developed a blister on my heel that hurt so much that I had to hop on one foot. Many cars passed me, but none would stop to pick me up. By the time I got back to my home, I had missed my mother's birthday party and incurred the wrath of my relatives for doing so. To make things worse I found out that my cousins from High Level had come down and had basically taken over my bedroom leaving me to sleep on the living room floor with my dog Jessie who managed to get into the cheese dip after everyone passed out and released the worst smells a dog can, all night so close to my head that I could hear her stomach moving before the wind passed. The next day I got blamed for the truck, for the sick dog, and for upsetting my mother.

"To be honest none of that was so bad," Delroy continued. "What I feared more was going back to the Medicine Woman empty handed. I was supposed to bring back some snake grass for her but dropped it when I was running from the squirrels. Unfortunately there was no way around it; I had to go see her. So after I finished cleaning up from the party I had missed, and taking the dog out for a long walk, with my foot in much pain, I made my way over to her house to explain my story. As I reached her door a cop car stopped, and the two officers inside jumped out and ran up to me. Before I could even speak a word of greeting they had me down on the ground, my face so close to a dog turd I could tell that the Medicine Woman's dog had been eating food too rich for his stomach. I was being hauled off to the cruiser when she appeared, as if smoke had billowed out of the front entrance, her staff outstretched, pointing at the officers.

"'He is not the one you seek.' She called out. 'The one you want is next door. This one is too incompetent to be dangerous.' "

"Her words had brought a smile to my face as the cuffs were removed. My clean clothes were now covered in grass stains, my blister had broken open, and again the rain fell. Waving goodbye to the policeman, I walked up empty handed to the Medicine Woman, noticing that her television was very loud in the back ground, and on it some man was calling out for Jesus to save some poor soul. I was hoping that poor soul was me, but I knew better.

"Finding out that I had not brought back the snake grass, the Medicine Woman was about to whip me with her tongue, when she suddenly stopped, looked at me very closely and then shied away in fear.

"'Stay outside, Delroy! Do not cross this threshold.' She cried out before I had one foot on the steps. At this point that the man on the television started screaming louder and louder in words that were completely unrecognizable. A baby made more sense than he did, and that coupled with the look of horror on the Medicine Woman's face cast me into a great pit of despair.

"I begged her to give me some reason, to tell me why I could not approach. She looked away, her hand held out, her staff ready to strike me if I came any closer. Her head began to convulse back and forth, and I realized that she had induced a trance. Five minutes passed by as I stood in the rain. The Medicine Woman was dry, convulsing, until finally her head whipped around. She looked at me with all the kindness she could muster, told me to go wait at the crossroads where the Cowboy Trail meets the Crow's Nest Pass, and that there, a car with three white folks on a quest would pick me up and take me to see a man who could rid my spirit of the evil that has taken hold."

Carl coughed loudly passing around another fat boy. "No shit!" He exclaimed.

If you believe that one force can exert influence upon another, then a coincidence like the one developing in the Toyota was of no big surprise to a fatalistic mind. It was meant to be, that familiar saying when the unexplainable happens. This kind of convergence creates its own well, a well in the fabric of space time that begins to exert a pull on other bodies that come within the event horizon. Try to escape it all you want, but the pull becomes so irresistible that even casual encounters become memorable ones.

The Medicine Woman had been attuned to the pull, her vision had been drawn towards the well. Delroy's discovery of the jar had been part of the alignment, the one that allowed the well to form.

The surprise ice quake in Ontario had set it all in motion, the release of energy sending ripples outwards across the sands of collective consciousness, aligning positive and negative particles.

Chapter 14

'A stale cake is not something to trifle with.'

The passing of an age sometimes goes unnoticed until future generations are able to analyze the data, and then pinpoint the moment of the shift. All new ages begin with cultural movements, forward or backward. As far as movements go, some are slow building, decades in the making, and because of the snail like pace, the change invoked barely registers simply because it has already become the norm. Little by little, burrowing into the minds of the masses. You can always recognize a good movement by the fact that it is in no hurry. Time will be the lever that moves the boulder.

One particular rock began to roll slowly down a gentle slope, a slope with such a negligible grade that without that initial push, the rock would have remained in its place a lot longer than it did. The land resists in the beginning, but only slightly, and the pace quickens over time. Soon the boulder moves with ease as it carries its momentum further and further, until the land levels out, where the forces that permeate the entire fabric begin to exert their will again.

"When you do set out on your quest, there a few things that you must remember." Nuna had said back in the monastery as the guests feasted on a very lovely curry dinner. Fresh unleavened bread, homemade chutney and jasmine rice with hints of green tea flavoring had kept the three too busy from talking. Listening was much easier at this point.

"The world has been influenced by those who have no desire to find a common good," the monk informed them. "They care not for the inhabitants who live here. It is quite obvious by the way we as a species continue to neglect the people in real need, and turn our attention on those who would be better off left alone. It has always been this way, though; it is the curse of mankind, in the never ending quest for power. Perhaps we will never shed this way of going about business in our lifetime, but in the meantime there are things that we can slowly do to set pieces in place to make the outcome of the game more favorable in the end for those that do care. Perhaps not a full on victory, perhaps just some ground gained in anticipation for when the game is played again. We have to think in increments, not in losses and victories as we navigate the cycles. So when you are out there on this quest you will most likely encounter those who carry negative vibes as if they were badges of honor. Do not succumb to their temptation, or their need to control. Maintain your balance by remembering, increments.

"What may feel like good, positive vibrations, may not be so. Those who stand by such notions of judging so strongly, should be looked at with one eye open, and one eye closed. We travel the middle of the road, The Order of the Righteous Dude. We are Bards, poet warriors who collect information, telling tales, but never allowing our biases to interfere with our pursuit of Dudeliness. This quest is a trial of sorts, a test for you to see if you will be able to the abide the truth that lives within the self, and a test for us to see if you will discover your faults and use them to grow into examples which others can follow."

In the Camry, Willow remembered these words as she studied Delroy in the backseat with her, wondering if his presence was a test of sorts. The coincidences were too real to ignore. She wanted to believe him, his natural vibe loose and free, but there was definitely a darkness surrounding him. Trust, it was something she had to learn how to do. Julius was obviously going to trust anyone who smiled, and Carl was cynical, likely to dismiss people out right, but without telling them so. Nuna's words were there, specifically floating through her thoughts. If this was really all predicted by some mad hermit, then she would have to develop some faith in her ability to know herself.

"So how were you planning on crossing the border

without a passport Delroy?" she asked, thinking through all the complications the new addition to their party might add.

Oblivious to Willow's scrutiny, the native man turned smiling. He was higher than the mountains they were navigating through, eyes completely bloodshot. He fumbled with a bottle of water, taking a drink in an attempt to free his tongue that had become stuck to the side of his mouth.

"Um, well, I never had a plan beyond going to the crossroads," he said with an almost comical deliberateness. "I just assumed the Great Spirit would give insights into my path as it revealed itself."

"Perhaps we could let you out somewhere close to the border, let you cross through the wilderness and we could wait for you somewhere on the other side," Carl suggested. He took out a map. "You know, give you a couple of hours or so? I imagine you are comfortable in the forest, no?"

"Why, cause I'm a native?" Delroy responded.

"Why, yeah?" Carl said as if it was obvious. "The story you told us when you first got in the car involved you out roaming in the forest."

Scratching his head, Delroy had to laugh. He had never smoked this much weed before. He was beginning to wonder if this was all a dream.

"Oh yeah. I forgot," he said. "Yeah, you could drop me off close to the border. I will listen to the wind and it will guide me," he said, pounding his chest with his fist.

"Okay then, great," Carl replied, opening the map. "We were planning on crossing over here at Kingsgate, and through to Eastport. There is a river that runs along the south end of town; if you follow that across the border we can wait for you here at the Howlins State picnic park. It looks like a couple hour hike at least, so we'll just chill there without creating any suspicions. After that, it's just a hop, skip, and jump until we meet up with a fellow dude who lives in Bonner's Ferry. We can rest at his place for the night. Apparently it is an acreage, and the Monk vouched for him, saying that he was a solid cat." Carl showed

Delroy the map and they went over the plan one more time before finding a good spot to let him out.

Armed with seven joints, two liters of fresh water, and a tuna fish sandwich, Delroy watched the Toyota speed off towards the border town, happy to be in the company of nature once again. He located the river by listening to its roar, stepped into the woods, and carefully began climbing down the steep embankment. As he neared the river he could hear other sounds, voices in particular, and right away Delroy went into defensive mode. Making it through this journey without any human encounters had been a big part of the plan, and already he was being tested.

"Why Great Spirit?" he asked the sky. In answer, thunder roared in the near distance, and the once blue skies began to cover over quickly with a fast moving cloud bank.

"Oh, I see how it is!" he muttered as he crept slowly along. To his credit Delroy was a real natural woodsman. His ancestors would have been proud of his stalking abilities as he edged closer and closer to the source of the voices. Only twenty meters now from the river, he could see two figures standing along the bank, fishing rods in their hands, casting out into the fast moving waters. With no way of avoiding a meeting with the two, Delroy emerged from the bush with his right hand raised in the traditional greeting of peace. On cue, rain began to fall, a few drops at first then a slow trickle that edged forward with the native man.

The fishermen looked over at their new guest with apprehension, for he had one hand raised aggressively, and by the way he was walking across the very rocky bank, he appeared to be drunk.

"Not another drunk Indian," George spoke to Luke.

"Jesus Christ, can't these motherfuckers go a day without hitting the bottle?" Luke replied to George.

"Hello there!" Delroy called out.

George looked to Luke. Luke looked to George.

"What is it that you're looking for?" George called out in reply.

Delroy realized that he needed a story. He didn't

want to raise suspicions with the border so close. He thought hard and fast, the weed helping him formulate something plausible.

"I'm thinking about doing some fishing in these parts. Was just wondering if the catching is good?"

Luke shot George a suspicious glance. George returned the look.

"Ah, nothing biting around here." George replied just as his line went taut from a hit. From the way the rod bent over it was a big hit at that. "Ah, must've snagged a rock." He lied.

Delroy was almost upon them and the rain now started wetting the two men who looked up in disgust at the sky. The forecast had called for clear skies over the next six days. Goddamned weathermen were good for nothing.

Feeling nervous Delroy reached into his pocket and pulled out a pre-rolled joint, deciding a peace offering was in order.

"Hey man, you can keep that hippie shit to yourself. Not everyone in British Colombia approves of smoking that brain rot." This time it was Luke who had spoken. George nodded in approval.

Quickly stashing the joint back into his pocket, Delroy decided to start walking up and around the two. He felt it best not to say anything else, and just to pass as quickly as possible. Apparently these were the kind of white men that made it difficult for his people to get a fair shake. Knowing their kind, the next thing he could expect was to be chased off into the river, to drown. One less redskin around to dodge paying taxes.

George and Luke both watched the native man closely as he circled around them and then made his way further downstream.

"Goddamn drunks and drug addicts," Luke griped.

"That's what the world is reduced to Luke," George said, struggling to reel in the fish. "Next thing you know we'll be praying to Allah."

"Not this asshole."

"Or I."

"I don't think our boy there is really interested in fishing," Luke said, giving Delroy a sidelong glance. "I bet he's heading for the border. Goddamn dope fiend gives the rest of our province a bad name. Watch my gear for a moment. I'm going back up to the road where I can get a signal on my phone."

Chapter 15

'Dude for a day, happy for a lifetime.'

Sunnyside Grove was the kind of hell that inspired writers to dream of ways to die early on in life. No one would willingly want to be subjected to regimented care, would they? Dining hours, scheduled activities, scheduled doctor's visits, etc., etc, etc. Life devolving back to when one was dependent, like a child. A place where caregivers talk to you like you were a child, using special voices they created when communicating to you, asking you questions that weren't really questions at all, but in fact were statements of what was planned for you. Example, "Is it okay if we put you in the bath now?" The caregivers were on a timed schedule, and they were going to put you in the bath regardless if you wanted to go or not. They would try telling you how much better you would feel after one, lying in bed, your wet head getting your pillow wet, making you uncomfortable for the rest of your nap time. Everything was planned, and everything was non-negotiable for the most part. No wonder children threatened their parents with, "We'll put you in a home." In this western world, old people were put out to pasture. People in general had lost sight of the potential, of using all that wisdom to help others who lacked the necessary wisdom to be useful in society.

Loki had left Odin angry and feeling very vengeful. There was a time when Odin would have dismissed the boy's mischievous ways, knowing that the other Asgard would balance out the natural flow. This trickery, though, was outright betrayal. The boy had conspired with other fiendish souls, helping to convince humans that there was only one god! What kind of crazy notion is that? Who in their right mind would believe that there would be a singularity operating in a universe, all alone, with no equal, or with no one else in which to share the experience? There wasn't one single example of a truly unique person, force, particle, dimension, anything that would give people this notion. There was always a twin somewhere: like Zeus, Odin's brother. Two cut from the same cloth, with the similar goals and desires. Another being who could appreciate one's work.

One god! Ludicrous.

Undoing the damage that had been done for sixteen hundred years was going to be difficult, but Loki, in his selfish need to boast, had given away clues in which to right some wrongs. This modern world had ways of allowing people of like mind to connect instantaneously, and Odin knew that if he could find people who still believed in the old ways, that he would be able to convince them that he was their god. Their faith would restore him in his glory. A god's power came from his followers. Gather the sheep, and tend to them, and your powers would return and grow. All Odin needed was someone to get him out of this god-forsaken place.

Serendipity walked into the room just as Odin completed that thought. It was her first day on the job, and the other health care aides decided to let the newbie have her first fun fill trip with the crazed loon in room 707. Her dreadlocks were tied back, her nose ring removed during working hours, and her sandals were safely stowed in her locker. They gave her little warning, snickering as they tended to do.

The usual grumbles arose as the door opened into Odin's room. A visit from a nursing aid almost always meant some kind of disruption to his world. They floated around liked they owned his space, and treated him like a child. In his mind he could already picture his retribution upon all the people who had thrown away their parents. When he regained his strength he would free those who had been trapped in this artificial little world, (except that heinous lot who actually looked forward to pub night); they deserved to be here. Their treacherous voices should never be unleashed on Earth again. Better to keep it contained.

The new nursing aid was much different than the other lot. The others were all short, foreign women who spoke with thick accents. This one was of European decent, perhaps even Scandinavian, though he had never seen hair worn in the style she was wearing. Blue eyes, strong broad shoulders and the type of hips one would expect from a potential mate that could birth a future generation. She wore glass spectacles over her eyes and sauntered around the room as if she held no care.

"Obviously you have not been warned about my temper," Odin announced. He began to assume that the young woman was paying no attention to him on purpose, as she puttered around tidying up. He groaned and grunted as she completely ignored him.

"Okay now, woman," he went on. "The house midgets usually can't stop their chattering. They roll me around the room and disturb my peace. Why are you trying to be invisible when I can plainly see you?"

Serendipity stopped and smiled.

"My grand papa prefers to be left alone," she said. "I was doing my best to do my job without disturbing you. I've got to feed the monkey and you don't seem to appreciate having company."

"Feed the monkey? What does that mean?" Odin wondered. "The last thing I need is one of those little creatures roaming around in here."

Another smile from the girl.

"I need to earn my keep," she explained. "Make money, bones, clams, whatever you call them. Support myself. That's what it means."

One of the rituals was, of course, the tossing of the sheets and the bed being made. Odin slipped back into silence watching the young lady as she continued feeding her monkey from the comfort of his mobile chair. As she bent over to pick up a pillow lying on the floor, her shirt hiked up enough to reveal a tattoo on the small of her back. A Norse Rune to be precise.

Odin's eyes lit up, a sudden gush of strength filled his limbs. "Are you a Valkyrie, lass?"

"Excuse me?" Serendipity asked.

"The marking on your back. The word Valkyrie."

"Oh, that," she said, continuing with her work. "I've always pictured myself as a strong woman, unafraid to walk side by side with any man. I loved the way it looked in the parlor, and was sold on it when the artist explained what it meant. So in some way I guess that I am, but I haven't carried anyone off a battlefield yet."

Now standing yet trembling, Odin said very calmly:

"Once your kind served the halls of Valhalla, and did so with honor. It is time for the feast to begin once again, and I am requiring your services once more, Maiden of the Spear. Too long have I slept, and too much has happened in the meanwhile. You must help me get out of this wretched place and find my son so I can lift the veil that has been thrown over the eyes of the people. Will you accept this charge?"

How does one answer such a bold statement without wondering if the marble bag had just spilled its contents? On one hand, Serendipity was responsible for the care of this man and others on this floor, so should she just break this illusion he was conjuring here and now, or had she made a break through where others had failed? Was this a chance for her to help the poor old man finally come to terms with his life? Her silence was drawing concern as his face twitched.

"Exactly what is it you require of me?" She asked politely.

"I need you to renew your vows to me, Odin, father of the gods, and help me find more of the faithful who still inhabit this world," he proclaimed. "I've heard that this internet may be the key, and that it is protected by a password. This would be your first quest. After that, when my strength has grown we shall leave this foreboding limbo, and save the people of Earth."

"Do you have a tablet?" Serendipity considered this first request as a modest by most accounts. The rest of his requirements were a bit delusional though.

"I possess only what you see. I am in need of your

strength. Your reward will be beyond your wildest imagination."

Like a spark that can never be contained, Serendipity pictured herself roaming a field in a mountain hollow with a log cabin at her back. Here, far away from the trappings of society, she could work on her poetry, sing at the top of her lungs, never wear an accursed bra again. She might have a love, she might not. It did not matter to her.

"If it is freedom from these wretches, I can give you that." Odin said in all seriousness. He had been able to get a brief glimpse of her dream. He smiled.

Not knowing what to say to that, Serendipity nodded, confused.

"I have a tablet in my locker," she said. "I will bring it to you on my break, and will show you how to navigate the web."

Chapter 16

'It never gets easier without a change in perspective.'

"What do you mean, I need some piece of identification? My name is Thor, peasant man."

The two Boston police officers who had pulled over the Yugo looked at each other, wondering if this was about to escalate. The Russian was already spread eagle on the hood, his wallet opened up, his money falling one coin at a time on to the pavement.

"Sir, if you do not start co-operating, I'm afraid that we are going to have to restrain you!" Officer One announced in a very stern tone.

"Restrain me? You? Ha!" As angry as he was, Thor found this very amusing indeed. Both men were no taller than his chest, and though they looked big and bulky, he guessed that it was their armor that made them look so.

"One last time, sir," Office Two said, taking the lead this time in trying to intimidate the big fellow. "Identification, please, and hands on the car."

Perhaps he wasn't as quick as he once was, not to mention the effect all the beer had on his present state, but Thor reached out grabbing cop number two and in one motion flung the man easily through the air at number one who had no time to raise his arms in defense. The ensuing entanglement gave Thor enough time to climb over the pile of men and clang their heads together with a sickening thud. The lights went out quickly.

The Russian, never questioning, quickly picked up his belongings and put them back his pockets. He motioned for Thor to return to the passenger seat of the Yugo as he grabbed a bottle of vodka from the trunk. He tore a strip of cloth off rag that he used for checking the oil, and stuck into the opening of the bottle. Next he lit the rag and threw the bottle at the cop car. With a loud whoosh, flames engulfed the vehicle. He hopped back into the small car, and turned the ignition. Old faithful started on the first turn, and the two fugitives sped off down the road.

"Good thing they never had chance to check my ID," the Russian smiled. "We ditch the car when we get far enough away. The license plate number will get them nowhere. I took it off a parked car at the shopping mall."

Thor smiled. He was feeling alive. His first little taste of battle had awakened a thirst within.

"They act like big men but crumple like sheep."

"You threw, man, very easily. You are feeling good, no?"

"Yes, very good, Russian. The beer has loosened up some of the tethers holding me in this weak body. Let us go now and find these dudes you spoke of."

Tyler Johnson was perhaps the luckiest man in Massachusetts that night. The police car that had pulled him over was now in flames, and the two cops who were about to discover the smell of weed emanating from his person, were now unconscious on the ground. To add to all of this he now had a video of a man throwing a police officer as if he was a bag of trash destined for the curb. For a split second there as the big man was hefting the cop with one arm, there was a peculiar glow around him and his features shifted slightly. Until he could get it on a bigger screen, he wasn't really sure what he had just witnessed, but he was just thankful that he wasn't going to be spending the night in jail.

The Yugo ended up in the harbor with a prayer spoken in Russian. As the car disappeared into the gloom, bubbles rose up, a last gasp by old faithful. A small tear held its place in the Russian's eye for he knew that it would be very hard to find a Yugo, mind you a, reliable one, ever again.

"Your metal chariot meant a lot to you?"

"Yes, Thor," the Russian said, sadly watching the last of the bubbles surface and disappear. "It was a symbol of all that was great about my country. So much different than America. Now in Russia there are foreign cars, foreign businesses, and foreign attitudes. No one remembers the struggle of the people. Now thugs rule the country with an iron fist. Men of money who drink power from Coca-Cola cans and wear blue jeans to formal dinners. The Yugo was a symbol of how everyone could afford a car and that no one had to look more important than another."

"Your nation will be freed, just like all others when the gods return, Russian," vowed Thor. "We will vanquish these usurpers and let the people remember a time when their plight was known by those who would see justice done."

"When you do vanquish the evil men," the Russian advised. "You must remember that the snake has many heads. There will be those who will wish to take over as soon as the others are removed. Such is the way of man. There is no shortage of power-seeking snake men."

The night disappeared into a morning fog. The city was hidden under a blanket of gray gloom. Sounds of life, forever present, were muffled by the thick air, and only the rising sun could part the skies again. Thor stared out of the Russian's apartment window. Looking down on the street below realizing for the first time that he was not meant to know this place. His place should have been secured in Valhalla, long ago, with his brothers and sisters. He had defeated the mighty serpent and had died on the field in his memory, but another memory also arose. This memory showed him falling to the ground, his strength fleeing, his awareness disappearing into the ether. In this place a fear had gripped his soul, it had terrified beyond, and sent him into shock.

How could it have been possible for a god of his stature to succumb to such a fate? How could the Asgard just disappear?

"Well, I have message from a man in Minnesota," the Russian said happily. "He claims that the faith is strong in the Twin Cities. Many there worship the Vikings, and would welcome you, but like all assholes today they want some proof of your claims. I told him that we would make video and send to him. From there he could show others."

"Whatever is needed, Russian. Make it happen." Thor was in a dark place. His head had sunk into his hands as this memory of being torn from the world and into a place of perpetual darkness haunted him. Limbo was worse than the Seven Hells. It would drive you insane faster, and leave you perpetually wondering, "What if?"

"Okay comrade. We need to show them something that only a Norse god could know or do."

Pulling his head away from his hands Thor, reached out with his mind to Mjolnor, desperately trying to find the magical hammer, and to call it back to his person. He felt a slight tingle but nothing else.

"Seven Hells!" Thor bellowed loudly. It reverberated through the walls and woke up Mrs. Karzak next store, who nearly had a heart attack as she thought for sure the world was ending.

"Until I regain my power, how am I to show these mortals that I am, who I am?"

"I think I have something," the Russian called Thor over to show him a video in which a man throws a police officer with one arm fifteen feet through the air, and into another officer. In the midst of the event a slight glow surrounded the giant, a faerie light of sorts.

"Well, that is me! In this body! Seven Hells, how is it possible? Is this some kind of crystal that shows the past?"

"No, Thor," the Russian explained. "Someone videotaped the incident with the police yesterday and posted it on YouTube. It is getting many hits, and many comments. I will send this man in Minnesota a link, and tell him that here is your proof."

"Do what you must, Russian, but I am growing weary of this," Thor grumbled, rolling his eyes at the ceiling. "These Minnesota Vikings do not sound like they have descended from the blood lines of old. I fear that in our absence they have become frail, and weak minded like this America that you have told me so much about."

The response was quick and to the point. The

Minnesota Vikings would not take any interest in a criminal incident that was obviously embellished after the fact by adding in the glow, the distance the cop flew, and the voice over Norwegian accent, of a man who was of obvious Irish decent. It was of their opinion that the man in the video should turn himself in immediately to the police and pray for mercy.

"These are not real Vikings!" Thor roared. "Who in the world would wear purple and claim to be warriors! I thought you said that this 'Dude' was living by the old ways?"

"Well, I always assumed," the Russian furrowed his brows. "He talks about Vikings all the time on the chat line. I did not know that he meant the football team. The good news is that the video has given us some real potential to find believers, oh mighty God of Thunder and War. I posted your real identity on the video, and many have replied believing it to be you. If we could just get another video of you performing another feat, then I am sure we could get you the followers you need."

"You'll have to explain this Facebook thing to me again," Thor scowled. "I am having a hard time understanding the concept. I now have a place where I virtually exist?"

"That is correct. And you are starting to get followers," the Russian exclaimed. "Soon, with another video some might actually believe it to be the real you, and then the virtual you, will become the physical you."

He smiled at his thunderous friend.

"You see? Simple!"

Chapter 17

'When you shine a light, aim it away from your eyes. You may not like what you see.'

If you don't like the weather in Washington State, then just wait ten minutes and it will change. Of course, that could be said of anywhere, and has been, as long as toothpicks have been mouth accessories. To the north, a bank of dark clouds held close to the border threatening to cross over any time soon. To the south clear blue skies truly believed that nothing would change. To the east, the rising of the moon meant that all was as should be, and to the west…well, no one really cared what the east thought.

Howlins State Picnic Park was empty of people except for three members of the Order of the Righteous Dude. They sat at a picnic table, aged, dirty, and infested with small black ants that ran around in circles aimlessly. The passing of many birds marked the top planks, right beside carved initials of lost lovers. Perhaps the park was just forgotten about, or perhaps there was no funding for upkeep, as weeds grew in the cracks in the aged pavement that meandered around the giant trees.

"I wouldn't want a park named after me if it looked like this," Carl commented, flicking a black ant off of his arm.

"No need to worry about a park being named after you," Willow snickered. As much as she wanted to open up a little more to her companions, she had that feeling that when their paths separated, they would never cross again. Investing in that kind of future seemed pointless.

"I'd rather have a boat named after me. Or a pub," Julius exclaimed.

"The only thing that will get named after any of us will be our children," Carl proclaimed loudly. He stood upon the table as he did so, his arms held out wide. "The path of the humble Dudeist Monk will keep us from seeking out the limelight. Make us shadows in the darkness, and most likely forgettable characters in any tale."

"Now you see Carl, that's just like you opinion man," Julius countered. "I mean someday I am going to singing to thousands of bloodthirsty woman who'll want to tear off my clothes, and ravage me right there on stage. When my band, 'Suns of the Fodder' release our debut album we are going to take the world by storm!"

He performed an amazing impromptu riff on his air guitar.

"Rock on, dude," Carl laughed, sitting back down beside Julius.

It was easy for Willow to drift off when the two boys started talking to each other. Holding the staff of the Wandering Abider had become a source of comfort for her. The aged wood, said to have been carved from an arbutus tree, felt like a natural extension of her arm. She wandered around in circles, using the walking stick to support her weight even though she didn't need it. It had been held by a humble monk and a mad man, and she wondered which path lay in her future. The call of abandoning society was great at times, it was reflected in her drawings and in her poetry, yet when she sang, she sang for others to hear. Open mic night at Winnipeg's Lost Libido Lounge was the one thing she had looked forward to every week. Tonight would have been her thirtieth appearance.

With the voices of the guys in the background, Willow's circles grew larger and larger until she came to the edge of the river. The sun was starting to go down and a cool mountain breeze was teasing the leaves on the trees that lined the banks. The river bubbled and gurgled against the sea of boulders that lined the bottom of the bed. A raven, with a six foot wing span was staring at the girl curiously from the grass. It had no intention of moving as her circle drew nearer, its head just tilted so one eye could fix upon her.

"Something is wrong boys," she called out. "Delroy

should have been here at least an hour ago." Perhaps it was the raven's appearance that filled her words with confidence; regardless, deep down she had felt it. The natives had their spirit allies, and perhaps this was the missing man's.

In a jail cell one can never quite feel comfortable. Too stark, too impersonal and far too cold, even on a warm day. Perhaps all that concrete held in the cold, or perhaps it was filled with lost hope which would provide no compassion. The flickering of the florescent lighting would give any person a headache within hours, and the hum from the bulbs would make you want to scratch your skin.

Patiently Delroy waited on the cold bench, his cheeks growing numb. They had taken everything from him, including his lucky eagle feather which had been braided into his hair. When he had complained about it, the officer cited it as a suicide hazard, along with his belt and shoe laces. Why anyone in the world would commit suicide for being caught crossing the border illegally, made no sense to the native man, but not much did when it came to the white man's world.

He had hoped that his status as a native would have lent him some leniency in the matter, for he claimed his people were not bound by borders, and should be allowed to roam freely across the land of their forefathers, but the police in this state had been fighting a war on drugs for so many years now, even a couple of joints got the hairs to stand up on the back of their trigger fingers.

"But it is legal here. Your leaders made it law," Delroy protested.

"Only if purchased here by American citizens, or guests with a valid passport boy," the cop spat. "You can't just bring your own dope to our party. No siree. We've had enough of you Canadian criminals flooding our borders with your bud."

The angry police officer had left him in this cell alone for at least four hours now, according to the lengthening shadows coming from the small window. His ride would have left the park by now, away on their quest, and he would be cursed to suffer this increasing bad vibe that he had been exposed to.

"Well, we can't wait around forever," Carl was saying as they made their way to the Camry. "We should go back to the border and see if he was picked up." Glancing at Willow, he hinted, "And if a comely, innocent-looking girl was to, oh, I don't know, saunter in and ask, I imagine the police might be a little more forthcoming with info."

"Yeah, yeah," Willow said, not even bothering to argue the point. When they had entered the U.S., the two guards stationed there had stared at her during the entire process. It made her wonder if they had ever seen a female before, by the way they became so easily distracted.

It took a whole of two minutes for Willow to emerge from the border station. Her look said it all. A frown never lies, unless of course it is hiding something.

"Well we are back to three," she sighed, sliding onto the backseat and shutting the door. "Delroy isn't going anywhere. They picked him up crossing the border with illegal drugs. According to the desk clerk, it can get you up to fifteen years in prison."

"But it's not illegal here, anymore." Carl protested.

"I know that, but do you think I am going to start arguing with them, get them suspicious enough to come out here and search this car? Do you have a receipt for that pound of weed you are carrying? Do you think they will treat you any different if they assume you smuggled it over the border?"

"No, but Delroy?"

"We can't help him now," Willow said, fatalistically. "I'm thinking that perhaps we are better off without someone carrying that much negative energy around anyways." She looked at Julius and Carl turned around in their seats to look at her. "We are on a quest, and we are going to have to make some big girl decisions, boys," she said. "So pull up your socks and let's leave Delroy to his own fate. He would have tried finding the Mad Hermit, regardless of our paths intersecting. Perhaps he will find a way out of this."

"Wow, that's cold, dude." Julius observed.

Willow could understand that. She would even normally think that, but she knew that someone in this trio was going to have to be thinking clearly, and these two were probably always going to have their heads stuck up their asses.

The drive was quiet. Leaving Delroy to his fate hung heavy over the heads of Order, a bad vibe had settled in. In all honesty, there was really nothing they could do, and if karma, or the fates had any good will left they would find a way to help the man.

The road to Bonner's Ferry wound along the wide valley, rimmed with snow topped mountains that reached into the sky. The sun disappeared quickly over the western range, and soon a vast field of stars filled the night sky. Soon they would meet up with the man Nuna had affectionately called Bear, and with the bad taste in their mouths they could not wait. A long-standing member of the Dude network, Bear was said to have more body hair than a wooly mammoth, and the ability to survive for days on end in the wilderness without the trappings of modern society to aid him.

A real survivalist, he was, with the spirit of the mountain men of old flowing through his veins.

Book II

Beyond Dudetopia and Reality

Chapter 1

'Sometimes it takes a little more compassion and understanding, and a little less opinion.'

The reports coming out of the First Union Media Corp., were not exactly positive. In fact they rarely ever were. In today's media blitz, civil unrest in several of America's most populated cities was the hot topic, along with who in the world hated America more. A few small riots had broken out, looting and property destruction usurping the force to affect peaceful change. Militarized police forces were marshaled. Carefully placed cameramen captured the mob mentality spreading like clouds of teargas in the streets. The leading causes of the riots were, of course, police brutality, racial inequality, and economic despair. It was all a good distraction, intentional of course, and quickly changed the focus of TV-shaped reality from the climate change issue, which was gaining too much momentum as of late.

Deflate the balloon, and then let them blow it back up all over again.

In the Middle East the kettle had been boiled dry for so long that even the plastic handle had melted off. War had spread across the imperialistically imposed imaginary borders of Iraq into Syria, Jordan, and even Turkey was dealing with unrest. With no shortage of bullets, guns, or tank shells, the fire of rage was burning, destroying the cradle of civilization.

But for a fortunate few, it wasn't bombs and guns, but business that was booming.

Between the Chinese, Russians and Americans, profits soared higher and higher as the merchants of death exacted their toll for the weapons they produced.

An outbreak of Ebola along the Ivory coast of

Africa lasted long enough for the foreign oil and mining conglomerate, Mega Energy, to buy up huge swaths of land in the regions thought to be affected by the disease. It always amazed some in the Star Chamber what a viral scare can do to real estate prices.

While the folks at home worried about what Russia was doing on the Crimean peninsula, China had its hands busy with a series of natural disasters that had taken a toll on its finances, slowing its economic growth by a quarter percent, which to western interests was seen a positive sign.

The Prince of Venice, Francisco Vocelli, lounged in the sun on his personal cruise liner, sipping a glass of fairy tears extracted from the last of the mystical beings he had held hostage in one of the below decks. With nothing but blue skies covering the Mediterranean Sea, he smiled watching his favorite concubine oil down his favorite prime time actress. It was a good day for the man who could have just about anything in the world he desired. Everything except the original knives used by the senate to cut down Julius Caesar. Pity. Rupert refused to sell them to him, but he was expecting him as a guest aboard his yacht soon, and would make him another offer. Perhaps this time he would offer up the magic bullet that had killed JFK, to entice the offer.

"Rupert, surely you must believe that in times like these that last thing we need are people expecting the government to do anything about anything." The Prince offered a glass of tears to his guest.

"Oh, not to worry Francisco. The last thing the citizens of the U.S., will ever believe is that their government is capable of doing anything. They swallowed that hook, line, and sinker with our boy Reagan." Rupert savored the sweet fairy tears he sipped from the glass. "Today, they all know that everyone in there is bought and paid for. It's no secret, which makes it so wonderful. What they don't realize is that the people that bought and paid for those people, are bought and paid for twice down the line."

They both laughed as they toasted the good weather and admired the glistening nude curves of the prime time actress.

"As you keep assuring me," the Prince said. "These policies have not worked so well over here you know. People in Europe, well, they still seem to think that their opinions matter." This caused both men to laugh again. "The way to do it with these old world countries is to create these economic unions, let them get angry at the countries not pulling their weight, and then let them have social referendums which really do nothing but stave off the banks for a couple months. After a while the wine will start to flow again, they will break out the cheese, and grow complacent. While that is happening we can milk the poor a little more, increase lending and criticize America for not setting a good example."

"Which brings me to my visit," Rupert said, clearing his throat. "America will be pulling out of the Middle East as we discussed, now that the unrest is more volatile than ever. We will need to point the Eagle in a new direction long enough to ensure that this civil war idea catches hold in the Deep South. I've been thinking that perhaps it's time to look at North Korea again now that China is in the midst of some fortunate and timely disasters. I think if we sank one more ship close to Seoul, perhaps one filled with school children, we could really sell it. By the time they invest what little credit they have left into another war, we will have the south playing good Ol' Dixie all the way to the White House."

"Are the others on board?"

"Well, of course, they are Prince. Even if it turned out to be a complete disaster, and let's say the boat doesn't sink, or there are lots of survivors, we can still sell it to the common morons who watch my news programs. We'll even get volunteers to go over there and finish the job their grandfathers couldn't finish."

"What about China, though," the Prince asked, peevishly. "They haven't exactly been interested in our vintage as of late."

"Well, we thought of that too," Rupert rejoined. "Perhaps it's time to give them Greenland. You know they have been looking long and hard for more real estate. We can make that happen I'm certain with the right block of cheese thrown the Danes way."

"Sounds solid to me, Rupert."

"Good, then I will count you as in."

In his Rolls Royce Manuel Juarez Ricardo Lupe Fernandez received the good news and was glad that everybody was on board with the North Korean proposal. With the dominoes falling with each state that passed more lenient drug laws, the revenue flow had to be subsidized. Nothing filled a wallet faster than a war, and with many former American factories now located in Mexico or overseas, the promise of falling bombs would bring the promise of rising profits. He held major stakes in almost every manufacturing company in his country, smiling every time someone gave the okay to fire.

The people of his country knew him as only a humanitarian, a force for change and for the removal of corruption. Little did they know that his cartel was now more powerful than any other in the western hemisphere, and that even the Colombian's and the Guatemalan's were paying tribute. He had people in place who acted as the bosses of the Los Amigo's, but every boss had a boss and he was the king. While others suffered the contempt of his government and the people, he collected respect like little trophies, using his influence to position his legitimate business into the most advantageous position.

In his little circle of five, he was perhaps the wealthiest, and could legitimately claim to own a country.

The village in which he chose to live, St. Juan, had the best living conditions for even the poorest residents of anywhere in Latin America. The streets were paved, housing costs were kept low, and all utilities were free. A broadband network was established to give all homes and businesses free internet, and even the grocery stores were subsidized to provide the lowest prices. Having been born and raised in the village, located one hundred miles north of Mexico City, Manuel had never left his heritage and past behind. As his fortune increased so did the well-being of St.

Juan.

There was no crime; the private militia that policed the village never had trouble with residents. Occasionally an outsider might cause trouble, but they learned quickly that they fucked with the wrong town. Working for this policing force was considered a retirement gig. The wall around St. Juan was monitored twenty-four/seven by the most sophisticated surveillance system money could buy. Even the Pentagon security staff had visited, learning how to improve things back in D.C. As his car passed, people waved. No one went hungry, no one lived in fear of violence.

"So tell me once again Roberto," he said on his phone in the back of his Rolls (he always added the "o" to the end of Robert Klein's name), "just how am I going to profit from buying bad loans?"

"Well to put it simply," said the voice of his fellow Star Chamber associate, "the governments in the countries where these companies are, cannot afford to allow the bankruptcies to go through without devastating effects to the overall economy. We are talking about corporations that employ over twenty thousand plus people. I've been assured that when the loans go bust, bail out packages will be offered, and we will get back all the money we invested plus the interest owed. Now because the loans will fall in to default, we will also be able to apply late penalties of two to three percent per month, which when you do the math will bring the actual interest on the loan up to the twelve to thirteen percentage range."

"I like those numbers Roberto. Who are we looking at targeting?"

"Well you know I have always been a big fan of GM, and their quarterly report is due at the end of the week. Things are still looking bleak in Detroit. Another sector I've been looking at is the Oil and Gas sector. We've got the Dutch ready to flood the market, which will drive the cost per barrel down dramatically to force Russia into returning to the bargaining table. This will also hurt Canadian production, Venezuela, and the U.S., where the governments are heavily invested and they will do what they can to alleviate the pressure created on their economies by opening up their pocket books. We've earmarked the most likely candidates and are just waiting on some papers to be signed."

"How will all this factor in with the North Korean agenda?"

"Perfectly, Manuel," Klein said with wonkish delight. "After the bailouts and subsidies, we will capitalize on low stock prices, wait for the bombs to start falling. GM, as an example, will likely convert some of its factories into war-time production. Oil will go up beyond the hundred and fifty dollar mark and we'll be poised to sell off the day before those commie bastards surrender."

"Beautiful, my friend!" Manuel said as the Rolls approached his villa. "Almost poetic in its symmetry. Count me in for a hundred billion."

Chapter 2

'Sincerity will irritate those who know on no such thing.'

Knowing the future and not being able to do anything about it could drive you mad. At least people would believe that you are mad, when you confessed to such a thing. No one wants to believe that things have already been set in stone. For most, the future should be a wild, mystical thing that will hold hope and promise. If you knew exactly what was going to happen would you really see it in any kind of promising light?

So the Mad Hermit sat across from the stranger who had come to Reality with the Pootles. Refusing to allow those parasites anywhere near his site, he convinced the soap box speaker to leave them behind. Left-Handed Larry was busy stoking the fire and smoking a cigarette he had secretly received from one of the kids named Corey. Above them, on the bridge, a mass of people had gathered to march on the city center to demand even more sweeping political changes. They had the right to smoke their stash, now they wanted it to be pesticide free. The target was the large multi-billion dollar corporation, Masseedo. Not only did they sell the pesticides to grow their genetically engineered crops, they also sold the fertilizer that ensured growth success. Without purchasing all three products, one could not use the other. With this policy they held many poorer countries hostage, countries that no longer received competitive bids from other companies which also dealt with such things on a global scale. Masseedo had bought out the bulk of their competition, then destroyed all but the office spaces.

"The people are rising." The stranger spoke.

"They are always rising and then they go back to sleep," Gerald replied. "For most of them, they will become bored, start looting and then burning. Happens all the time.

They come in peace and leave in a wake of destruction."

"Why is that, do you think?"

"People for the most part have the attention span of children," Gerald replied. "They get excited, start to participate, then soon wander off when they see something sparkly. Just look at the occupy movements. How long did they persist after the first occupation? Sure they held their ground for a while, but in the end there were no real changes made, except for giving us the '1% vs. 99 %' phrase. Otherwise, superficial promises. When you allow the poisoned tree to continue to grow you are going to keep getting poisoned fruit. If they took half the energy and desire they exhibit in protesting, got the education needed to infiltrate and rise high in the ranks, then they might affect change. That kind of persistence, and diligence, though, lacks in the youth today. Only the promise of love, fame or wealth brings it out."

The stranger removed a book from the inside pocket of his coat. It was rough looking journal bound in fake leather. He opened it to a page marked with a pink ribbon and began to read.

"As the hopes of the common man fall into the void of hopelessness, new ideals will arise. No longer will the people look to heavens above for their answers. No longer will they rely on the words of mystics to get them through. They will look for the common person who speaks their thoughts and lives like them. This will renew their hope."

"And your point is?" The Mad Hermit asked.

"My point is, Gerald the Herald, that these people have been motivated by the common person's thoughts and desires. They are no longer acting out the will of governments, lords, and religious folk. What began in the Sixties has continued to flourish, and everyday more and more people turn towards a brighter future free from this tyranny."

Gerald chuckled and Larry joined in. They shared another sip of whiskey and then offered some to the stranger. As the fire in the metal can grew stronger, the shadows around the three lengthened.

"Let's say for one moment that these movements are genuine, which may be the case," Gerald said, watching the fire dance. "You are still dealt the hand that has the laziest card in the deck, the joker. When you have this card in your hand, you, at some point in time, are going to be distracted by the show it puts on for you. In addition, the joker card will become distracted easily by the show the enemy will put on for you, distracting you from the hidden agenda. The secret motives that are never clearly defined. What you think is the real problem, rarely is." The reflection of the fire was dancing in his eyes. "Example: you ask your girlfriend if everything is okay. She tells you she is fine with you having a friendly relationship with your ex. Guess what? She'll never be okay with it no matter what she tells you. There will be fights, and it might be about the garbage pail being over filled, but I'll bet you a thousand dollars that it's still about the ex. You see, very few people can move on when they hide the truth. The enemy knows this. The enemy plays this card every time. When you think you should be protesting GMOs, you should really be protesting banking in general. When there is an unjust war, the people of this great country should hold a general strike so that the resources being used to build the weapons suddenly disappear. Up there, those people, they are doing exactly what the enemy wants them to do. Shares in this seed company may drop, but guess who buys them up? The same people who own the company. They sold stakes to increase the size of their business, set up these little stock market coups, then buy them all back at a lower price, and effectively have more control over what they do. Sure they might make a few concessions to appease the crowd, but they will never change the fruit they produce."

    The stranger was gazing into the flames, feeling the heat. "So having seen the future, Hermit," he said finally. "What do you suggest?"

    "The visions are long gone, and thankfully, written down and handed off to someone who will take better care of them me. As for the memories, well let's just say that a little whiskey, a little smoke, and this strange desire to forget it all has worked pretty well. I might not remember how she moved underneath me, but I do remember that she moved."

"Like yourself, I have been gifted with visions of the future, Hermit," the stranger offered. "I have seen the evil, entrenched in a tower in Atlanta, sitting around a five pointed star. Here at this table lives are discarded as if one discards a paper napkin after finishing a plate full of succulent, sauce covered ribs. In this chamber, the fortunes of nations are decided in between which musician is due to grace the top of the charts, and how to dumb the populace down even more. Behind the veil, there are five more veils, erected to keep the spotlight on others. To make hated men out of martyrs. To raise puppets instead of leaders, and to keep the world off balance. Haven't you ever noticed that the pendulum never swings back?"

The voices of the protesters on the bridge of above could be heard now. Chanting, hollering and clapping, colliding into one epic confusion of noise. Gerald looked up at the struts supporting the concrete and smiled.

"You should really try and tell me something I don't know, if you are going to share my fire and drink," he said. "Larry here doesn't say much. He shares silence with me. He lets me speak my thoughts aloud and never questions why. You, though, have so far given me nothing. This chamber you speak of was the first vision I ever had. Everything else you have said, part of the same dream. Now, stranger, tell me why you are really here."

Chapter 3

'When I focus my positive light, it burns through negative shielding.'

As fast as someone can think of something, someone else is posting it online in another part of the world. The connected consciousness was, of course, still in its infancy, but having a world wide web had helped it along tremendously. Language barriers, a thing of the past. Physical distances, not a factor. As it continues to grow, the more the people become aware.

"Now I know why this is a thing to be feared," Odin grimaced as he watched Serendipity give him a tutorial on using the IPad.

"Oh, there is nothing to fear here, um, Odin, sir." It felt uncomfortable giving into his delusions, Serendipity thought, but calling him by the name he preferred was a key to gaining his trust. With a little patience, she would help the old man adjust, and hopefully help him learn to find some joy in life again.

"Ha! Nothing to fear you say," Odin declared. "I can tell you that the evil that infests this world will look upon this network with disdain, and will do everything in its power to gain control of it. In fact I imagine they have already set many measures in place that would allow them to shut it down at a moment's notice if people begin to realize its full potential."

"Well, the internet is the last bastion of freedom, Odin," Serendipity said. "It isn't controlled. Monitored? Yes, but it is still relatively untouched by the governing bodies." She showed him how to scroll just using his finger and the old man yelped.

"Give me your hand child," he said. "I shouldn't be doing this, it might just burn out what little strength I have, but it will speed up the process to that of a galloping stead, and then I will be able to show you for certain just where this evil I speak of lies."

With nothing to fear from the weak, old man, the caregiver offered her hand up. Odin's face contorted into a prune with two tufts of hair sticking out where his eyes once were. His lips quivered as he shook gently, rocking back and forth. Serendipity smiled, wondering what could possibly be going through the man's mind as he put on this act. After a minute of this, he finally released her hand, sank back into the pillows and sighed.

"Okay," he groaned. "Let me see the device again." He could barely raise his arm as he pointed to the IPad. Serendipity passed it to him wondering why he had performed that little exhibition. He looked like he was ready to pass out.

Odin slid his hand across the interface screen, and his index finger quickly began scrolling through various pages. At first it appeared that he was just randomly searching and typing in names, but after a minute of this, Serendipity realized that there was a pattern, and that the old man was looking for something specific. Apparently, he had been playing her all along as he navigated the web with ease, but she didn't feel slighted by it. A barrier of trust had just opened up in front of her, and the man who called himself Odin was accessing skills he denied having. She smiled as the old man looked up at her and pointed to screen.

"There you go," he said. "This Patriot Act. There is your monitor. Here on this other page is a company by the name Logistics Far and Wide. They are responsible for maintaining the power supply to the internet on the whole continent of North America. They are a subsidiary company of Global Tech which oversees the continual power supply in Europe and Africa. Private companies owned by other companies that are owned by other companies. There is a trail a mile long, and it all leads to one place where with a word spoken, the power can be shut off. Even if you look at all the redundancies in place, they all lead through other veils that circle around back to some corporation in Atlanta, Georgia, U.S.A."

"Not Walmart?" Serendipity asked, frightened.

"No girl. Not Walmart," Odin said. "The company in question is just a registered number, and has no name." It was the way his hand drew a circle in the air, that caught her attention. He was mimicking her gestures. Come to think of it, even his choice of words had changed. His emphasis placed on different syllables. More Canadian, less foreign. Serendipity was amazed by her breakthrough. She truly believed that she had reached some place inside of Mr. Olsen that had everyone else had written off.

"So why would they fear the internet so much?" she asked.

"A collective mind of the people cannot be bent over the forge and formed into a blade," Odin said. "The key to ruling people is too keep them ignorant, every would-be king knows this. Your internet allows you to unite over great distances. Without great warriors to lead you, this is your only salvation, without the help of the gods. Thankfully, though, I have returned, and you are going to aid me in putting an end to this."

"And exactly how am I going to do that?" Serendipity wondered. The breakthrough had apparently been short lived as Mr. Olsen slipped back into his fantasy personality.

"We are going to need to reach out, connect to a network of people who can aide us, but who will not question our intentions," Odin asserted. "The last thing we need is to alert the enemy and have him shut down the net before we are able to muster out forces."

Sometimes the answers are there before the thought even occurs. It is in these moments, one questions the grand design, the big enchilada, the purpose to it all, and realizes that there is more to the picture then what can be seen.

"Let me tell you about the Dude," Serendipity started. For some, the Dude was merely a character in a Coen Brothers movie. For her and many others, he was an epiphany.

She gave Odin an in-depth lesson into the slowest

growing religion in the world centered on the Dude (Dudeism) and the kind of people it attracted. Educated, spiritual, blue collar, atheists, Christians, even people who dabbled in Eastern philosophies were paying homage to the Dude these days. The idea that one could relax, not get too worked up about the things they could not control, and find the positive even in the negative, was attractive to many who were tired of the way the world just raced on without any heed of enjoying the experience. Elements of many different philosophies were rolled into the Dudeism carpet, threads that made perfect sense for those who just wanted to live their life, their own way, without all the judgment that past generations had relied on to measure their worth. Dudes just rode the train and were happy the wheels were turning.

"Sounds like a boat load of fools!" Odin exclaimed.

"Far from it, Odin," Serendipity countered. "These are exactly the kind of people that fly under the radar." Odin looked puzzled. "I mean, don't draw attention to themselves, and believe it or not, there is a very large network of them. The last group in the world to be monitored by these evil men you speak of would be the Dudeists."

Odin considered this. He needed silent warriors, not lazy daydreamers. As he considered her proposal, he decided that he could live with subterfuge and leave the attracting of warriors until a further date.

"Okay, let's get in touch with these Dudeists," Odin said. "We will have to use subterfuge and cunning in our contact with these mortals. Under no circumstances can we allow our plan to become public knowledge."

"First, we'll set you up with an account," Serendipity began, creating a Facebook page for the old man. She really hoped that helping him communicate with the outside world would tear him away from these fictions he had created. Either that, or it would just allow him to sink deeper into them.

"What do you want your profile name to be?" she asked. When she saw his puzzled expression, she said:

"How would you like to identify yourself?"

"Why, Odin of Asgard, of course."

"Hmm. That might draw the attention you were wishing to avoid."

Again Odin heeded the wisdom of this female. She was an old soul, and her logic had so far proven to be sound.

"Okay then perhaps I can be this Olsen fellow everyone around here calls me," he relented.

"Excellent idea," Serendipity said, tapping away at the keyboard. "Thomas Olsen it is, from, let's say Toronto, Ontario. No need to add a phone number or anything else. A profile picture is needed, but we can use a picture of something instead. Any ideas?"

Sometimes the thought is two seconds behind fate.

"How about a raven?" Odin answered.

Laughing, Serendipity agreed, pulling a picture of a raven off of the internet, drawn in the tribal art style that matched her tattoo. She added herself as a friend, and then showed him his virtual makeup.

"Now show me where those followers of the Dude are," Odin said.

Chapter 4

'There is no light at the end of the tunnel because there is no tunnel; it is a merry go round.'

Time is tireless, that is its most enduring quality. Ticktock, with precision, life moves to its beat. Even the heavens and those free to roam them are subject to it.

As Loki walked amongst the protestors in Seattle he found himself becoming quite bored with this whole game. Humans had become so damned predictable that he could no longer be surprised by them. There had been a few moments in the past hundred years when he was genuinely surprised. The Assassination of Gandhi was one. While everyone was sure to blame the militant Hindus, Loki could see the weaves of other forces at work. As hard as he had tried to discover an alternate truth, his trail grew cold in London, behind veils of names and corporations, all leading to dead ends. What he wanted to discover just for pure curiosity's sake, he had to let go.

These protestors were no different than any others. Eventually the peaceful demonstration would turn to looting and violence. The police would crackdown with force. Of course, Loki may encourage a little chaos, but it was their own attachment to the mob mentality that would take it to the next level where reason would be trampled on and left for dead on the slippery pavement.

The weather here could truly be dreadful. Days of rain on end, and that was perhaps why he liked it so much. In amongst this sullenness, strange and interesting humans arose. Some could really tap the essence of life by living in such a place, and many artists had. Still to this day he promised himself that he was going to skin the person responsible for killing Kurt Cobain. It wasn't going to be pretty, and it was going to add some closure for the god.

"You really do get around, Loki."

The voice was not audible; it was a telepathic connection from someone nearby. A harpy, trickster, who only showed up when the game was moving too slow.

"Well if it isn't one of the fates," Loki smiled. "How are you, my love? As horny as ever I imagine."

"You know, Loki, the fates do not engage in sexual relations," the female voice responded. "We have no desire towards it and are physically unable to as well."

"Of course," Loki stood corrected. "Your gods had no sense of humor, or did they?"

"Our purpose is not one that you will ever understand, Asgardian," the harpy said. "While your kind only worries about justice, battle, and honor, my kind delves into the mind, inspiring thinkers, poets, and heroes alike. Beautiful word, 'inspire,' don't you think? From the Romans' *inspirare*: breathing the divine into. That's what we do. We breathe the divine into mortals, help them find the right path, then leave them to their own devices. What did the Asgardians do? They left their people blind and without strong direction. How quickly they converted, how quickly they adopted the god of the Jews, and discarded their own."

"I'm sorry, love, but you seem to forget that I wasn't born of Asgard," Loki countered. "My relationship with them is complicated at best, you see, but still, I am a little fond of them. If you continue to pester me with this obvious ploy, I will discover which of these bodies you are inhabiting and I will sever you from this existence. There you can try to live out your life in Limbo, where no amounts of imagination, destiny, or fortune telling will ever make it bearable."

"Oh, Loki, do not be like this," the harpy said. "We know that you had a hand in the downfall of your own people and your allegiance to them is paper thin. We know you conspired with others that chased out Jupiter, Mars, and the rest of the flock. We still remember hearing Zeus cry long into the night as his mind collapsed under the indignation the humans threw at him. Those spirits left, but as you know they are returning and they are going to be looking for someone to blame. I would not want to be you when Thor discovers the truth of the matter."

"To the Seven Hells with you, Fate," Loki said. "Thor is not going to return. Odin was powerful, his spirit enduring, but Thor was too brash. Too much ego to survive such a thing."

Loki was scanning the faces around him, looking for the possessed body. His frustration could clearly be seen in his frown as it deepened.

"Oh, but he is stronger then you thought, and has returned," he heard the Fate taunt. "Right now he seeks out followers to help rebuild his strength. With the right nudge he may even discover the truth. That is to say, if he was to find his father. As you are aware, Odin is not very happy with you, and I am sure he would like nothing better than to have his true-born son smote you from existence."

There was a small smile that appeared on the face of a girl with dyed green hair not ten feet from him that drew his attention. Without hesitation he snapped his fingers and the protestor fell to the ground dead before even hitting the pavement. Her soul energy remained frozen as Loki studied it looking for the right color patterns associated with higher beings. To his disgust it turned out she was just a human who had smiled at the wrong time. The Fates can be cruel.

"Be careful, Loki," the Fate warned. "Using such force will draw unnecessary attention to you. There are men who can see things you thought only possible by gods. They have unlimited resources and the ability to find your weakness. This is fair warning, star child."

"Okay, you have my attention," Loki conceded.

"We have watched you for a long time," she said, "influencing events with a nudge and a pull, here and there, interfering with work that normally falls into our territory, and we did so out of curiosity more than anything. There have been times you have amused us, and there have been times we feel that perhaps you took it a little too far, but we understand how easily these people can be swayed. Sometimes a little push turns into a rogue wave that cannot be stopped. Example, Napoleon. Who could have foreseen how that man would generate enough hatred for three major wars on continental Europe? As it is, we have been observing, working with your efforts at times, working against them others. Now though we have reached a critical stage on this world where we need to have an awakening before the children ruin the planet forever. We know you are trapped here, something you could have never predicted, but when you sent Odin away, you also closed the rainbow bridge."

    Loki's eye darkened with acknowledgment as the harpy continued: "We could have warned you of that consequence long ago, but your ego would not listen to reason. Now we are giving you one last chance to let go of your ego momentarily and help us."

Chapter 5

'If you believe what you hear, then you will hear what you believe.'

Delroy wasn't able to sit up. His stomach felt as if someone had punched him the guts. It was just his luck to get food poisoning while in jail. He should have known better then to trust the white man when he said that the hamburgers were always served medium rare in the good ole' U.S. of A. There wasn't a joint in his body that didn't ache, and even though he was in obvious discomfort, the border guards just kept feeding him water, telling him to stop acting like a baby.

As his head swam in the gutter with his guts, he could hear the Great Spirit outside his window. Crawling up to the caged glass, he pulled himself erect, and could see a large raven making one hell of a racket. The bird turned to look at the man behind bars, and let out another screech.

"Why Great Spirit? What have I done to deserve this?" Delroy implored the dark bird. "How could I have known that the jar was full of such evilness?"

The raven bellowed again.

"I was doing the bidding of the Medicine Woman. She told me to wait at the crossroads. I was supposed to ride with the dudes."

Again the raven responded with a call.

"Is it part of the grand design, that I become a prisoner of the white man? Am I to feel the fury of his law?"

This time the raven moved closer. It hopped, two bounces at a time, and stopped, bowed its head and picked up a nickel that was sitting in the grass.

"Curse the white man and his money!" Delroy spat. "Curse his jars full of evil! Curse his terrible cooking!"

The raven picked up the nickle, danced around with

it, much to the chagrin of Delroy. The Great Spirit could not help him here. This square building of concrete held no power, no connection to the mother underneath it. Cringing from another spasm in his intestines, the fear of another movement kept the man very still. His knees pulled in closer to his chest, his heart raced loud in his ears. Through the window the raven stopped its dance, dropped the coin and flew up onto the little ledge outside the bars. It screamed out loud and watched the man inside. Moments later it flew off, and Delroy crawled back closer to the toilet.

"The Great Spirit has no power," he muttered. "That damned Medicine Woman is really to blame." She had sent him out to find the grass, sent him on this silly quest, had treated him like a child when he was a full grown man, and had even kept him from moving to the city to live with his cousin where he could have gotten a job detailing cars at Budget rental. It was foolish to believe that his people could hold on to the old ways. It was foolish to believe that the world would allow them to wallow in their sorrow of everything that they had lost. Once he was free of this curse he was going to leave his reserve and get on with life. The jar wasn't the only thing that had brought this negativity into his life. Being surrounded by his extended family that did nothing but blame the past did him no good. They would not accept that things would never go back to the way they were. As a people, they had to start taking advantage of the very few things they had going their way. They had to use their warrior spirit for strength, their relationship with nature to persevere, and their tax breaks to start amassing communal wealth.

"You are free of my continual harassment, Great Spirit," Delroy sighed, closing his eyes and rolling onto his side. "Go on, and tend to the animals. I will shed the wings of despair and fly on my own."

Two days later Delroy was feeling good enough to walk around again. He paced in his cell and only ate the starches and vegetables provided with is meals. He no longer cursed the guards when they came to check on him, he thanked them for providing him with shelter. There had been some delay in the proceeding, apparently there were bigger things happening elsewhere. He heard talks of riots in the streets, and the pressure being applied on the Governor, the Feds, and the local authorities, to get it under control. With all this going on elsewhere, Delroy was deemed to be less of a priority, and to be held at the border until further notice.

"Hey Delroy! You want a burger for supper?" the guard asked laughing with his partner as they brought in lunch.

"I'll just have the bun with lettuce and tomato if you don't mind too much?"

"Aw, just kidding buddy," the guard chuckled. "

"How about some fried chicken. Your people like that, don't they?" the other guard asked. By the look of him, he hadn't missed a meal with second helpings since they day of his birth.

"Who doesn't like fried chicken, sir? Even the white man does. They even made the person famous for cooking it, a Colonel." Delroy wasn't going to let the racist guard get under his skin. The tall thin one was much nicer and never made fun of his ethnicity.

"Yeah, well, between the Indians and the Blacks, you made that Colonel one rich man."

There is a point when even a mildly racist person can get offended by a true diehard racist. In this case it was the tall, skinny guard who had enough of the taunting by his overweight cohort. Delroy had been pleasant, even forgiving. A real model prisoner.

"Lay off the racist shit, okay, Henry?" he muttered. "Delroy doesn't need to think all Americans are complete assholes."

"Well, shit. If it isn't the fucking Democrat from Ohio, showing his true colors, now. No wonder they moved you from patrol on the real frontier in New Mexico. That kind of sympathizing only encourages more assholes to come into our land, and steal our god given jobs."

"I'm just saying, Henry, that we can treat the

prisoner like a human being until he is processed and taken off of our hands. No need to start with the racist shit. Everyone knows that when you resort to that level of degradation, you are showing just how uneducated and ignorant Americans can be."

"Fuck you, Ohio!" the corpulent guard exclaimed. "Let me guess. Fancy education at a fucking university where they teach you that you can be all that you want just by getting out there with your education and trying. Well, I'll tell you that nothing can be further from the truth. I served in the military, where we learned discipline, how to work hard, and how to identify the enemy. You see that piece of shit there in that cell? That's the enemy. Sneaking across the border, high on drugs. Probably looking to find work that pays cash so he doesn't have to pay taxes. This piece of shit right here doesn't know a thing about hard work. He doesn't want to fit in. He just wants the government to hear his cries every time someone cuts down a goddamn tree to build themselves a home. You think that I don't care about him! Well, I'll guarantee you that he cares even less for us. Goddamn bastards want to live in the Stone Age, while we walk on egg shells around them."

Delroy stood up and walked over to the cell door. He looked at the tall guard then looked at the fat guard.

"He is right," he acknowledged. "My people have not gotten down with the times. We have spent too long in sorrow. We have not seen the possibilities, only what has been taken. The evil that has gripped us will never go away until we come to terms with it."

Both guards stood silent, stunned. The fat guard wanted to say something but found that he had nothing to say. His lips trembled, he realized that this savage had taken away his fire. After a moment the tall guard smiled.

"Henry, go get the rest of the food orders. I am going to let this savage get cleaned up."

"Yeah, right," Henry mumbled. "Okay. He does smell like shit."

After the other guard disappeared around the corner, the tall guard opened up the cell door and led Delroy to the shower room. He gave him soap, a towel, and a scrubby.

"Normally, I'm supposed to stay in the room while you shower," the guard said. "But you are still weak from your sickness, and probably don't have the strength to escape out that back door that was unfortunately left unlocked by captain fatso there. Being as weak as you are, you won't be able to stumble that five hundred yards across the field and back onto Canadian soil where we would have no way of retrieving you." He opened the door, winked and closed it once Delroy was in. The door on the other side of the shower room was unlocked, just as the guard said it would be. Opening it quietly, Delroy peeked down the hall. There was no one there. At the end of the hall was an emergency exit door that was propped open with a chair to let some of the early spring heat out of the building.

Without looking back, Delroy took off at full speed and raced back to Canada.

Chapter 6

'You usually get what you pay for, but with me you get a bargain.'

Sometimes, expectations can live up to themselves. As a species we fall prey to expectations so often that it has made us weary, and sarcastic. Too many times we have discovered that living up to the hype was harder than creating the hype. Boxing matches touted as The Big One become the big bore. Movies with actors who never fail to entertain, sometimes drop a bomb. Even fast food chains, with all their stop place measures to ensure consistency can sometimes ruin a sure thing. Nothing was ever meant to be a sure thing. The element of human failure, the unexpected circumstance arising, or even the lack of care and concern, all play a part in what is to be expected when expecting.

The Bear lived up to expectation. He was hairy, and lived on a plot of land nestled in between two mountains. His home, a log cabin that boasted a working waterwheel, turning with the running of the creek that ran along side. The yard was unkempt, but obviously efficient, as planter boxes covered the entire sprawl. Everything from pumpkins, to green beans were growing, and the greenhouse located in the backyard had a wide variety of peppers shooting up from the dark soil. Mrs. Bear chased Bear around the yard with a switch she had cut from the fringes, laughing as she cursed the dude for feeding the dog Horace a bowl of home brew oat soda. This is the sight the Dudeist travelers on their stupefying quest were confronted with as the Toyota pulled up in the driveway.

Willow, Carl, and Julius waited patiently for the chase to end before coming forth with the staff of the Wandering Abider, held high to signal their arrival. At the first sight of it, Bear stopped, took the switch in the back, ignoring the inconvenience it provided, and smiled. His beard parted like the Red Sea before Moses, and his arms raised high in the air forming a giant arc above his head. Mrs. Bear stopped her attack on the hairy man when she noticed that they had guests, dropping the switch to her feet and performing a curtsy in welcoming.

"Behold!" Bear proclaimed with a wide, welcoming smile. "The Staff of the Wandering Abider as foretold by my friend Nuna the Monk. You have reached the sacred grounds of Dudetopia, aspiring members of the Order of the Righteous Dude. In your honor we will have a feast and discuss your travels. Oat sodas for everyone!"

Horace, a massive St. Bernard, came lumbering over to the newcomers. If a dog could smile, Horace was wearing one as he stopped in front of the three, sniffing the air.

"Don't mind him. He began the party an hour ago." Bear called out. "He is completely harmless unless you are a mountain lion. He hates mountain lions."

Beneath the starry sky, a grand feast of vegetables prepared in more ways than one could count, was laid out on two adjoining, handcrafted picnic tables. Candied yams sat beside mustard cauliflower. Sugared snap peas shared a bowl with wine soaked dates. Spiced pistachios complimented a colorful spinach salad and zucchini stuffed with goat cheese went well with the raspberry relish. Three loaves of fresh bread, still warm from the wood fired stove, were coated with smear of fresh butter. And oat cakes chalked full of raisins were set beside a bowl of butterscotch sauce.

For Willow this was a dream come true. Five days of road food consisting mainly of fast food take out, had made her innards very unhappy. Her two companions had fared much better than her, their diets had not strayed far from what they would consider the norm. Eagerly everyone ate, and occasionally Carl gave Julius a look of wanting, wondering when the meat would be served. Alas, in Dudetopia, there was no meat. The only time meat was served was if Bear went hunting, otherwise it was a strictly vegetarian diet.

When the feast concluded, the real drinking began. Insisting upon full glasses, Bear made the rounds with an ever full pitcher of honey mead, made from the honey collected from the hives they kept in the back, beyond the greenhouse. Mrs. Bear popped in and out to check on the guests, but spent most of the time inside the modest home working on various art projects that she had on the go. Bear would beam when he talked about the love of his life, his second wife. Together they had been looking for a way to live off the land, and together they had made it a reality.

"So you seek the Mad Hermit?" Bear asked, finishing off another glass of honey mead. Of course he knew why they had come, but it was an opening line to begin conversation. His guests were rather quiet, trapped in some kind of retrospective funk.

"Nuna the Monk said that you would be able to help us with that," Carl responded. He was rolling a big fat joint with some of Bear's weed grown in the greenhouse behind the peppers. When he had first laid his eyes on the bud when Bear took them around the grounds, Carl had actually started to salivate. Deep purple veins ran through the thumb thick buds.

"Well, that I can," Bear said. "There is a dude in Seattle who looks out for the Herald, as a favor to me. Guy's a plumber, well connected, and a true dude. We have to do it covertly, you know. Gerald is sensitive about his independence. The only gifts he will accept are secondhand goods, or whiskey. He has abandoned the normal lifestyle that brings with it all the trappings of society. Instead he prefers to be on the street with the people."

"He chooses to remain homeless?" Willow asked.

"That he does. He says he likes to keep it real, his finger on the pulse, so to speak. What you have to understand about Gerald the Herald is that he wants to be considered mad, but the truth is that he is far from it. In fact, he may be the most sane man you will ever meet. He never lies, never lives with expectation, and would rather starve then become a ward of the state. You'll see for yourself, soon enough."

"It must be hard to live on the street like that." Julius noted.

Bear smiled. He had spent some time in Seattle with the Hermit, visiting him while on a training session with his previous employer. They had drank by the fire, talked of many things, and not once did he believe that the man across from him was suffering in any way.

"For most people it would be, Hawk," Bear said. "You don't mind if I call you that. It's a great last name and it rolls right off the tongue." Julius lit up with appreciation. He had tried several times to get people to use it as his nick name, but unsuccessfully. "You have to learn to see life beyond the material realm. All these things that people work for, drive for, and kill themselves for are often superficial, have no real effect on the life experience. I myself used to be a slave to the corporate world, working for a company that built planes, bombs, and other various destructive tools. Immersed in that world, I spent my money on things I didn't need, was trapped in a relationship that was bleeding out love faster than when I cut off my baby toe in a motorcycle accident." He poured himself another glass of honey mead after topping off Willow's glass. "I wasn't happy, as are most people out there who are caught in the same boat. The Fuck It moment came soon after I discovered Dudeism, and started chatting with people online. I realized that living like I was, I was heading in one direction. A cold, birth in the ground. Dig it! The wild was calling." He motioned to their surroundings and the arc of starlit sky. "I gave up everything without a fight, met my special lady and moved off the grid. It's not the same as living on the street, but in essence it is rooted in the same beliefs.

"Do you dudes realize that you are the first dudes to visit this little slice of paradise!" Bear laughed. "It is a time for celebration. Nuna tells me that all three of you are musicians. Just happens that I play a mean harp and can even hold a beat on the drums. What do you say we go into the barn and let loose?"

High and a little tipsy, the Order of the Righteous

Dude moved from under the clear skies into the barn around back where a PA system was hooked into the two large stage speakers. A drum kit, several guitars, and microphones were set up as if jamming in here was a common occurrence, and judging by the pile of roaches in the ash trays, it was.

The music they made filled the void of the deepest night.

The next morning there were many heavy heads, as there always was with such celebrations. After a wonderful breakfast of fresh berries, cream, and granola, Bear lead the trio into the forest for a nature hike. He claimed it would cure them of anything that ailed them, including a hangover. With pre-rolled joints, a couple flasks of blueberry wine, and fresh cinnamon loaf, they headed into the old growth with Horace leading the way.

"That staff has been here before," Bear exclaimed, nodding to the Staff of the Wandering Abider Willow used as a walking stick. "When the Mad Hermit was making his way to give Nuna Monk the *Dude See Scrolls* he stayed with us for a night. I can tell you this much, he isn't much of a singer."

"That seems to be a running theme with those who possess the scrolls," Hawk remarked. He savored the way the fresh morning air cleared his head.

"These trees have been here longer then the white man has been on this land. The further we climb along the ridge we'll come to some that are wider than your arms. It cost me a pretty penny to buy this property, but there hasn't been a day gone by that I haven't fully appreciated the beauty."

"It's too bad Delroy wasn't here to see this place," Hawk mused. "The trees don't grow this big in Alberta." He told Bear of the native man, the negative vibe jar, and the unlikely coincidences that had brought them together.

"Well, fuckin' A, man, it is too bad that he didn't make it," Bear agreed. "I do know how to perform a Dudercism, and a friend we are going to meet would have been able to help him find his path again. The spirits can abandon you if your hopelessness becomes overbearing."

"There's someone else living way out here?" Carl asked, a little winded. He saw no signs of roads, or civilization what so ever. In fact they were following what appeared to be a dear trail. Having lived in the city his whole life, this experience was starting to open his eyes up to the world of nature. First with Nuna, and his monastery in the foothills, and now this place with moss covering the entire forest floor like a soft, cozy, carpet. The trees themselves extended so high that he could barely see the sky.

"Oh, yes," Bear said, breathing in deeply. "Why do you think Nuna sent you to see me? I could have given you the directions in an email. This, though, well, this you have to experience."

Suddenly the trees gave way to a mountain. A glade, the size of football field opened up in front of the hikers, with a small lake hugging the base of the sheer rock face. A rivulet of water ran down the mountain and fed into the lake which was surrounded by blossoming wild flowers of all colors. Bees were busy flying from one to the next, doing nature's most important work. The sun reflected off the water and lit up the rocks in behind, showing the compacted layers, now broken and thrust up out of the earth.

"Do you feel that?" Willow asked.

"I'm so high I can barely feel my feet." Carl responded, which earned him a knock over the head from the staff.

"I feel like I could fall asleep," Hawk answered her query, his eyes looking heavy.

"This is a very calm place, dudes," Bear said, his as solemn as a mountain. "This is where we can find our inner being." He walked over to the edge of the small lake and sat down with the mountain to his back, facing the way they had just come.

"Come join me," Bear told them. "It's going to take a while for our guest to arrive."

Following suit the three sat down facing the trail

they had used. Horace lapped up some water, did a circle of the perimeter then plunked himself down amongst the flowers and fell asleep. Apparently the humans where not the only ones feeling the effects of the night before.

"This place is a sacred spot," Bear told them after a moment of silence. "Here Ley lines meet, connections of the earths energy. Here a shaman can tap into the power that flows all around us, and consult with the spirits. I come here every other day to do so. Meditation, and a limber mind allow me to open up to the great will, and to feel the power of life. It is here where I met my friend, he came to me in a vision first, then in person."

As if on cue, a shimmering appeared at the forest edge and large, hairy, man-like beast emerged. With impossible grace and quiet, the beast strode forward, its gigantic green eyes staring at the people sitting by the water. Half terrified, half amazed, Hawk, Carl and Willow sat frozen, wondering what was in the weed they smoked to cause such hallucinations. It wasn't till the creature was within ten feet, that they could feel its presence and knew that this was no apparition.

It looked at Bear, smiled at the sleeping dog and spread its hands out in a peaceful, welcoming gesture.

"Dude." It spoke with a definite male voice with a noticeable German accent.

"Dude." Bear responded, jumping up and hugging the beast.

"Sasquatch." Hawk was somehow able to mutter.

"Actually, my name is Hen," the creature corrected him. "And I've always preferred the term Yeti. Has a much nicer tone. Sasquatch sounds like something big and bulky. Clanks around the woods making all kinds of noise. I mean, you think that you'd hear me coming with a name like that, but you didn't, eh?"

All four nodded their heads in agreement.

"So tell me Bear, who are your friends?"

Formal introductions we made, and Hen insisted that each hug him in greeting. One could smell honey, flowers and something else completely foreign in that embrace. It was a new smell that lingered on the nose, pleasant yet strange.

"Ah, I recognize that staff," Hen remarked fondly. "It seems that someone was wise to pass it on to you Miss. A good choice," he said.

Willow blushed and loosened the grip on the staff as she realized that she was in holding too tight. The Yeti posed no danger to her, she could feel that instinctively in her bones. In fact she wanted to hug the creature again and again, it had felt that good.

"You are heading the wrong way, I'm afraid," Hen said to Carl, who still was looking at the creature, then at the joint in his hand, and back at the Yeti.

"But,..., I.., huh?" was all he could manage to get out, before concluding: "Dafuq?"

"Your path is not aligned," Hen told him. "You are out of your element, and will probably feel better once you get back to your natural home. You see this," with a flick of a finger two brilliant beams of light appeared the exact spot where they were standing, intersecting, each going off beyond sight in all four directions. "You normally feel attuned to stationary living, I'm guessing. See how the light vibrates around you. It knows that you are out of place here. Your friend, Hawk, well he is more attuned to traveling. See how the light grows calm in one direction. It's pointing him towards his destiny. Now with the young lady, as you can see, the light envelops her. She is a master of her own destiny, and is probably the only one who is really meant to be here. I'm sorry to say it, dudes, but paths diverge here."

Of course, this was not news that Hawk or Carl wanted to hear. They had invested a lot of their time on the road in this quest, and now some hairy, hypothetical, yet oddly articulate beast was telling them that they were no longer meant to be part of this adventure.

"Sorry, Mr. Yeti, but I'm not liking this whole line of thinking," Carl finally managed to say without stumbling on the words. "I mean, like who are you to know where we should be?" Although he hated to admit it, though, Carl really was out of his element and did not feel at ease.

"I am sorry, sir. I don't mean to offend you," Hen replied, his creaturely eyes showing compassion. "I am just telling you the truth of the matter. You see the Yeti have existed longer than man has. We roamed this world when the dinosaurs ruled, hiding, being hunted, evolving quickly in order to survive. During our evolution we became in tune with nature, the forces that govern everything you see. In order to survive we had to become one with our world, as we were listed on the menu more often than not. It was this dedication to living in tune with nature that we learned of the Ley lines, learned how to listen to the wind, and discovered that this world you see was not the only world open to us.

"Discovering the mirror worlds," the Yeti continued, "we were able to survive the great doom that befell the dinosaurs, and the ice ages to come after. We were able to thrive once the world righted itself for a time, when your original ancestors first learned how to build fire. We taught the Neanderthals how to live in the cold climate, imparting the wisdom, and voice of nature to them. For thousands of years we were able to remain on this world without the fear of being hunted until your people discover the arts of war. This senseless turn from nature created a rift between our species and once again we feared for our lives. As time passed, your kind became increasingly more violent, more aggressive towards all other species of the planet. We returned to the mirror worlds where once again we await for the world to become safe for us."

"Trans-dimensional beings!" Hawk said in amazement. "Holy fuck!"

"Exactly."

"So nature is telling you that we are not on the right path?" Carl was still not convinced. He wasn't even entirely convinced he was talking with a frickin' Yeti that wasn't part of some pot-induced hallucination.

"Yes, indeed," Hen nodded. "Like it or not, my friend, all life is interconnected on this world. The Earth as a whole, is much a part of you, as you are a part of it. At one time we were all star dust, then the forces that bind, brought us together."

"Well, fuck me, man." Carl was not pleased. "I wish I had of known all of this earlier. I could have been making money instead of just wasting it."

"Carl, the adventure is what brought you out," they Yeti said. "The lesson was to learn that you are not an adventurer. Not many people get to learn lessons so truthful in their life. Do not look at this as a negative, turn it around and find the positive, and you will enrich your own life."

"Yeah, I guess, man," Carl said, still unconvinced.

"Well, I'm still going on," Hawk spoke out with confident defiance. "It is my car after all, and someone has to get the lady here to the Hermit. Right?" Of course, he still harbored a secret hope that he and Willow might be something more than just traveling companions.

"Yes Hawk, I see your path in harmony with this quest a while longer," Hen agreed. "There will be a time, though, when you will realize you were never meant to be a member of the Order of the Righteous Dude. With the unfolding of time, your band will require most of your attention."

"Yeah, well we do have an album coming out in a few months, actually," Hawk admitted.

"And I, for one, look forward to listening to it." Hen replied with a big Yeti smile.

Chapter 7

'You can find the most amazing things when you stop looking.'

The sixth annual meeting of the Fellowship of the Tabard was being held in the Four Seasons Resort and Spa, located in Lake Placid, New York, this year. Four hundred online members gathered for what promised to be a fun filled weekend of jousting, mock sword battles and medieval feasting. Yes, it was the excitement of comic con rolled into a LARP session, as the procession of people entering the dining hall proved that crushed velvet would never fade away.

Coats of arms and banners had been erected around the circumference of the room by the hotel's maintenance staff using a man lift, on behest of the organization. Countries' flags from all over Europe were represented by their distant American cousins who truly believed that they still held ties to the Old World, though very few had ever crossed the Atlantic. In this gathering it was good enough to quote Shakespeare, *Brave Heart* the movie, or the television show *Vikings* on the History Channel.

A small contingent of Norwegian enthusiasts sat in the far back corner doing their best to provoke the Francs, who were doing their best to compete in a drinking match. They were louder than the rest, more into their roles than the rest, and definitely drunker than the rest. Some of them had even come from Canada to participate, where they had built a complete Viking settlement on the banks of the Ottawa River to show their devotion to the old ways.

Striding into the hall as if the world was his, Thor was followed closely by his follower, the Russian. They tramped past the damsels, the wenches, the barons, and the dukes. With heads held high they marched up to the head table where an elaborate throne had been placed for the sponsor of the feast, King Henry Smith. Seated comfortably with his queen at his right, and his concubine at his left, the king watched the two guests approaching, frowning at their twentieth century garb.

A man, dressed as a herald holding a long horn stepped in front of the two newcomers. His purple tunic was stitched with silver thread, his leggings black, with silver doves flying in circles.

"Who comes forth to speak to the king dressed like beggars?" the Herald asked with his hand raised.

Thor's lip quivered at the sight. He looked around, many of the guests had stopped everything they were doing, now looking at the mountainous ruffian and the Russian. Many snickered, and whispered, behind lacy cloths.

The Russian, sensing impending danger to the Herald, put a hand on Thor's shoulder and muttered something to him in his thick accent. Begrudgingly, the giant man allowed him to speak before laying waste to the flop who had the audacity to mock him in public.

"Before you stands the God of Thunder and Strength," the Russian announced. "He is the son of Odin, killer of giants and undefeated in battle. I give you Thor!"

In the back corner of the room, the Viking contingent stopped chugging their mead long enough to hear the proclamation. They looked at each other in disbelief, then studied the giant Irish man as best as they could from the distance. Ivan the Forgotten stood up and jumped up on the table, kicking over a couple of pints along the way, yelling at the top of his lungs:

"Long live the son of Odin! Forever may his enemies flee in terror!"

His call was answered quickly by the rest of his contingent just before he tumbled backwards on to his chair which collapsed into a pile of kindling.

"And who may you be then?" The Herald asked the Russian over the voices of the Vikings.

"I am simply the Russian," he shrugged. "I am guide for the returned god."

In a quieter tone the Herald leaned forward and spoke to the two.

"You know we really frown upon street clothes, guys. Yeah, um.., we kind of have rules about this sort of thing."

"I am Thor, I do not follow your petty rules!" The big man bellowed. This brought about another round of cheers from the Viking contingent. Even a couple of the Danes in the other corner knocked forks to their cups in appreciation.

A slight flicker in the lighting drew everyone's attention for a moment. It is funny how people always look up when the lights flicker, figuring that they are going to see something that would explain the inconvenience. When the flickering ceased, they looked back to the spectacle unfolding in the center of the room only to see that the giant Irish man had suddenly donned a wig of golden locks and that his shirt had disappeared completely to show his impressive bulk. Many of the wenches sighed in admiration, and a few of the fops could barely contain their appreciation.

Baffled by the quick costume change, the Herald still looked as if he had his doubts, for the Russian had not followed suit, and still looked a soldier in the Red Army preparing for winter.

"Well Thor, may I introduce to you then," the Herald spoke loudly, bowing and moving backwards, to his left. "King Henry Smith, the slayer of the Doomsday prophet. The lesser of two evils. The unjust hand of the just. The declarer of declarations, and the host of this fell gathering."

"Come forth Odin, and tell me your tale." The King announced.

"You do not command me mortal," Thor growled flatly. "No matter how long your list of deeds may be, I am the son of Odin and I care not for your petty kingdom. I have come here for them!" Turning, he pointed to the table of Vikings in the back who began to holler so loud that the Francs nearby bent away trying to cover their ears.

Again the lights flickered and this time when they stopped Thor stood as he had once stood over a thousand years ago, in his armor forged from dragon's breath, back on Asgard. The cries of excitement from both the Vikings and the Danes threatened to disrupt the food service, as the serving wenches were forced to stop with their heaping platters of mutton and head cheese. It was unfortunate for them that the Vikings occupied the table closest to the kitchen, as they were all standing now, banging their wooden swords on their wooden shields.

The Russian moved in close to Thor, he had been filming the entire event on his phone.

"It is working. You should see yourself now," he marveled.

"The power of faith, mortal. That is what gives us gods our strength," Thor said, feeling emboldened. "This is not enough for more than a show, but I am happy to be myself again."

The Vikings came running up with the Danes in pursuit, surrounding their god, patting him on the back and cheering. With the power surges subsiding, and the lighting in the hall stabilizing, the Herald raised the horn to his lips and let out one, long note. This silenced the crowd as the King rose from his throne.

"If you are who you claim to be," said the King, "then you should be able to best my most victorious knight, Sir Ragland!" On cue, the King's devoted followers started chanting Ragland's name over and over until a man who was standing behind the King came forward, dressed in ceremonial armor, a long sword sheathed at his waist.

Thor laughed. "Him! This is your best warrior! I will turn him into a cup from which to drink."

"So be it then. A battle before dinner, mead goes to the winner." The Herald proclaimed.

Sir Ragland unsheathed his sword, strapped on his wooden shield that his squire carried over. Painted on a green back field was a large, golden serpent. Bowing to his king, he turned to meet the giant man, who stood bare chested, in his golden radiance, with no weapon.

"How appropriate that he has a serpent on his shield." Thor remarked to the Russian. He then turned to the Viking horde behind him, asking to borrow a weapon. All eight members of the group nearly tripped over themselves trying to give the god their weapon. In the end it was war hammer that he settled upon. As he tested the weight, he looked at the Russian, confused.

"Remember, this is all fake," he whispered. "Even the weapons. These people are just pretending. Even this battle you are about to engage in is just a dance, really."

"Oh, Seven Hells," Thor sighed, his massive shoulders dropping. This world really was too much. "How am I supposed to fake battle? These fools will never believe who I am if I play as if a child."

"Well, you can make it convincing, but still remember these are not real warriors. Defeating them really proves nothing, Thor."

"Okay, Russian," Thor grimaced. "We play it your way, then."

The combatants met in the middle of the dining hall, face to chest, for Thor was a good eight inches taller than Sir Ragland. The Herald stood in between, while minstrels in the back ground fired up their lutes, and a Hurdy-gurdy to add flavor to the occasion.

"The first to strike what the King deems to be a mortal wound, wins," the Herald announced then backed away. Standing beside the King, he assured his lord that Sir Ragland was bound for victory.

"May you find honor on the field of battle," the King called out. This statement brought a smile to Thor's face. Perhaps these fops weren't so bad after all. At least they respected the idea of honor and combat.

Sir Ragland bowed to his king and then to Thor. Thor grunted and hefted the fake hammer with one arm. The wooden head, made of what felt like cork, whirled in great arcs, gracefully.

"Fight!" The King shouted.

Sir Ragland was no fool. He knew that the big man was a lot quicker than one would guess of a large man, so he circled slowly, not attacking straight on. Thor watched, letting the man have a moment of hope. It took every ounce of his will not to throttle the knight quickly, but the Russian had been right on many accounts so far, and Thor was beginning to trust him.

Sir Ragland's sword slashed out quickly, the attack aimed at severing an artery in the leg, to end the battle quickly, but Thor parried the attack with a down swing of the hammer, then stepped back. He would give the man three attempts before he would end this charade.

This time Sir Ragland made as to come in low, but at the last minute went for a neck strike. Again the giant man turned aside his wooden sword with ease. This time Thor could not help but laugh. In reaction, the Vikings watching from the side line laughed along, which brought a stern frown to the King's face.

"Okay, Sir Ragland, finish him!" The King called out.

Before he could even move, Thor struck out with the hammer, its speed blinding and impossible to follow. The head of the weapon connected with the serpent painted on the shield, splintering the protective device in two. The hammer head itself exploded into a thousand little piece of flying cork. Thankfully for Sir Ragland the blow was so precise that all of the force behind it was absorbed in the destruction of the shield. A tinge of anger rose up as he realized that over one hundred hours of crafting precision was lost. His arm was completely numb, but unhurt, unlike his feelings. By some unknown instinct that he possessed his sword lashed out only seconds after the hammer struck and he caught the big man across the stomach with what would have been a disemboweling blow had the sword been real.

Thor looked down at where the sword blow landed. Amazed by the speed the man had exhibited in his counter attack, noticing that something had changed in his opponent. There was a light in the eyes that wasn't there before. There was a confidence rising from the darkness beyond the iris. Even the air in the room had become charged with an unknown current.

"By the gods! Who are you?" Thor asked.

Shaking his head, as if coming out of a daze, the man rose. "By the gods I am Aries, son of Zeus, and I thank you Thor, son of Odin for waking me up."

Chapter 8

'Sometimes it is easier said than done.'

"You are never going to believe it, Mad Man, but there are more of those Pootles in Reality." Left Handed Larry said, returning with more pallet wood to burn in the barrel.

"They can wait." Gerald replied. "Our guest was just about to tell me why he is here. It's something I'd like to hear before I do anything else."

Beneath the tattered clothes, the stranger removed a chain. On it was a pendant, a Yin/Yang sitting upon one side of a scale, with the world sitting in the other. In the fire light it appeared to be gold but Gerald knew that it was silver. He also knew the origin of such a pendant.

"Oh for the love of Christ," he moaned. "Not a member of the Taoist West Society? You bastards just don't know when to let sleeping dogs lie."

"Come now, Gerald. You must have known that eventually our paths would cross. Didn't you see this in your vision?" The stranger smiled peeling off his tattered clothes to expose the robes of a monk underneath.

"Well hell no! If I did, I would have had Larry here throw you in the river. Christ, when I left West Chapel, I told you fools to never bother me again."

"We were willing to honor that agreement, but then the visions came," the stranger said. "I saw you leading a woman down a path, the rise of Dudeism, up on par with Taoism. I have seen violence erupting all over America and I saw the symbol of the Dude rising above it all and somehow bringing about peace. You know Sandie would never let that happen."

"That woman is wound tighter then a nickel plated guitar string," Gerald said. "I could care less what she thinks about Dudeism, and its place in the world. She is going to have to accept the fact that it's not just some gang of surfer dudes who walk around all day saying, awesome man! Or, cool! It's about looking at life through the same set of eyes that originally conceived Taoism, Buddhism. She's just jaded and set on repeat, man."

The stranger shifted uncomfortably on his milk crate. He apparently didn't approve of anyone slandering the great and noble leader of the Taoist West Society.

"She has sent me with a special offer for you that I think you should hear out before you attempt to slander her any further," the stranger said. "It was with great reluctance that she sent me, but so far all the visions have come true, and it was this one she fears the most.

"If you were to leave Reality now, come with me, you would be welcomed back at West Chapel, given your own room, and allowed to continue your studies in whatever way you wish, as long as it didn't interfere with the balance we maintain. Sandie has told me to tell you that she is personally inviting you back, and that she apologizes for removing your group discussion privileges.

"You'd be happy to know that the entire premises now has high-speed wifi, so you would be able to keep in close touch with all your dude buddies. You could get back to writing that book you always talked about. We wouldn't hinder you in any way."

Gerald specifically remembered using the Australian term "Daft Cunt" to Sandie's face. It wasn't a proud moment of his, but it was a moment that would live on in infamy. There is no recovering from something like that. There is no forgiveness, even if it is offered.

"Listen closely, stranger," he said. "Daoism is spelled with a T. Even auto correct on the computer knows that, for fuck's sake. You new age assholes run around in your robes like you really understand what the Asian world has to offer, yet you discard some of the basic tenets like balance. Not everything from the past is going to help you now, and the reason we evolve and continue to study new ideas and new thinking is so that we can find a way to help all of humanity, not just those who spend all their time translating and deciphering books and scrolls written two thousand years ago. I mean, after two thousand years if you haven't got it figured out, worded in simple plain language so people will naturally gravitate towards it, then it isn't complete. You adhere to this old way of thinking, allowing it to turn you into pretentious pricks." Gerald was just warming up. "I mean, half the people there never listen. They have an answer before a question is even asked, and when they do answer, they are just repeating something they read. They can't think for themselves anymore. They've become these mindless robots that wander around appeasing people like Sandie, who need constant worship to keep their ego afloat. If Lao Tzu walked into that temple, he'd leave running and would probably turn to Buddhism."

"I think you are being a little harsh and petty," the stranger answered back.

"Do you! Wow, if that's all you've got to say in defense, then you know what I am saying rings of some truth. Of course I am a bit jaded! Who likes being thrown out of a public forum, while others are watching? I was trying to keep myself in check for the group's sake, keeping most of my opinions to myself, but I still felt that being honest would be accepted in a group that should abide the laws of balance. Those meetings are like listening to a one-sided argument where everyone is agreeing yet arguing. Do you know how frustrating it is to listen to that? I know you do, 'cause I can see it in your eyes. Back and forth they go. Every topic becomes the same discussion. Black is black and white can be gray, yada, yada, yada.

"Boil down the basics for me and tell me how Dudeism and Taoism are so different," Gerald challenged the stranger. "We both believe in seeing life for what it is. We both believe in balance. We both feel that one should take it easy, one wants to gain a greater perspective of things, and we both believe that things are the way they are, and they always will be that way until they change."

"You know, she is a bit uptight," the stranger admitted.

"I know, dude. Trust me, I know."

"Some of the members still talk about you when she's not around."

"Well that is promising. There were some good folks there who were just better at holding their tongues then I was."

"Look, I can see this is a pointless endeavor," the stranger said with resignation. "The future can have you, if it wills it, and perhaps in that future we can find some reconciliation between our two philosophies."

"I wouldn't hold my breath, stranger, but so say hello to Sandie for me. Tell her that I am attending counseling to get over the trauma inflicted upon me during my time at the retreat. Also let her know that I was content to remain on the sidelines, but if the opportunity arises to push Dudeism up onto a level playing field with Taoism, that I am now all over it."

"That might be pushing it a little too far, dude." With that, the Taoist monk left, taking his milk crate and knowing that he had done what was instructed of him and that he could do no more. Changing a rock to sand took time without the proper machinery.

"By the way," he called back to Gerald. "My name is Nigel, and thanks for sharing your fire. Abide, dudes."

Left-Handed Larry led Gerald to a small gathering of Reality citizens who were busy mingling with another six Pootles. They had arrived with cigarettes and liquor, making them even more popular than the original six that were still mingling about. With those calling cards, it was easy to bribe their way past the gates and quickly find friends. Sitting around a fire, one Pootle, Radley, had brought his acoustic guitar out and was strumming a few notes making sure it was in tune. As the party below began to take shape, the protest above on the bridge had slipped into the dark side, morphing from a protest into a riot.

"Anyone is welcome to join along," Radley offered as the group focused all their attention on him. He started with a Neil Diamond song, a classic sing-along one, "Sweet Caroline." The Mad Hermit heard this as he entered the circle, his face turning thirty shades of scarlet. Left-Handed

Larry accepted two cigarettes from a girl who wore an Anarchy Luvs A Sycophant t-shirt.

"One more note and I swear I'll through you in the fire!" Gerald yelled over top of the crooning crooner.

All eyes now turned to the Mad Hermit as he stood there in all his rage, his beard sweating, his tattered clothes steaming, the flames burning hotter.

"Hey bro, like what's you prob?" Radley asked, winking at the girl who was giving Larry cigarettes. She smiled in return, rolling her eyes at the homeless man who dared to intrude on their musical interlude.

"Not another goddamn note from that song, you hear me boy!" Larry was now smoking a cigarette and standing beside his friend, eyeballing the Pootles as if daring one of them to challenge the amputee.

Radley, sensing that the man was not in complete control of his faculties, decided just to play it cool. He had spent a lot of time around children and knew exactly how to deal with rowdies.

"That's cool man," Radley responded using his teacher aide voice. "I know other songs too. You don't have to get down on the vibe man. We just came to hang with you all and have a good time."

"Go ahead!" Gerald shouted. "Play 'Brown Eyed Girl'! I dare ya. Let's see how far that guitar will fly. In fact I'll start it for you. Hey, where did we go?"

Now Radley was standing, and so were the other Pootles. They were all quite confused by this turn of events. Shouldn't homeless people be grateful to have the youth out supporting them?

"Listen here, Pootles," Gerald had regained some of his composure now that he had successfully interrupted the song, though the boy's tone was bordering on a beating. "I realize you think it's hip to be down with the people and all, but you are fooling yourselves believing that this is all cool! Many of the people living here are doing so because of circumstances beyond their control. Many of them have had life slap them in the face and tell them to fuck off, but you know what? They are not going to. If any of these people had the choice, they'd prefer to live under a roof, where their parents don't understand them! Not one of these folks would even consider coming down to a place like this pretending to understand the suffering, to take selfies to show off at high school. Who in their right mind would ditch their perfectly good clothes to throw on dirty clothes, trying to fit in with folks they pretend to care about?"

"Yeah, well if you just chill, bro, I think you'd dig us, man," Radley replied.

"Listen here, fucktard," Gerald popped that bubble fast. "If you are trying to pick up chicks like this little cutie over here with the t-shirt, by playing your campfire songs, then go do it at a Starbucks, and explain to her all your wonderful theories on life. I can guarantee that by the time you run out of smokes and liquor, this little love in session you have going on here will dissipate real quick. You are going to find yourselves cold, hungry and wanting mama. My suggestion is go, come back some time without the bribery, and try to really get to know the people, unless of course this is all just a ruse to impress a girl."

There was no response. The Pootles looked at each other, nodded, and packed up their things. They didn't bother to take their liquor; they left it behind. Radley was at the front of the group as they left but the girl with t-shirt stayed behind for a moment.

"You're not as old as you look, are you?" she asked Gerald.

"Nope. I am a spring chicken." He replied admiring her shirt.

"What caused you to be homeless?"

With the Pootles on the run, his head cleared of negative thoughts, he laughed at her question. It wasn't a mocking laugh, it was a hearty belly laugh that brought Left-Handed Larry and the girl along for the ride.

"I choose to live here," he said.

"Do you mind if I stay awhile and just talk?" she asked.

"Come back tomorrow," Gerald said. "This rioting above us is going to get out of hand soon. Trust me when I say I know it will. If you still feel like talking, then yes you are more than welcome to come by my place and have a nice conversation."

"Okay, you can expect me." she replied.

"It's okay to wear you regular clothes."

"These are." She smiled and ran off to catch up with the rest of the youths.

Chapter 9

'You are not alone in your thoughts.'

It is almost impossible to get away with anything in this modern world with cameras capturing almost every person walking the streets. Smart phones have not only revolutionized the way people communicate, they have also revolutionized the way are able to keep the world informed of events as they happen. As tensions mount, more and more transgressions are recorded and released onto public virtual networks. It's this collective world evolving, so fast, adding logs to a fire that had always had heated coals.

Videos of police officers in American cities beating detained victims were no longer shocking. People came to expect such things. There was even rumors, unconfirmed at this writing, that a show similar to *America's Funniest Videos* was being pitched in Hollywood featuring the week's best beatings. Bombs blowing up in London subways were caught happening on camera, whereas in times of old, one would have to wait for the television news reports to air. Be-headings in the Middle East by terrorist factions was an internet event, desensitizing the populace more and more each day. Violence was so intertwined with what people were viewing, becoming focal points of life.

For the majority of the planet's inhabitants, though, this just wasn't the case, as people managed to live peacefully. In the entertainment sector, though, peace was boring.

The average person may witness violence, but rarely does one witness the kind of violence that really enrages a whole city. Women, who have long suffered under the violence of men, must look upon some of these acts which enrage so many and say, "Why not me? Why has no one burnt down a drug store in protest of the abuse I have suffered at the hands of my husband? Why hasn't the city burned to the ground when a child sex offender has been released into the populace, and committed the same crime again? Why haven't the people who say that they belong to a religion of peace walk the streets in defiance of their leaders until the terrorists who have killed innocents have been chased from the bushes, caught, and punished?"

There is no anti-violence movement, just individual causes that flare up, then die away.

Odin had come to the conclusion that humans were not very good at looking after themselves. In his day and age, there were atrocities, yes. Vile acts which had been looked at with a blind eye, and it was with great regret, as he sat in his bed, knowing he could have helped steer the human condition in a different direction with his influence. A series of tears were wiped away, as he continued to scan through the history of the Earth in the past thousand years.

Glorious battle was no longer imaginable in times when a man could kill another without even seeing him. Mass graves of innocents filled because of ethnic differences. There was no honor in any of this. This was not the path to the Great Hall, where in the afterlife, one could tell their tales with great pride. Men would not speak of the things they now did. Men were ashamed of what they were capable of and it had tainted society. An invisible finger lurking on the shoulder, forever in judgment.

Perhaps, this is why he had returned after so many years of being trapped in Limbo. Perhaps it was the humans turn to teach the gods a lesson. For a god, realizing that your way was never quite conducive to a harmonious society, was a lot to admit to. The ego of a human was pathetically small to that of a god.

"Tell me Serendipity, is there a way to make this right?"

She rubbed his back, stopped, surprised by the emotion that he was showing. They had spent the last hour just looking over the images and articles he had saved, having her explain the events. This change in demeanor threw her for a real loop, as his fictional personality seemed incapable of allowing Mr. Olsen to resume control even under duress.

"There is always time," Serendipity said. "I admit it does seem hopeless when you are bombarded by all the negative images of the world. The media, the entertainment industry, and even mainstream culture has all had a part in keeping this in the forefront. Creating this wall of hopelessness."

"It does seem futile to think that it will sort itself out," the god sighed. "In my age, we would march to war, celebrate victory, and prepare for the next battle with a sense of purpose. This, though, has no apparent purpose. How do they make men march into the fire without any promise of glory?"

"There is no glory, and there never was," Serendipity asserted. "In your time, it was an illusion. Many of those who died at your feet did not do so gloriously, they died with fear and regret filling their souls. If you had filled your halls with them instead of those who welcomed death, you would have seen just how wrong you were." She kicked herself for feeding into the delusion a little too much, but she was committed to making a breakthrough.

"Aye. It began so long ago. This need for blood."

"We need to move away from the need for blood," Serendipity said thoughtfully, rubbing Odin's back again. "We need to find other ways to resolve our conflicts. Look at where this path leads. It leads to living in world that is dying by our own hand. The resources that could be used to heal our great mother, are still used to destroy her. We must, at some point, come to the understanding that we are all part of this whole. Each of us is needed to create a healthy, viable world. It's not too late, but we are running shorter on time."

The next video to pop up was one that made Odin catch his breath. There, surrounded by a company of armed warriors was his son, Thor, battling another man in armor.

"Do you know this man?" Serendipity asked seeing the reaction the video had produced.

"Aye. That is my son."

Thinking that this could be the breakthrough that she had hoped for, she paused the video and zoomed in on the large, blond-haired man who wielded a war hammer.

"This was recorded by one of the dudes in the network I belong to," Serendipity said, recognizing the Russian's screen name. "You know, the one I showed you yesterday. This is a role-playing gathering where people pretend to be figures from history."

Odin watched as Thor toyed with the mortal. He could see that he was taking his time, allowing the opponent to believe that there was some hope of victory. Serendipity's words barely registered as the hammer finally came in for a crushing blow.

"You say this is not real?" Odin asked puzzled after seeing the hammer explode into thousands of little pieces.

"Well, it's real, but they are just acting out the battle. The weapons and armor are not real, they are replicas fashioned to enhance the experience."

When the mortal fighting Thor thrust his sword so quick that even the camera could not catch it, Odin knew something had changed very quickly. He could see a slight aura rising around the man in armor. The same aura surrounding his son.

"See that, that aura!" Odin said excitedly.

"Well I see something," Serendipity squinted at the screen. "Spotlights focused on the combatants."

"No, the glow is coming from within. You just witnessed two gods battling."

Every step forwards became a step back with Mr. Olsen, Serendipity thought. Perhaps the other nurses had been right about him, believing that he was a dementia patient. So far the doctors had ruled that prognosis out, but perhaps with her assessment they would consider changing their diagnosis so that the old man could get some help. Believing that men who participated in Live Action Role Playing were real gods was just beyond the realm of reasonable thought. Believing yourself to be one, on top of it, was a sure sign that not all of the squirrel's nuts had made it home to the hollow in the tree.

"Hey, where are you going?" Odin asked as Serendipity started to leave the room feeling as if all hope had been lost. She had really believed that she could reach the man, make him come back to the real world. It was naivety on her part. She was just a nurse with aspirations of becoming a doctor someday.

"I've got to finish my rounds," she replied, managing to conceal her sullen mood as she had been trained to do as a nurse. "I'll be back to get my IPad later. You keep it for now." She kept her back turned to the old fellow. She didn't want him to see the doubts she was carrying.

When Serendipity was gone, Odin stared at the image frozen in front of him. Reaching Thor was of paramount importance now, before his son regained his strength. There was no telling what that boy would get up to without his guidance. Quick to temper, born and bred for war. This was a real dangerous situation, doubly now that he had met up with Aries, his Greek brother. He had to reach the person who posted the video back to the Dudeist site, so Odin typed a message.

"Tell my Son, I need to see him. Odin."

Chapter 10

'Keep it simple to avoid misinterpretation.'

Carl left with Hen through a portal that was invisible to the naked eye.

As compensation for being given the bad news that he wasn't meant to be a member of the Order of the Righteous Dude, Hen had hoped to cheer up the distraught man by giving him a quick tour of a mirror world. This was a once in a life chance for the internet blogger to really see something that could quite possibly transform his whole perspective. Anyone with half a brain would dive at the chance, and soon the all thoughts of being cast aside disappeared, along with the man and his stash of weed. Few, except spirit walkers, medicine women and men, and the occasional acid tripper ever managed to successfully find their way into the mirror worlds.

Bear led the remaining two members back to his home in this world.

Upon returning to the homestead, Hawk was able to use his smart phone again, picking up a weak signal from a tower, located in town, just a few miles away. Like most of his generation, the need to be constantly connected had been nagging at his thoughts the entire time they were in the wilderness. It disturbed him to think that he was craving something so unnecessary, yet he could not pull himself away from the device.

All over Facebook, people were posting videos of Seattle protestors clashing with police. Things had spiraled out of control over the past twenty-four hours, and the Governor of the state was calling in the National Guard. Some stores had been looted, homes burnt, and six people dead as a result. This made the whole prospect of getting into, and out of the city, more daunting.

"There are a lot of liberal minds in Seattle. A lot of

people not afraid to protest," Bear conceded. "This whole Masseedo thing has got people really swinging from the rafters. To tell you the truth, if I was there, I'd be protesting too. Those bastards have been killing off the bee population on purpose, forcing farmers to buy their self-pollinating seeds. Shit, without bees, the world dies, man."

"This is all part of it," Hawk said. "It must be. I mean the whole reason that we have been sent to find the Mad Hermit. Nuna hinted at some of the grave tidings in store for the world, but we don't need a translator to tell us just how important these protests really are." He was standing now, dipping his pita back into the hummus. "Perhaps there is something the dudes can do."

Bear scratched his beard, Willow gripped the staff tightly, and Horace covered his face with his paws. Reaching behind him and opening a drawer on the baker's cabinet, Bear pulled out his laptop computer with its mobile stick, and connected to the internet. Moments later he was on Facebook, searching for chatter about the riots in Seattle, and came across a Sister Helena Dudeski, whom had been posting updates every five minutes. From her vantage point, living in a condo downtown, she was right in the thick of things.

He sent Sister Helena Dudeski a message asking her about the likelihood of the violence ending in the near future. Her prognosis was grim. Next he messaged Paul the Plumber, the dude who kept an eye on the Mad Hermit. His response was along the same lines. Bear informed him of the Order's need to bring Gerald the Herald out of the city. The Plumber suggested he attempt to pull the Hermit out before the plane crashed into the Alps. Knowing how stubborn and difficult Gerald could be, the Bear could only hope he would go along. As quick thinking would have it, he snapped a picture of the staff and sent it, asking the plumber to show it to the Hermit, and explain to him that it was on the way.

"If this works, it is going to make your life a lot easier," Bear mentioned to Willow and Hawk.

"Is he that hard to reason with?" Hawk asked.

"Who, Gerald the Herald? Reason, no, but if it isn't his idea, then you'd have better luck convincing a cat to wear a leash."

"Old men are always stubborn," Willow pointed out.

"Old? Oh no dear. Gerald is young. Probably twenty-four or five. It's hard to say. His whole history is some kind of mystery. All we know is that he is Canadian by birth, grew up on the west coast, but after that, your guess is as good as mine."

"Why does this seem to be a theme with people associated with the *Dude See Scrolls*?" Hawk pointed out.

"Well, dude, we're not really sure," Bear said. "He is just a man and some things are beyond explaining. The best theory that I have is that the scrolls contain information so important that one must make them appear so full of shit, and fake, so that no one will ever be tempted to hunt them down."

"Ah. I get it. A veil over a veil." Hawk drew a hand over his face so only his eyes were showing. He then got up and began dancing around the room. Horace looked up, then looked down, apparently uninterested.

"Well, obviously we believe they contain some kind of vital information or else we wouldn't be out on this quest," Willow pointed out.

"Too true, my lady. I guess that makes us crazy." Close enough to swat, Willow tagged Hawk in the gut, and he doubled over, laughing hysterically.

"There are only two people who know the truth," Bear reflected. "I trust one of them, the other is a wild card like our friend here, Hawk. If Nuna says we need the Herald, then we need the Herald, and all the crazy baggage that comes along with him."

In the mirror world Carl walked beside Hen, passing a joint back and forth with the Yeti. As far as he could see, this world was just like his world, but without the people and all the construction. The sun, of course, seemed a little brighter. The air tasted fresher and birdsong was so loud at times he almost wished he had ear plugs.

Almost.

Here the Ley line was visible to the naked eye, and one could easily follow it as trees, flowers and other plants grew around it, but not directly over it. Quartz stone lined the trail floor, slightly glowing with energy infused into it, allowing travelers to follow it even at night. For hours they walked slowly, sometimes leaving the path so that Hen could show Carl animals long extinct on Earth, such as a flock of Heath hens and Passenger pigeons. Even a Californian golden bear came on the trail briefly to rub nuzzles with the Yeti.

"It is amazing what a different feeling the world has without men," Carl commented.

"Indeed. On this world, species still die off, but according to natural selection, and changes in habitat. No one hunts here to the extent that entire populations are killed off over night. Here, things happen naturally, and us Yeti observe and maintain the balance only when necessary. Some causes become hopeless of course, but other causes are important for maintaining the integrity of the whole."

"So, you are just making judgment calls?" Carl asked.

"Oh, no," the Yeti said. "We listen to the Great Spirit, the wind, the heartbeat of the world, and from there we know what is required of us. If we upset the balance, in time, our usefulness would become obsolete, but because we keep in harmony with the Great Spirit, we maintain a strong natural bond."

"I really wish you could have met Delroy," Carl said. "He talks of the great spirit all the time. Poor bastard has had an unusual bad run of luck, though." He went into more detail and explained the jar, the negative vibes surrounding the native man, and the visions the Medicine Woman had. "He was convinced that he had to come with us. Even our initial meeting seemed fated."

The Yeti pondered this for a moment as they rested beside a glacier-fed stream. One sip of the water breathed new life into Carl's tired legs.

"Perhaps it would be best if you wait here a moment," Hen said. "Do not worry, nothing will hunt you as long as you stay on a Ley line." Without waiting for a response, Hen disappeared. Alone, and completely out of his element Carl glanced around nervously and made sure that not even a toe left the quartz path. In a world where there were no humans, animals would have no need to fear them, making him quite the exotic dish.

An hour passed, and the occasional woodland creature would cross the path, somewhere in sight. A mountain lion the size of a small Volkswagen Bug, sent chills hurtling through Carl's spine. He had never felt such raw fear before, not even when he had been mugged, walking alone in Montreal on a summer night, two years past. This was a raw, primal fear. He shivered, moved to the middle of the path and didn't take his eyes off of the feline until it left, several minutes later. Carl could envision it circling around, through the pines, creeping in. He scanned the forest, even getting down to ground level to look around when Hen returned, this time with a guest.

"Hi, Carl," the new person announced.

"Oh, hi, Delroy."

Chapter 11

'The devil you know, probably knows the devil you don't.'

The great feast of King Henry Smith was a smashing success. The battle that had taken place before the meal service would be talked about for months to come. Some even began planning the next year's battle, having Hercules return to do battle against Vishnu. Imaginations were running wild and the mead was being consumed faster than it could be poured.

Given a table of honor next to the King, Aries and Thor argued over who would win a rematch if proper weapons were available. The Russian sat with them, nodding his head while pounding back the drinks. He was still considered an outsider by the gathered faithful for not wearing a proper costume, but it did little to dampen his mood. He sat with gods, his mind was convinced of the fact. Standing so close to the battle he had witnessed things that would be unexplainable if not for divine power. No one could move that fast, no mortal could create the aura that surrounded the two.

As for the other guests, the battle was still considered staged. Many felt that King Henry Smith had really raised the bar by hiring professional actors to take part in the feast. Autographs were being asked for, and under the tutelage of the Russian, the two gods were making their marks with some efficiency. With each autograph, their aura increased in intensity, their appearances altering slightly.

"I know little of what befell us, but I know it was not the Ragnarok as foretold by my father," Thor reflected. "I never tangled with the serpent strangling the earth. All I remember is a great sorrow and disbelief overtaking me, and then I was gone. Suspended in Limbo for so long I that I disappeared inside of myself. I relived a dream to which there seemed no end. A dream where I was as helpless as a mortal."

"It was the workings of that damned Christian movement, brother," said Aries. "I know, for I witnessed their rise in our lands. One by one my brothers and sisters disappeared as faith in this one god spread like an unstoppable plague. I was the last to go, for man will never lose his taste for war. It was shortly after the sack of Rome by the Germanic tribes that my end came. Like you, there was this overwhelming breakdown, my mind shattered from it. I receded into the darkness and lay awake, but in a dream."

"Mortals are so easily swayed, brother, and here we are again on this crazy world!" Thor thundered. "This Russian has tried to explain how the world has changed, and so much of it makes no sense. Wars are started by cowards now, and fought by people who have no desire to fight! If that is not the most ludicrous thing you have ever heard, then I do not know what is."

Aries accepted another flagon of mead from a very cute serving wench who hovered around a little longer then need be. Her long lashes flickered, and she managed a twirl of her hair before setting off to bring drinks to the next table.

"It was inevitable that the weak would rise, Thor. It happened in Greece, it happened in Rome. Wherever men are allowed to rule themselves, this happens. They no longer consult the gods, or make offerings, or show respect to the traditions of old. Power corrupts them, for they are unable to wield it as we can. They have no respect for it, they become sick with power, and allow it to turn their souls black. If their world is in as poor shape as you would have me believe, then I say good on them.

"The Christian god never made his presence shown," Aries drank down the rest of his mead. "He cast his son to the wolves and watched them devour him, and yet he did nothing. Had that been Zeus, the world would have burned. These people, whom we looked after for so long, were so easily swayed, and perhaps that was our great failing. Did we demand too much of them, whereas this new god asked so little? He sacrificed, instead of asking them to. Unheard of, really."

Thor was less of a philosopher then his Greek counterpart. He listened, but he really didn't care about the how's and why's. He wanted to return to Asgard, return to his rightful place amongst his brothers and sisters, find glory in battle and wield Mjolnor once again. Humans were weak and pathetic in this modern age. Once he had his full power back he would destroy the evil that had infested this land and then leave for good. He would find those that had ruined a paradise and send them to the Seven Hells where they belonged.

"I need to find my father and consult with him," Thor stated.

"Perhaps, that might not be so difficult." The Russian, who was checking his messages, showed Thor the note on the dude's website, right below the video of his battle with Aries. The message said, "Tell my son I need him. Odin." Thor demanded at once to know where he was.

"Sunnygrove Retirement Facility in Toronto, Ontario, in Canada."

"Is that far?" Thor asked, his hands clenching.

"Not really, but we have to figure out a way to get across the border. I don't imagine you have a passport, do you?"

Confused by his question, Thor looked at his traveling partner with stone cold eyes.

"No worries, we can figure it out," the Russian reassured Thor. "Canada is much easier to get into than United States. There is a big border, and very little of it is guarded."

"Aries, will join us on this quest?" Thor asked in all seriousness.

The god pondered the question but then shook his head. He wasn't prepared to go off in that direction when there was a force calling him from further away. Over the seas somewhere, in an ancient tomb, there was a beacon sending out a vibe he could not shake.

"I am sorry Thor, but I am needed elsewhere."

Chapter 12

'Follow the road to where it leads and you will find another road.'

  The seeds of discontent grow rampant in the unkempt field. As the roots take hold, the soil becomes a partner, not caring whether or not the new species is invasive or not. The sun has the same sort of relationship, always giving, never being prejudicial. The wind will tell its tale, as it tells all others, and it is only the farmer that comes along, cursing, deciding what gets to live and what does not.

  Left to grow, the seed of discontent spreads through the field, using more and more of the earth's energy, feeding into the ever vibrant vibe. It now has the power to become contagious, the power to replace reason with cause. The fertile conditions allow the spark to consume, and soon it blossoms outward.

  Seattle had become the most reported city in America over the past three days, as rioting, protesting, and civil disobedience ran amok. What started out as a protest against a corporate entity, Masseedo, soon blossomed into a protest against the government, other corporations, and financial institutions, as underground organizations merged together to keep the pot boiling. It was spreading quickly across the country now, and even the smaller Midwest cities experienced the surge of anger.

  Forced into action, the governments did what they always do, they brought in more force. Soldiers, sent into the streets to walk along the side of police officers, did the best they could, but the vibe had been building for far too long. It had sat dormant since the early Eighties, in limbo, adapting, poking and prodding, still feeding off the power infused into it by a generation of hippies who wanted social change. Every now and then it would surface in the face of ripe conditions, only to sink back down into the sub cultures. This time, though, it felt that it had enough traction to sustain itself.

The Star Chamber sat in an unscheduled meeting, one of necessity. They had too many interests at stake to not pay close attention to what was happening in the streets of America, and this sudden flare up was ahead of their planned schedule. When stocks took a beating, they could improvise, capitalize, and come out better than before, but when the whole, always-volatile market threatened another major crash, well then an intervention was needed.

"The problem as I see it, is there is just no way to profit from this." Robert Klein opened with. His banking interests overseas were beginning to get the old jimmy leg, with America in chaos.

"Well we are doing our best to downplay the situation," Rupert scowled. "I've got all media outlets focusing elsewhere as best we can. Is it possible to advance our plans ahead, and turn the south on the north? Are we ready for that kind of commitment yet?" He had been overseeing the building of his safe house in Fiji, and this disturbance had spoiled his mood.

"If we were to go ahead, at least we could find some way to profit from this," Manuel Juarez Ricardo Lupe Fernandez pointed out. "As it stands right now, there is nothing to profit from. One side is fully armed, reluctant to start opening fire, and the other, barely able to spell correctly on their signs." Even drug trafficking was taking a hit as the streets became war zones instead of drug zones. The Mexican cartels were seriously considering taking to the streets along the border states just to open up some of the flow again.

"The problem is the right catalyst. What will it be?" Robert asked.

"The race card always works well over here," Francisco pointed out.

"Religion is a more volatile subject these days," Sir Richard countered. "We get the South beating the Christian drums and the North playing the liberalism card. And perhaps if we were to have our Muslim Congressman present a gun control bill laden with restrictions and regulations…"

"No, that won't work," Rupert shook his head. "How about we have a northern Congressman attempt to have any reference of God removed from all federal and state legislation. We can start out by having the song 'God Bless America' banned in public arenas due to the fact that some find it offensive."

"That just might do it," Sir Richard said. "The religious card, I mean, the erosion of free speech, and with the right advertisement campaign portraying the South as a bunch of banjo-playing god freaks, we might have something. We could throw the occasional log on the fire, and soon these coals won't simmer for long, they will explode into a bonfire."

"Okay, so if we move ahead with this plan, who will win in the end?" Robert asked.

"Well, we can't have a bunch of banjo-playing inbreds running the country, can we?" Rupert replied. "No, we will ensure that in the end they will run out of resources. Eventually, we will have this whole god fascination removed from this land. Then, maybe, just maybe, we will be able to salvage something useful from this wasteland."

So it began. In a room, decided by five men. A phone call was made to one puppet, then that puppet called another puppet and in the end the trail disappeared completely. In Massachusetts a member of congress drafted the bill that would set fire to a nation. Of course, it would have to come from that hotbed of liberalism. New England had been a thorn in the South's side for generations, at least since the abolitionists ruined its economic model.

There was no way a bunch of liberal, hippie types were going to throw a wrench in carefully constructed plans. The future had been glimpsed, and it did not have a socialist handbag hanging off the left arm of some moderate wannabe. No, this slight deviation only encouraged the Star Chamber into action. With chaos already finding itself a home, the need for order was stronger than ever. Controlled war could do that.

A general call to arms would not happen overnight, that was a given. First the kettle would have to boil dry, over heat, turning the metal red hot. Then you add water and watch it explode on contact. Within a week, people would have forgotten about protesting big business, and the inequalities that kept the world poor. Now their attention would be turned on their government. Voices rising up, decrying the audacity of such measures, while others would finally feel that their thoughts had found a voice. Why was god involved in the making of laws, cried the atheists? Why were the people of America beholding to superstitious powers, like the people of the Middle East where it had created nothing but unrest, and misery for centuries.

In California, the people were the first to stop playing "God Bless America" as it was written. In its place the people sang, "I Bless America" during a Dodger, Braves game. A game that was broadcast live across the country on Sunday night's game of the week. It did not sit well with the Atlanta fans who hit the internet immediately, posting their fury. A viral thread that spread like mold in an unplugged refrigerator.

In the northern states, liberals took to the streets in droves supporting the separation of church and state once and for all. Fueled by media reporting, speculation, and the occasional railroading of the facts, the kettle was set to full boil. It was easy to rile those who had opinions. It was easy to play on those beliefs. The media machine understood the human mind better than most would give it credit for. Angering people who liked to flaunt their beliefs was as easy as typing a single word on a viral feed.

Chapter 14

'Sometimes there isn't enough coffee or cookies to make it worth getting out of bed.'

Gerald took the coffee from Bob the Plumber and thought about his request. With the city ready to explode, there was little reason to stay. As far as chaos goes, it's only fun when you are on the outside looking in. Larry was circling behind the box mansion, talking quietly to himself, and Gerald knew his friend would have to be part of the deal, one way or the other.

"Okay, Bob," Gerald said. "You've shown me the staff, with a pretty thing attached to it. Bear and Nuna are calling on my help, and the world is about to go into the biggest shit storm since 9/11. I'll go with you, but Larry has to come. He can't cope on his own anymore. His nerves are shot and I'm the only one who gives a shit if he wakes in the morning or not."

"Whatever you say, dude," Bob said. "I'm going to get you outside of the city and far enough away before all the roads in are shut off to the outside world, but we got to go now."

Looking around at Reality, a tinge of regret seeped into the Hermit's veins. He quickly chased it away with a shrug. Attachments only held you back. If the visions were really coming true, this would be the last time he would roam these cardboard alleys. It was time to take to the hills.

"Larry, grab your things," he said. "We are out of here."

Larry came around the corner, his left hand scratching his head. It was apparent that he was deeply distressed, and anxious.

"Um, Mad Man. I.., don't think I can leave."

"Of course you can leave!" Gerald encouraged his friend. "This shit is going to get heavy, man. People are going to turn into savages and they will burn everything to the ground before they smarten the fuck up."

Larry shook his head. His hand was shaking. "I know Mad Man, but this is my home. Your home is where ever you want it to be, but I don't have that option."

Gerald looked at his friend. His heart fill with pain, for he knew that there would be no changing his mind. Too much trauma had marred his past. This was his home, the only place he had found comfort. To him, Reality was where he belonged. Forgotten, left alone to battle his demons in private.

"Stay low, brother," he advised Larry, consolingly. "Keep off the streets and don't let any assholes try to move into that Maytag mansion, you hear. It's yours now. I've got to go sort some shit out."

The embrace was quick, and soon after the plumber's van was weaving through back streets, avoiding all the potential hazards that the main thoroughfares were experiencing. Behind them, flames jumped up into the sky, as the city started to tear itself apart.

"All this hate Bob, its coming to the surface," Gerald shook his head. "The fools tried so hard to keep it buried beneath the shit pile, but now they can't contain it. This is going to be worse than the shit storms of the Sixties and Seventies. This time it's being fueled by some real negative dudes."

"It's in the air, Herald," Bob agreed, swerving to avoid debris scattered on the road. "The mega vibe that will turn friends against each other."

"No jar will be enough to contain this one," Gerald said. "Hopefully these so-called Righteous Dude will have enough in their tanks to see this through to the end. I know we've got the right people in place, but do we have the right vision to see it through? I mean, I wrote those scrolls over a period of six months, two years ago. To me it's a hazy memory, and I might not be able to make any sense of them. Shit, the weed I was smoking then would knock the Dude himself on his ass. I should have stayed away from that experimental shit, but you know how it is when you get free dope. Party time.

"Even if we do find some kind of answer in there," he went on, "who's to say that we'll have any chance of acting on it. After spending my time in Reality, I've seen just how much of this land lies under a cloud of darkness. It's everywhere. No regard for the future, little regard for the past. and the present is in the hands of children who squabble over who has what. Even marriage would be easier to figure out then this shit show. It's going to take some extraordinary help, I'm thinking.

"Who knows though? Maybe this is exactly what the world needs. Perhaps we've got to reach the bottom one more time to realize that we're just treading on the surface. There really is no finish-line to race to. There is no prize, other than creating harmony. Try to get some people to bite that lure, though. Too busy competing, too busy fighting, and too busy staring at what the other fellow has. What the hell do I know, though? All the truth ever did for me was get me labeled as mad."

"I've got to believe there are better times ahead, dude," the plumber replied. "I mean it can't be all meat and no gravy, can it?"

"Well, we'll just have to see. I'll tell you, though, that this power we are fighting against has been concentrating on its advancement for a long time, dude. They have invested more time and energy into the smallest of details than we have on the basic question."

"What question is that, Herald?"

Gerald snorted. To him it was so obvious. The First World populace cared little for such things.

"How do we achieve absolute equality?" he asked. "The follow-up to that is, 'What is stopping us?'"

A convoy of National Guard passed the plumber's van on the out skirts of the city. The main arteries were now blocked to incoming traffic, though people were still allowed to leave. Armored personal carriers were bringing in volunteers from all around the state who wanted to help put down this leftist uprising. Might would make this right. It always worked before, and in this instance a couple of bloodied noses would have those dirty hippies running back to their Volvo's and VW buses. Fifty miles from the city limits, at a busy rest stop filled with transport trucks loaded with wares bound for the city but now held up, the van pulled up beside a Toyota Corolla, which contained two passengers sitting patiently, waiting.

With a handshake, Bob left the Hermit in the care of the two young Canadians, and immediately sent a text message to Bear, proclaiming that the package had been delivered. He Turned his van around, prayed to a god that he really didn't believe in, hoping that he could somehow find a way back into the city, and back to his family. His house was in the suburbs, far from the hot zones, but still he worried.

"So this is the Order of the Righteous Dude!" the Hermit proclaimed. "Two Canadians in a Toyota, out trying to save the world." He walked towards the two, who got out of the car when they watched the van pull up.

Willow was the first to speak up, raising the staff.

"I think this belongs to you."

"It used to, but I gave it to someone more dedicated to the cause then myself," he replied. "You must have really charmed the pants off of the monk, for him to let you hold his staff."

Hawk laughed at the innuendo in the Hermit's statement. Willow just frowned. It was a look that Hawk had become used to, and feared at times.

"Now don't get all tense, dude. I know what a pretty face can do for a person. It's gotten me this far in life." Gerald goaded.

"Look, I don't care who you are, just get in the car," Willow replied. "We've just driven across the country to find you, and I've had it up to here with all this macho shit that men cling to like their mother's tit. So get in the back, and have a puff of a joint, and mellow out until we get you back across the border."

With her fists at her side, Gerald could see that there wasn't going to be much bantering with this one. He smiled a genuine smile, seeing that Nuna had chosen wisely here.

"You bet, dude," he conceded, climbing into the Camry. "But I don't toke anymore. It makes me social, and that defeats the purpose of being a hermit."

They blazed north with the fury of a thousand suns pushing them on. The mountains around them on all sides blocked the sea from spilling into the plains beyond, while banks of clouds remained trapped on this side of the divide. Ahead of them was Canada, their home and refuge. Behind them America was tearing itself apart.

A calm fell over the Herald. His hand had steadied, his heart stopped racing. It had been some time since he had felt at ease around strangers. These two acolytes appeared dedicated to this wild cause, enough to be considered crazy. The long-haired driver was living in the moment, his heart fueled by the promise of the future. He talked of his band, of his mates, of his city with great pride. He recited Dudeisms with every second breath, and the Hermit wondered if he was doing it just to impress him.

The girl, on the other hand, said very little. She stood behind a shield of solitude and deflected any attempts at reaching her on a personal level. Very business-like, counting the miles ahead, her eyes scanning the darkness for any unforeseen danger. In her hands, his old staff rested comfortably, the worn hand holds seem to wrap themselves around her fingers. These were interesting times. He was beginning to have a little a faith in the Dude network, something he never thought would happen. Mistakenly he had thrown them in the same hole with the rest of the modern world, believing that this movement was all a fad. He had truly believed that the upstart religion would fade into the mists of yesterday. That was part of the reason why he had given away the scrolls. That was why he had given away his staff. That was why he had abandoned every part of his previous life.

"I'm going to level with you kids," Gerald said, interrupting the silence that had settled over the Camry after Hawk had played a home-made recording of his band. "I never expected this day to come. Sure, I had visions of it, but everything is subject to change, yet here we are."

"What are you saying, dude?" Hawk asked.

Gerald confided. It felt good to let it out. He explained his need to separate himself from anything involving Dudeism. He explained how he purposely abandoned the scrolls with the first person he thought might actually believe in the nonsense contained within. It was his own lack of faith in anything that sent him into hiding, where he could ignore the world and the future he had seen. In the back seat of the Toyota, a closet opened up and all the skeletons came out.

"So you're not really a Dudeist?" Hawk tried hard to contain his astonishment.

"No, dude. I'm not. Or at least I haven't really been thinking along those lines for a while. There was a time though, when I was really into it. I was online, chatting, writing, posting. Things sort of started to slip for me though when I realized that no matter how hard I tried, the world wasn't getting any better. Shit was still getting fucked up, and people were still walking around with blinders covering their eyes. I got frustrated, I stopped believing with my heart and I turned to my brain. Logic called me like horny stripper and I fell into her bed. It became easier to stop giving a fuck, but I took it even farther. I took it to that place of apathy, where I no longer cared either way. Let the world go to hell, let the bastards ruin it for everyone else. At least I found a little peace by distancing myself. I ran but I guess I could not hide."

There was another moment of silence following the Herald's confession. This time it was Willow who turned around, looked past the scraggly beard, the creased forehead and the haggard eyes. She smiled, opening up her inner light and letting a little bit of it warm the homeless man.

"It's time to believe again," she said. "It's time to make a difference. The network is alive and well and growing fast. That change you were looking for was always coming it just took a little longer than anticipated, in true Dude fashion. I was as skeptical as anyone, until I read between the lines in all the conversations happening online.

Beyond the usual regurgitation of movie quotes I discovered a real spark, a place where people cared. Strangers who had never met in person, were wishing each other well. Offering sound advice in times of need. Showing compassion when others would make fun of the everyday trials we endure. Love, unusual, yet real, was filling the posts in places where one would expect to find sarcasm and negativity. Like anything, there are a few bad apples, but in truth it's the best thing I've come across in all the soul-searching journeys that I have under taken."

"Well, you know after living in Reality for the past year," Gerald reflected, "I've had a chance to realize that even in the depths of despair, people find happiness. Left-Handed Larry knows no other life now, the war took his ability to adapt, but it couldn't steal his happiness. He had to look a little harder to find it, but he opened himself to the possibility and it found him. I understand why he wouldn't leave that place, even with the fires threatening to burn it all. I, on the other hand, know only fear. I've been running for so long now that it's all I know. Maybe by doing this, breaking my comfort zone, I don't know. Maybe I will finally find some peace."

"It will come if you allow it," Willow offered.

"You know I clean up pretty good." Gerald remarked, smiling with a twinkle in his eye.

Chapter 15

'It never gets easier without a change in perspective.'

  Mirror worlds are forever copying each other. No one is quite sure which was the original world copied, but everyone in the multi-dimensional realms agree that it was not the Earth we know. Apparently the world we know was a byproduct of another, a fart so to speak. The wolves believe that it was men from another Earth who decided to test the theory that humans could run on ten percent of their brains, and do so successfully. Even making it as far as they had, it was viewed as quite an achievement throughout the various realms. The Yeti assumed that most humanoids ran around the ten to twenty percent mark, for on several of the Earths they knew, the laws of reason and harmony just did not exist.
  When you flaunt the fact that you operate at only ten percent, and are able to do more things then other species can do at a hundred, you tend to have few, sympathetic, friends. Dogs and cats for the most part were the only other beings capable of living around people for any length of time. Most of them willingly, thriving in life with the bipeds. Others, especially birds, had an immense hate on for humankind. They poisoned all of their favorite places, the air, the water, and cut down swaths of perches. The most they could do to extract their revenge was to shit on the human's possessions from above. Birds operated at one hundred and ten percent for the most part. Their little brains working harder than anyone else. So hard at times, that they don't even notice the big whirling blades the humans erected into the skies, at their ten percent, in their attempt to find cleaner ways to produce energy.
  The biggest problem with operating any system at its minimal output, is that there is a severe carbon build up in the parts that remain dormant. Heads filled with non-

firing pistons tend to find the easiest way to operate, live, and make due. Stepping through into a mirror world does something to the human mind though, something that hadn't been fully researched because so few had made the journey. Standing on the Ley Line path, both Carl and Delroy could feel a tug inside of their noggins.

Now, it is easy to dismiss all of this and say that humans don't operate at ten percent and that all of this has been written off by the scientific field as bull, but how do you explain some things like Donald Trump, reality television, and daylight savings time without wondering?

"I can almost feel myself existing," Carl said, smoking another joint.

Delroy looked around at all the lush vegetation, and let the breeze tickle his face. He had removed his shoes, thrown them into the woods, along with his socks. A great energy was surging up through the ground and stopping around his knees, where it was met some kind of resistance.

"The Great Spirit! For the love of God! I can almost feel it!" He began to weep silently.

"Yeah, well that is great, man. I am glad that, you know, you can feel free to express yourself so openly around me." Carl replied, lying. He felt very uncomfortable around tears. It was one of the reasons he rarely dated, that and he was an ultra-geek.

"Yes, brother," Delroy beamed. "This place is the place my people spoke of. The place beyond the clouds. A place where the great medicine still holds power. Where the mother cares for, and the father teaches. All these years I was beginning to think that everything my family and the Medicine Woman told me was nothing but a load of shit. Years of running through the forests, collecting this plant, that bark. It was all part of the great circle. Oh, what fool I was to deny it! To think I was ready to give in to the white man's world, once and for all. To start believing the lies that keep you from growing as one, with the planet."

Two coyotes appeared on the trail ahead. One, with an orange hue to its coat, came closer to the humans, wanting to see for herself what all the hoopla was about. As the coyote inched closer to Delroy, she suddenly sensed the darkness that surrounded the poor being, and in response bared her teeth. The hairs on the back of her neck rose, and she backed away ashamed that she could not help.

"Goddamned negative vibes!" Delroy cursed. "I must be free of this curse."

"Don't worry, dude," Carl said, releasing the smoke he had been holding in after a toke. "I think that's why Hen brought you here. I told him your story and he seemed to think that he could be of some help. Perhaps just being here will chase away that cloud. I honestly don't know, but I think a pull off of this bad boy will help put your mind at ease." Passing the joint over to the native man, Carl waved at the coyotes as they jumped back into the bush.

"You're weed is better than I remember," Delroy commented.

"Yeah, I think it's this place," Carl said, looking around at the humming hues. "Everything probably tastes better in such a pure environment. Even the water I got from a spring a ways back seems to have given me more energy than I ever remember water given me, and I've been on a strict bottled water diet for three years now. No more fluoride going in this machine. Mind control shit, you know. Poisons the soul and makes it easier for the government to sell you shit you don't need. I tell you this place has really limbered up my mind, man, got me thinking. I'm going to get back to what I do best, blogging. I'm going open a big ole' can of worms and set me some hooks. Aw, look at me. I've started rambling. This weed is killer shit."

There is no hole opening up, with special sounds accompanying the distortion in space time. One minute there was no one there, the next a Yeti wearing a frown. He scratched his head as he walked up to the two high men, as they sat on the Ley Line trail, staring into the forest.

"I'm sorry to say Delroy, but I was unable to find someone who could perform a Dudercism for you. Humans are always too busy these days, and others rarely wander off into nature where I can intercept them."

Carl patted his companion on the shoulder. Carrying around this negativity would wear even the strongest of men down. No amount of weed or drink could save someone from such an affliction. He looked at Hen, his eyes searching out for another answer.

"There is of course a spirit walk," Hen mentioned reluctantly. "It is possible that if you were to come across your soul guide during such a journey, the combined powers of your energies, might just drive this curse away. It's all speculation, of course, otherwise we might just have to wait until this other thing that has taken priority back on your Earth has run its course."

Immediately, Delroy snapped to. He turned to the giant furry being and grabbed one of his hands. Inside a sudden urge to explore, deep rooted from the blood of his ancestors, called out to accept such a journey.

"Tell me how I begin."

The Yeti walked in circles for a moment, conflict obviously eating at him. For a human to enter into a spirit journey on a mirror world would bring about great danger. Many of the creatures of this realm had never encountered a human and would instinctively fear this negative aura that surround his spirit. A few would even be tempted to kill him just to rid the world of such things.

"It's not something to be taken lightly, or accepted without knowing the risks," the Yeti warned.

"My father's father's father walked the path of the spirit," Delroy explained. "He came back with an eagle feather and lived longer than anyone else in our tribe. No man since has been allowed to undertake such a thing. The Medicine Woman says the reason is that men come back from such journeys with useless things like feathers, when they should be bringing back the hope of a nation. She says leave it to a man to find himself when he should be finding others." The eagle feather still hung above his parents' bed beside the picture they got in Florida of themselves standing at the gates of Disney World. Beside the picture was a Swordfish's sword that they had purchased at a gift shop in Cape Canaveral.

Preparing for such a journey really required little preparation. Already high as a kite, Delroy's mind was limber enough to accept what was to come. All he needed now was to be pointed in the right direction. He stood facing east, his hands at his side as he was told, and closed his eyes. Hen winked at Carl then moved in behind Delroy and gave him an incredible shove in the back, sending the man flying off the Ley Line trail and into the forest.

Chapter 16

'You have two hands, so lend one once in a while.'

When hope is renewed, it infuses a soul with the power to heal. Like water to a parched plant, hope raises the dead, or the semi-dead, and throws them back out into the world of the living. Blues become warm, greens become vibrant, and black just becomes the outlining border, giving the other colors more definition. This spring that erupts within an individual can become a contagious thing, spreading quickly into all those around them.

Finding such hope was not an everyday occurrence at Sunnygrove.

Odin was walking now, a cane helping him along the way, supporting each step. He escaped the confines of his room more often, taking meals with the others in the dining room, occasionally sitting in on the local news assembly in the television lounge. His sudden turn around surprised the entire staff, and all of them had gone out of their way to congratulate Serendipity on her amazing feat. Even Doctor Schobel had pulled her aside and gave her the praise she deserved.

Apparently the shell on this nut had been partially cracked.

Odin, on the other hand, just decided to play along for now. His son was on the way, he could feel him, sense his presence getting closer. Hope had made it easier to forget just how ridiculous this whole setting was. A pasture, for the elderly to await death. Fill them with routine until they can take no more and let their spirits go. In the new world he intended on creating, the elderly would never be treated like such again.

Feeling their pain and acknowledging their plight, allowed Odin to converse, hiding his true identity for the moment. He just wanted to experience what wisdom and knowledge of the world lay in such a place. Many had seen wars. Many had survived harsh economic times. Many had experienced the purest love. He had to learn this human experience quickly if he was to be of any use in this modern age.

    In the midst of a Sunday buffet with friends and family in attendance, Odin discovered that loneliness was the biggest killer of all. All of a sudden these aged spirits suddenly sprang to life when their kin entered the front foyer with gifts in hand. Such rare visits allowed the ones teetering closest to the edge to hang on again for another month or two. It was a cycle for some. A small amount of hope, followed by the pain of loneliness.

    "Hello, stepfather," Loki announced as he sat beside Odin and handed him a jar of pickled herring. He appeared as a well sculpted, Wall Street-type this go around, with blond hair parted to the left.

    "Seven Hells! What are you doing here you miserable, piece of..." Odin replied, watching his rising spirits take a turn down a dark road.

    "Okay, I get it," Loki said, raising his manicured hands. "You are angry. You might even have every right to be, but I wouldn't have come back unless it was really important, knowing full well that there was a real possibility that my life would be in imminent danger. So please hear me out." He watched the old man swallow his anger before moving on.

    "Thor is never going to reach you here," he proceeded. "This world has things called borders, and at those borders they had guards who only allow people in with the right paper work. Now, knowing my brother like I do, I'm going to assume he'll just try crossing over and will quickly find out that he cannot, and in turn, it will create a great ruckus which will land him in a cell for a long time. Instead, I propose that you allow me to take you to him, for I have the know how of this age, the ability to go where I need to, and the resources to spring you from this country club. I only have one request, and that is you do not tell Thor who I really am when I get you to him. I fear his rashness would only create a conflict that would not work in my favor."

Odin reached out and grabbed Loki's arm. His boney fingers dug deep into his tailored suit, wrinkling the fabric.

"What kind of trick is this?"

"No trick, father. I, like all of you, sometimes must obey the Fates, and this time they point me in an unusual direction. Believe it or not, I am really here to help you."

"The fucking Fates!" Odin grumbled. "Those Greek bastards! I won't trust one of them with my flagon of ale, as I pissed on a cedar tree. They have been playing at being a god, without ever really knowing what it is like to be a god. To listen to them, is to listen to a goddamn goat. Stubborn, willful, and always believing to be right. You must think that I have become a bigger fool as a result of my time in Limbo."

Calmly and carefully, Loki removed the hand from his arm. He sat down in the chair next to Odin, smiled at the elderly lady who was sitting across the table from them and picked up a glass of water, from which he sipped.

"Believe what you must, Father of the Asgard," he said. "I, believe it or not, am telling the truth this time. Think it through logically. I obviously know where Thor is. If my intent was to do him harm, then why would I come here and pester you. Second, even the shadows must sometimes borrow from the light, in order to maintain their balance in the universe. I, like it or not, have a debt to you that must be paid at some time. I would prefer to choose that time and place, and as such, I choose to do so now. One cannot carry around such a thing for too long without it slowly working against you. There is no gain for me here. If I wanted either of you dead, or back in limbo I could do so with the snap of my fingers. My power is not derived from the belief of others, such as yours is. My power is derived from their disbelief, and trust me when I say that there is enough skepticism in this world to make me the most powerful god to ever tread on the soil. Be thankful that I choose to be benevolent for the most part."

Sometimes a leap of faith is the equivalent to jumping a chasm. When there is a hurt so strong that it can totally dominate your thoughts, one must have to wonder when one can let go. It's easier said than done, everyone knows that, but for a god, letting go was a monumental task. Perhaps the past would always linger, perhaps a small amount of forgiveness could be useful in the short term. Going against his better judgment, Odin decided to allow a handful of trust back into his relationship with the master of lies.

"Get me the hell out of here," he muttered.

Loki allowed Odin to use his arm for support and guided him towards the front entrance. There was nothing in his room that was needed, it all belonged to someone who no longer existed. As they passed by the front desk, Serendipity looked up from her computer console and stood as the two neared. Odin smiled. He liked the girl, even if she was truly barking up the wrong tree. He was too old for her, at least by a millennium or two.

"I see you have a guest," she beamed. "That's great, Mr. Olsen."

Loki smiled; it was the charmer's smile that could woo the strumpets in a tavern, but would instantly turn off an educated woman. A small frown appeared in the left corner of her lip, threatening to take over.

"Ah, yes," Odin said. "This is my nephew, Luke. He surprised me by showing up today. As far as I knew, he thought I was dead." Odin wanted to proceed quickly but the nurse came out from behind the station to meet this relative that no one knew existed.

"That is great," she said. "We all believed that Mr. Olsen had no relatives, or at least any that would ever come visit him. He was always very adamant that he had no one to get in touch with. Except, there was that video though, with a man he claimed to be his son."

Loki was fully prepared to deal with this distraction quickly, but Odin squeezed his arm tight, letting him know that he had this covered.

"Well, that man in the video is my son," Odin

explained. "Luke here knows him well and since we sent that message on your little magic machine, my son requested that Luke here come visit me, and see that I was fine." Loki nodded.

"Oh, that is wonderful," Serendipity smiled. "I sense that you are a busy man, Luke. You have that look about you, as if you'd rather be anywhere else then here." She was digging, something did not feel right about this. Her gut was grumbling, refusing to be ignored.

Again, Odin intercepted the jab.

"He is a very busy man, and by all accounts not very fond of me, nor I of him, but we are family. Some ties must be maintained, even when the taste left on the tongue is sour."

"I suppose so," Serendipity said. "I have an aunt, Kerry is her name, and she just ...." There was flicker in the lights, a sudden gust of wind and Serendipity was back in her chair, head tilted back, fully asleep. Loki looked at Odin with an apologetic glance.

"I cannot stand listening to small talk," he apologized.

"Okay then, get me the hell out of here."

Outside in the roundabout, Loki had a black Saab waiting. He used the keyless remote entry button and helped Odin into the passenger seat. He then walked around to the driver's side, climbed in and started the car. The motor hummed quietly, the air conditioning revved up, and a Roy Orbison song, 'Only the Lonely', came on the radio.

"So I suppose this is your first experience in a motor vehicle, other than an ambulance," Loki chuckled at the old man's wonder. "This is what the Vikings now build. All and all, it's a nice ride and handles the road quite well, though I must admit that the Germanic people have really mastered the essence of quality. This, unfortunately is going to be a long ride, so feel free to have a nap if you must. I promise not to get into any mischief."

Chapter 17

'Each thread is important to the weave.'

  Invisible lines divide us. They are everywhere. Rules define these imaginary borders, places people take claim over. On one side, somethings are okay, on the other, no. There is no unified set of laws governing the inhabitants of the world, each side seems to think they can do it better than the other. Secretly, we all believe in the same basic rights, yet we want to hide behind a banner of nationalism to give our own self-worth a boost. We want to belong to something, and we want our something to be better than theirs.
  These markings on paper, in people's minds, create divisions that keep us separate, untrustworthy, and eager to defend. The common belief is that it takes backbone to stand up for what you believe in. We want strong leaders, before we want wise ones. We look for strength in our faith, before we evaluate its merit from end to end. We are more likely to believe in the unbelievable, due to the fact that it is the more popular outlook, and requires less thought on our part. In numbers we look to find strength, but we sometimes give up our rational sense of basic right and wrong by following the crowd.
  People are paid to stand and protect these invisible lines. Lines that wars have been fought over. Generally speaking, the root cause is based on resources. One side has something the other doesn't and when brief negotiations fail, the general discourse is to turn to violence. From the playground to the United Nations headquarters, when words fail, fists are raised. Guards watch for people who attempt to cross the lines without all the hassle of identifying themselves. The earth was meant to be roamed, and yet man does his best to prevent others from doing so because of the fear of losing something that they cannot

bare to lose.

Until leaders, backed by the people, the world over, turn away from violence as a choice to resolving conflict, the cycle will perpetuate itself. People still see it as a viable option. It is still a card in the deck. It is easier to follow old habits than to create new ones.

The Russian watched the border guards at the crossing and noticed that on the American side, they were much more thorough in their inspections. People were asked to leave their cars, dogs were led around, sniffing, and some people were even forced to unpack items from their vehicles and place them on the ground. Voices were often raised, tears were sometimes shed, and some folks were refused entry. Thor started to believe that these Canadians must be very deceitful, and untrustworthy.

Traffic heading north of the border seemed to flow quite steadily. Very few cars were pulled off to the side, and very few people were forced to explain themselves beyond a sentence or two.

"I don't know why you insist on waiting, Russian," Thor said. "These Canadians are obviously too untrustworthy."

"Yes, I know, but we must be careful. We do not have papers for you, and coming from a country that is big on papers, you do not try to bluff your way across no matter how naive the guards on the other side are. If you try to force the issue then you might end up in a gulag, and there you never see your father again."

"No more excuses, Russian," Thor shook his head. "We have been here a day, scouting as you wish to call it. I grow weary, and soon I will take action."

"No, wait, just a little longer," the Russian urged. "I think that I have a plan. We will wait for a big truck to stop at that diner over there, climb in the back of it when the driver goes into store. Next thing you know we are across the border. We will then find a way to Toronto, and reunite you with your father."

When the perfect truck came along, under the cover of shadows, the two raced across the street and hid behind the back of the long haul trailer. The trouble with the plan became clear immediately when the Russian realized that the door latch was on the outside, and could not be replaced when the two climb in. Leaving it unlatched would lead to curiosity, and increase the chances of a search.

The Russian cursed. He knew that there was no way to make this work. He thought about climbing on top of the trailer and laying low, but there were many mirrors at the border station that would give away any such hiding spot. He kicked the ground and started to think quickly. Thor was losing his patience and would eventually resort to something foolish and brash. With the cool night breeze keeping them alert, they were both well aware of the black sports car that pulled alongside of the truck and inched its way closer to them. It came to a halt once it was directly beside them. The passenger window slid down and old man stuck his head out.

"What in the Seven Hells are you doing, Thor?" Odin asked.

Shocked by the appearance of his father, and slightly embarrassed at his attempt at subterfuge, Odin grabbed the Russian by the arm and dragged him over to the Saab.

"You've looked better father," he offered.

"And you have been braver! Sneaking around in the darkness like your brother! This age has effected all of us differently, I guess. I thought I'd save you the trouble of trying to get over that border. Being thrown in prison would not have helped our cause."

Thor bent lower to look into the vehicle. Loki sat patiently, smiling at the big man. He turned off the car's lights to arouse less suspicion in the parking lot. The scene had the makings of a drug deal going down, and with so many American trigger-happy guards only a couple hundred meters away, there was no need to attract attention.

"Hello, Thor," the blond man at the wheel said. "My name is Luke. Your father has told me a lot about you."

"It was a long trip and I had to keep my man servant occupied along the way. Tales of valor always inspire better dedication," Odin offered.

Thor motioned the Russian ahead, making him kneel before the elder god in due respect.

"This, Russian, is my father, Odin, King of the Asgard. The skinny man beside him is his manservant, Luke."

"It is a pleasure to meet you both," the Russian replied.

"Russian, my ass," Loki said, smirking. Where are you really from? Boston?"

"But what do you mean?" the Russian replied.

"I like to bet, you see, and I'd wager a million dollars that you have never set foot in Russia."

Odin shot a warning look at Loki. He was supposed to be invisible in this quest, and yet here he was sticking his neck out. It would only take one wrong word before Thor would sniff out the deception. Thor, on the other hand, wanted to assure his father that he still held true to the old ways.

"Show him your proof, Russian, and then you may beat this man for his insolence," said Thor.

The Russian looked at Thor and could see that he was serious. He then looked into the car and could see that the two men in there were waiting on him. He shrugged his shoulders, reached into his pocket and pulled out his driver's license and handed it to Odin.

"Andrew McDonald, Boston Massachusetts. Doesn't sound very Russian to me." Loki commented looking over Odin's shoulder.

"Ya, so what's it to you. I'm from Boston, born and raised," Andrew said, with a full Bahstan lilt to his voice. "My father was a Scot, my mother a Ukrainian. You guys are running around pretending to be gods. What difference does it make if I pretend to be Russian? I like it."

"Pretending to be gods!" Odin roared. From behind, Thor grabbed the Russian by the back of the neck and pressed him closer to his father.

"Well, you know, I've seen some incredible shit that your son here has done," Andrew said. "But I don't know if it really qualifies as godly. I'm just saying, you know." There was no mistaking that this Bostonian accent now as the Andrew spoke quickly to save himself from his companion's wrath.

"You are going to need him," Loki commented.

Odin sighed; my, how the world had changed. To get the mortals to truly believe the gods had returned was going to take more than just stating the fact. The people of this Earth had become very cynical, lacking of faith, and devoted to this belief in science. How could the Elder God blame them, though, after being trapped in Limbo for as long as they had been?

"Let him think on it, Thor," Odin counseled. "If he cannot accept who we are after I demonstrate to him our power, then feel free to do whatever you feel necessary as punishment for his deceit."

Holding him firm, Thor watched as Odin laid a hand upon Andrew's head. His other hand secretly reached over and touched Loki's, who funneled a small amount of power into the Elder God. In a bright flash within the Russian's mind, he could see Asgard, Odin and Thor as they were in their splendor. He showed him the epic battles that spanned space and time and eventually he showed him Limbo, the most dreaded of places. Even more so then the Seven Hells.

"No shit," Andrew whispered in awe. "You really are who you say you are. I'm sorry, Thor, for pretending to believe you, it's just, you don't know what kind of crackpots roam around this world. I mean, you've got a Jesus on every corner, a fucking bunch of aliens running the White House, and kids that will kill for crack. I mean the world is pretty fucked up."

Odin held his hand up, preventing Thor from answering.

"My son has not had the visions I have had," he told Andrew. "He does not know your world. You, in your misguided ways, have helped him, though, and for that I owe you a debt, but for now, you are still needed in our cause. We will call you The Russian, out of respect for your choice, but do not deceive us again."

Odin opened the car door and stepped out. The small surge from the Russian's belief was enough to allow him to stand unaided, the cane remaining alongside of the seat.

"Now we have work to do," he said. "We are going to need the help of those Vikings in the video you posted."

"Those dudes?" The Russian asked.

"Dudes? Yes, I know of these dudes. Passive, laymen who claim that taking it easy is the root of life," Odin replied.

"Well, I did not mean dudes in that sense, but yeah," the Russian said. "A couple of them claimed to be Dudeists. That will make it easier to track them down. This one dude, Wolfgar Lawrence, helped organize that great feast. He'd be the first one we could contact."

"So it shall be. We will gather a small force, large enough to give us the strength necessary," Odin replied.

"Necessary for what, Father?"

"There are some evil men in Atlanta that we are going to find and destroy, Thor."

"Are they capitalists?" the Russian asked.

"The worst kind," Loki answered, smiling.

Chapter 18

'Before you can relax, you must abide.'

Beneath the canopy of the virgin forest, sound was amplified a thousand times, or so it seemed to Delroy. Birdsong lay over top of a steady beat provided by a nearby river. Crickets added to the high notes of the forest's tune, and squirrels lent the occasional backing vocal tracks, as they went about their business collecting nuts.

The sky was impossible to see, for the trees had grown unimpeded for thousands of years in this forest. The moss surrounding their trunks, centuries old. Ferns as tall as a man could easily hide a large predator, yet the noisy forest meant that none were around. With every step a vibration of the Earth's energy shot up through the soles of his feet, and he felt as if he had to force his way past an invisible barrier. It was as if the forest itself was resisting him. Perhaps it knew what kind of destructive force people possessed.

"I come in peace, Great Spirit," Delroy intoned. "You can see my face and know that I tell no lie. You can see my heart, and feel that it is unburdened. You can feel my spirit, and know that it wants to fly on the wind."

Delroy walked slowly. He did not want to disturb this place any more then he had to. He walked with soft feet, being mindful of where each step landed, and with flowing grace. The song continued on, though he could sense that the tune had changed slightly. Everything alive was aware of his presence. The good part of it, and the bad.

"Great Spirit, I come seeking your help. I come humbled by your power and your beauty. I come in awe of your kindness, and in fear of your wrath."

He was following a trail, perhaps created by deer; it was hard to tell for the moss was very spongy and tracks disappeared as fast as they were laid down. Rays of sunlight cut through in places, bright shafts that almost appeared tangible. Slowly he crept forward, the river getting louder and louder.

"Great Spirit, I have been beset upon by a viscous lot of thieves. They have stolen my good energy, and replaced it with something devised by men who know nothing of your touch. Help me rid myself of these negative vibes, and let me return to the forest, pure and proud."

Nearing a slight rise, Delroy looked down at the ground below and discovered a vast mound of mushrooms growing alongside a rotting tree stump. These mushrooms looked very familiar to the ones in the forest that he knew. Excitedly, he wandered over, getting very low to the ground to check the underside of a large one that had a slight bluish tint in its coloring. Under the cap, was a series of ribs that ran vertically around. Bingo!

Grabbing a couple of smaller ones, he sat back on the trail and chewed them up. The taste was revolting, and he had to keep himself from throwing them back up as he gagged. Shivers went up and down his spine as he did everything he could to shake the taste, but no mind trick would work. Knowing the river was somewhere up ahead, he walked on, hoping to get a drink to wash away the taste.

The river was a series of small falls that climbed further and further to the west. To his right the land leveled out and the fast-flowing water snaked its way between the massive trees. It wasn't a very wide river, or deep for that matter, but a lot of water moved along its course. Delroy knelt on a mossy boulder and cupped his hands. He pulled some of the cold water out and lapped at it quickly. After three handfuls the awful taste subsided and his thirst was quenched. He decided that this place would be as good as any to see if these mushrooms had any magic in them. He sat quietly for fifteen minutes, and then fell backwards, onto the soft mossy cushion.

To Delroy, it felt like his mouth was sweating. He could do nothing but lie there, and run his tongue back and forth across his teeth. The sky grew brighter by all accounts, and the air temperature soared. In the corners of his eyes, waves of barely visible air fluttered, removing his peripheral vision. His head felt like it was lifting off of the ground and his stomach was churning something fierce. He had been down the mushroom road before, knew what to expect, he just didn't expect it to happen all at once.

"Spirit! I'm opening myself up!" He yelled. Or at least he thought he yelled, but it was really just a whisper. The river banging against the rocks only meters away was now a deafening roar. He couldn't hear his thoughts anymore. He struggled to rise, doing his best to let his floating head pull the rest of his body up, but to no avail. His vain attempts brought on laughter. Belly laughter fought hard to cleanse his soul, but met resistance right around the place where his mind's eye was.

"Holy shit," he proclaimed as he cried. Images appearing in his mind would set him off in fits. In one bout of laughter he managed to roll onto his side where he could see under the ferns. The air was alive, dancing, moving to the rhythms of the forests song. He laughed some more as he could see the plants swaying ever so slightly. Even the earth below was heaving and sinking with the beat. His arms curled in closer to his body, his legs were pulled up tight. He fought against this feeling that he was being pulled away, and for the longest time he barely managed to contain himself.

After an eternity of struggle, Delroy's mind pulled free, bolted down a shaft of darkness that eventually shot upward. Soon he was above the trees, then above the clouds, then above the planet. In an instant his mind started to understand things he would never be able to put into words. Visions of the inner workings of the universe came and went as he traveled on, until he reached the edge. Here he could see the mirror, the universe behind him. Here he could push forward into the beyond, but there was something holding him back. He could see it in the mirror, and there was a rope. A twisted thing of various threads that did not belong together. The rope moved this way and that, but never far from him. It encircled him and he reached out. He tried to grab it but it was elusive and escaped every attempt. He started to cry again, not from laughter this time, though.

"Why are you holding me back?" he asked himself.

Another voice answered.

"You are tethered by the will of others. You always have been, Delroy. These negative vibes surrounding you will stay with you until you let them go once and for all."

"Who are you?" his mind asked.

"I am your guide on this journey. My name is Rick. I take the form of deer mouse back in the material world. The Great Spirit has heard your honest pleas and sent me to help."

"Well, what do I do?"

"Let go Delroy. Repeat after me:

"I will abide. The power of the Dude compels me.

I will abide. The power of love guides me.

I will abide. Let me maintain my balance.

I will abide. Fuck it."

Delroy's mind reeled for a moment.

"The Dude?"

Rick laughed.

"The Dude and the Great Spirit are one, man. They are the same as milk and cream. I use the Dude, because I know who you've been hanging around with them in this journey, and I dig their style. Change it to Great Spirit if you want, but the results will be the same."

Delroy had never been this high before. He suddenly realized just how high he was, and that he wasn't even in his own body. He was at the edge of the universe, with an invisible deer mouse talking to him. The sudden realization was pulling him away from the mirror.

"Delroy, listen. Yes, you are tripping balls, man, but this is real. This is your shot to get free of those negative vibes, man. Hurry and just say what I told you to say."

What do you do when you are this high? Fighting it only leads to the point of no return. There had been many tales of people from his tribe who had never returned from such journeys. You have to go with the flow and so Delroy did. He forgot about his body. Forgot about being sane, and just let the now in. Again he was face to face with the mirror and he began to recite the words with Rick.

Chapter 19

'Ease into the moment and make a quick escape.'

Before the dawn, there is that moment when the darkness is darker then it has been the entire night. In this brief half of an hour, even nocturnal creatures return to their dens. It occurred to Hawk as they drove down through the Fraser Valley that our method of keeping time was all messed up. Why should the start of the day be in the middle of the night? It made no sense. He wanted to vocalize his thoughts, but the two passengers needed sleep. Someone was going to have to take over the driving soon, though, before they ended up in a ditch.

This period of the night, when even the headlights from vehicles do little to brighten the road, was a perfect time for the mind to wander. In fact, this small fragment of the day is when people are usually in the deepest part of their sleep. The thought of sleep was so enticing that Hawk had to really focus to keep his mind awake.

The day generally starts when people rise. Let's say the average human wakes at six am., according to work schedules and what have you. Make this hour one and then work your way up to hour twenty-four. This made a hell of a lot more sense than starting the clock at midnight. Two twelve hours! That just lacks any imagination. Repeating every hour in the second half of the day was just ludicrous. P.M., A.M. Nonsense, Hawk concluded.

Of course, thoughts like these rise in the night. They are unwelcome at any other time during the day by the majority of people busy conforming to the standards of society. Sticking to what we've been doing has been the unconscious human motto for ages now. A radical thinker will only be mocked when he tackles the bewildering with simplicity. Hawk was unafraid of straying from the norm. It had brought him out on this journey, shown him that his purpose in life lay somewhere along the life of a dude, but not bound to it. The Yeti had cleared a lot of things up in his mind about the future. Of course, his band was going to rock. Of course, his hair would continue to grow. He was just not dedicated enough to align himself with a full-time cause that didn't involve the pursuit of rock and roll dominance.

  The town of Hope was in the rear view mirror when the sun began to chase away the night. Thirteen hours from now and the mission would be complete, and then the journey home could commence. Hawk had a growing suspicion that he would be making this journey alone. Willow was becoming this Dudeist monk right before his eyes. Her firm stance had softened slightly since crossing the border. She was smiling more often than not, and she even commented on how terrible she looked from all the traveling, a comment he would not have expected from a vegan, Earth Mother, Dudeist, whose strong feminist streak would usually squash such statements long before they escaped the lips. The Mad Hermit had a strange effect on her. There was no doubting that he had a powerful aura. Even a casual horoscope reader could see that.

  "Look, one of you dudes is going to have to take over," Hawk announced loud enough to wake the sleeping two. Moans of anguish answered his plea, followed by stretching limbs and rustling clothes. "Preferably the person with a legal driver's license."

  Turning her head to look out, Willow rolled down the passenger's side window and let the cool mountain air rush in. Invigorating and refreshing, she stuck one hand out into the open, and let out a sigh.

  "I cannot wait until I see the outside of a car for a long time," she exclaimed. "Pull over and I'll take the wheel."

  From the back the Mad Hermit sat up and offered to give Hawk the entire rear seats to himself. It was an offer too enticing to ignore. He had been awake now for thirty-six hours, driving all but five of them.

  "Yeah, I think the next time we have to rescue a

Hermit who lives in a city surrounded by a million other people, we should really look into flights," Hawk couldn't help but take the jab. Gerald was a dude for the most part but he had a habit of rubbing the Nova Scotian the wrong way at times. This giving up of the back seat was just a ploy to sit closer to Willow, but still Hawk really did want to stretch out.

"Listen here, young-ling, I never claimed to be a hermit," Gerald said. "The name came to me by others. It stuck, and that's the way it is."

"Young-ling! I bet you are no more than two years older than me," Hawk asserted. "Just in case you didn't know it, Hermits are supposed to be removed from society. Not embedded in it."

"Ah! Enough with that you two," Willow intervened. "We are so close to finishing this quest. The last thing we need is a cock parade in the middle of the town square."

Both men laughed at this, exchanged seats and waited until the driver was ready to go. She stepped off into the bushes to allow nature to run a new course through the foliage.

Of course, it was the tiredness that had really sparked the hermit remark. When people are tired they say and do stupid shit. Hawk barely knew the man who they had come to retrieve; he barely knew why they needed him. In the tired haze, reality distorts and your mind can no longer be fully trusted to do the right thing. You have to keep a close eye on it during this stage, and never allow it to play with simple things, like latches or forks.

"So tell me, Herald," Hawk said, still a little too wired to sleep. "What is in the Scrolls that is going to help put out the fires that are springing up all over the place?"

Gerald leaned over the seat and looked at Hawk lying comfortably on his back. His green eyes glittered in the early morning light, and his smile stole the darkness.

"I do not fully recall what I wrote down," he said. "At the time it was coming to me so fast that I just started scribbling and didn't stop until it was over. I did not enjoy it. I do not recommend going through such an experience, and I hope to god it was all worth it. It would really set my mind at ease, Hawk. Believe it or not, there is still a little part of me that cares for the world. A part of me that wants to fit in more naturally and less selectively. If we are lucky, it won't be too hard to figure out. If we are unlucky, well at least we will be safe in Canada for a little while where we can hope the madness doesn't spread."

"Do you really believe that you saw the future?" This was the part Hawk was most skeptical about. Predicting based on theories was one thing, but actually believing you were seeing the future was another. Perhaps this is what Hen had saw in him. That little lack of faith.

"I do; I wish I hadn't."

"So why run from it? I mean the future is going to find you no matter where you hide. Under a bridge in Seattle, the future found you. Passing on the knowledge to someone else, the future found you. Seems to me that anyone who doubts destiny is in for the harsh reality that there is a pervasive will under it all."

Gerald earned a couple of respect points for the sprawled figure. The wild ideas and the crazy dreams were really all that kept things interesting. If the possibility of destiny really loomed over each of us, it would make accepting your fate a lot easier. Like microbes in a cell, we each had our part. We could pretend that we are the free radicals floating around trying to disrupt the whole, but in the end we are part of it all.

"Get some sleep, Hawk," Gerald advised with care. "You deserve it. The Lady Dude will get us there safely."

Chapter 20

'That moment, just as you hesitate, is your moment to fool them.'

The whirlwind of distortion ripped through the heart of the Midwest. It picked up fury as it neared the Mississippi river, flowing through the St. Louis Arch, and gaining speed. This wave of negative energy met little resistance when the people who came in contact with it had already given up on hope for the most part. It was easy to turn such apathy into anger. To stir the water back into the oil, and then let the fire burn out of control.

FOX television, of course, was the worst perpetrator. It took videos of the "I Bless America" rendition and inserted it into their reporting in fifteen minute intervals, making sure that no one forgot that people were forsaking god. It then attached totally unrelated footage to these videos, liberal Californians burning Confederate flags, scenes from a book burning at Satanist Country Club where the King James Bible was the first to go in. Dogs were shown walking people, and the Governor of the state was happily declaring his support of legalized gay marriage.

Put all together, it was almost too much for any true Tea Bagging conservative to take.

Other networks played along, to a lesser degree, though. Forgoing the in-your-face approach, they focused on the differences between the South, the North, and the West. Each post was another nail in the coffin, assurance that the sense of division would spread quickly.

To further things along, a couple of the major lending institutions of America had their hands out again, looking for bailouts from the government. Of course, the independently owned "Federal Reserve" supported the move, claiming that the decreasing housing market had been worse than the previous forecast, keeping the economic crisis from rebounding. Prices were still plummeting as full-time, permanent jobs were still hard to come by. Sure, there was lots of temporary work out there, but temporary work does not get you a mortgage and banks do not make money when there are no mortgages.

The seeds of discontent did not need to look far to find fertile soil. The riots that were aimed at banks and big corporations were soon turned around so that cousins no longer trusted each other. In the north Atlantic, two new super ports were announced, along with three new gas refineries. More funding for the ever-bleeding automotive industry and a sizable military contract for the aeronautical industries in Washington State. No money was heading south to help the faltering coal industry, the farmers who had endured a prolonged drought, or to rebuild the cities destroyed by a busy hurricane season.

"It won't be long now," Rupert reported to the Star Chamber gathering. "You can feel the surge against the barriers and in a month or two, the levee will break."

"I like this," Manuel chimed in. "For the first time in history, we have an influx of people *returning* to Mexico! Given the recent trouble with our government there, we will have people joining the cartels and moving on Mexico City within the year. Once we install our own person as President, we'll be able to use it as a base to land supplies for the South. My Chinese connections assure me that they can deliver, but just not on American soil."

"The IMF is prepared to support both the north and south, even the West, if a third party is formed," Robert added.

Sir Richard was a little less enthusiastic about the way things were going though. His holdings in the U.S. were bound to take a hit, and no mention of compensation had yet been brought to the table. He had brought the issue up a couple of months back, but still no one had given him a clear indication at how he would retain his property no matter which side ended up victorious.

"As to my concerns about my holdings over here,

chaps," Sir Richard began. "I am still looking for some assurances that in the event of a catastrophic fail, I will be able to recoup my losses, which will be considerable, even for someone as rich as myself."

There was a hushed silence as each member took a moment to consider this. In this room, global affairs were to remain the matter of discussion, and private affairs left to less formal meetings. The reason no answer had been offered to this point, was exactly for that reason. The other four felt that Sir Richard had been out of line in bringing up such pettiness. Everyone at the table would lose from such a venture in the beginning, but in time would triple their personal fortunes as the war progressed.

As acting chair of the chamber, it was up to Rupert to address this situation. He grunted as he readjusted himself in his seat.

"It has been well established in this chamber that personal affairs are to remain off the table until such times when we can be objective and free from group obligations," he said, looking at Sir Richard with an all-business look in his eyes. "Now, we understand that the housing market will suffer the worst from this readjustment, we also feel that in the end it could be the most profitable, depending on how we swing the war. Immediate compensation will not be considered, as a sacrifice must be made by all in order to advance our goals. So, I am hereby proposing that the matter be sealed, and that the honorable member in question refrain from such applications again until such a time that is more suitable."

A simple vote involving the raising of a hand was conducted. The motion was received with three approvals. Sir Richard bore it with the typical British stiff upper lip, though inside he was seething. He was in too deep, for too long, to ever consider pulling out with these tinkering fools, so he knew he had to lump this one.

"Understood, gentlemen."

With a keystroke on his smart phone, the message was sent to liquidate all American assets. This would create waves, no doubt, set off alarms, but he could not allow the other four the satisfaction of seeing his fortune dwindle by roughly twenty-five percent. He could live with fifteen. With another stroke, his people began the process of buying up deep harbor lands in Mexico on the Pacific coast, where any Chinese supply would most likely have to land.

"Now, can we get the President of this upstart country on board with officially removing God from mention in any political form?" Francisco asked.

"We are working on it." Rupert replied.

"I tell you, this is the thing. With this, you will have your South up in arms," The Italian mused. He had used the projector to see into the future prior to the meeting and it showed him a country divided and the war machine rising.

"Now, if there was only some way to speed up the drought. Desperate people take to arms quicker than women take to diet fads," Manuel offered. His phone then vibrated. He picked it up and read the message on the screen. He looked up at Sir Richard and smiled. Moving in on his own country was a sneaky move, but to be expected by a Brit. They had centuries of experience at it. He excused himself from the room, so he could call his brokers in Puerto Vallarta, and make sure there were no stones left unturned there.

It was the Italian who then led the discussion for the next half hour, explaining the keys to success in civil wars, having sponsored four in the past decade. Making sure weapons got to their destination was one of his specialties, utilizing his vast shipping network. Creating safe delivery zones was of the up most importance. Boston being far enough north, with its mega harbor project a go, was going to be a key site. For the South, Mobile, Alabama, would draw less attention initially than New Orleans or Galveston. His emphasis on allowing these cities to remain as free from attack as long as possible would allow for a prolonged engagement, which every party wanted. Quick wars were not very profitable, that is why very little is ever mentioned of the Falklands, Grenada, even Libya for that matter.

When Manuel returned to the table, he was all smiles. His evasive maneuverings had failed. Whomever

Sir Richard had on his payroll in Mexico was a well-connected, thorough man, who should be working for him in the future. It was of no matter, though. Eventually when the time came to get the permits, Manuel would be there controlling the flow of traffic. He could buy the land, but he could not buy the bought government.

Before the session ended, the four-dimensional viewer was consulted again one last time to see if things were still progressing as foretold. As with any foretelling, there was always a small part of the visions that were left to interpretation, but as far as the group was concerned, everything was unfolding exactly as they allowed it to.

Chapter 21

'Holding on to what is meant to be passed on, leads to independency issues.'

Along the Ley Lines, nothing grows in the mirror world other than tufts of grass. For miles one could look straight down the opening in the forest, wondering who would have cut such an exact trail. The truth was that on this world, nature took care of such things on its own. This particular mirror world was used for traveling by many of the creatures of the universe that knew of such things. This was the place where the unicorns had escaped to, leaving King Arthur to his predicted death. Here the gods of old would walk occasionally on route to their own worlds. The occasional human had crossed over here as well, completely by mistake, of course, returning with tales of strange and majestic creatures like pixies and elves. Of course, those faery fellows didn't inhabit this world, but they used the energy lines to travel.

Delroy wandered alone, his mind free of agony and negativity. He breathed in the air as if it was his first breath. The blueness of the sky both amazed and delighted. Fresh, fragrant aromas from flowering plants almost made him wonder if he had ever possessed the ability to smell before. Bees filled the skies at times, working away, collecting, pollinating, ensuring the growth cycles continued.

"Great Spirit, I see now why the Medicine Woman had me wandering the forests, all these years," he prayed. "I was too blind to appreciate all that was around me. I looked for reasons to distrust and to curse the woman, all the while she was trying to show that there was still hope for our people. We can return to the forest while we still have some of our land. Our way of life is not lost, it has just become part of the past that most want to forget. The pain, the misery is relived in the forest. We have betrayed and we have been shamed, but we must rise above it. Perhaps she truly held out hope for me when so many of my cousins gave in to the evils of the material world."

Rick had been following alongside in the bush, unseen by the native man. Hearing him call out to the Great Spirit meant that this was his cue to reappear.

"Not all is lost," the deer mouse said. "The world you come from is hurting, there is no denying that. What is needed is for the people to see that hope is not lost. Only when hope is lost will it all crumble, and the Great Spirit will abandon the world. With every generation that strays away from the wholeness of nature, the chances of survival decrease. You must be the example Delroy. This is your purpose. The Medicine Woman had visions, though she interpreted your meeting at the crossroads to lead to one specific end. The truth is that these people you met are different, they care, they listen, and they want to help. The problem is that they like to take it easy, too much at times, but they can be rallied for their hearts are still in the game. Do not let the labors of hard work slowly slip away with the tides. The negative vibes you encountered were a way to push you onto the path, to open your eyes. Now that you are free of them you will see that all has been carefully laid out in front of you. There are no chance meetings; there is always a plan."

"So I should somehow, reconnect with the dudes, when I get home?" Delroy wondered.

"Connect, and involve yourself," Rick offered. "Teach them, for they are open minded and will easily agree to help support a righteous cause. We have been watching them, and they show a great amount of compassion for one another. They do their best to keep things simplified, and to stay away from these silly religion traps that so many other organizations fall into.

"The Path must merge at some point. Your people are a lost herd and may never come back. Do not give up on them, but do not be afraid to introduce new blood. The Great Spirit has seen that there are many people out there, dudes and non-dudes, who have an appreciation for their mother, and wish an end to the harm being inflicted upon her. It is going to take great fortitude, but after your ordeal, I feel that you are ready to lead the way."

In his mind, Delroy began to see how the division between his people and the immigrants who now lived on the land had grown wider and wider with every year. Those that did leave to join the white man's world rarely came back to their people. They couldn't, for they would be marked traitors, and in turn, the changed man would look down on his own people for not accepting the changing world, as he himself had been prepared to do. Giving in wasn't the answer. Finding that inner strength to pursue a higher purpose would see him through the troubles ahead.

"You might want to prepare yourself," Rick cautioned. "Up ahead is a gate that you can use. It will leave you a little ways from home still, but at least you will be back in Alberta."

"Will you follow me?" Delroy asked the deer mouse.

"Are you crazy? That world's fucked for us non-car driving creatures. I'd rather just let a cat eat me now."

"Yeah, I guess we have let things kind of go," Delroy, admitted.

"Kind of! That's putting it mildly. The air is being poisoned, the water is being poisoned, the trees are all being cut down faster than they can grow back. More species of animals have died off in the last hundred years then in the past thousand. You can blame the white man all you want, but at some point everyone is going to have to take a united stand against this aggression towards the mother. Soon the only children she will give birth to will be the ones she walks away from."

"I know, I know," Delroy nodded. "I am going back with my path clear. It is time for the sleeper to awaken and to lead again. Maybe in time it will become the place you once remembered it to be. Maybe then you will come visit."

Rick scratched behind his ear with one of his hind legs. He wasn't generally the optimistic type of spirit guide;

how could a mouse really be? Death was usually lurking around the corner, food sometimes hard to find, and most things were bigger then you.

"Yeah, sounds good." The trace of sarcasm couldn't be missed.

They reached the junction point where two Ley Lines intersected. Rick led Delroy past the apex, and off into a small clearing. Ahead a temporal distortion appeared, very faint, making the trees behind look as if they were behind a thin sheet of water.

"Just walk through there," Rick said, pointing his nose with a little nod of his head. "The Line will recognize your energy pattern and take you back to your world. I'm thinking you'll be somewhere close to the crossroads in which you were picked up at. Feel free to take a trip sometime and visit me."

Without waiting for a goodbye, the deer mouse scampered off into the woods. Delroy took a deep breath and stepped into the portal, vanishing from the mirror world. He reappeared in a gully, filled with rocks, one hundred feet from a highway. He could hear the traffic above zooming by, and so he climbed up the embankment and up over the guard rail. The town of Frank was half a click to his left, so he turned the opposite way towards the rising sun.

Six hours later he was back on the reservation feeling very good about life. His heart was singing, his mind clear, and the wind was speaking to him. Instead of going straight home, he marched up to the medicine woman's house and knocked on the door. The wind chimes lining the porch came to life while he paced across the wooden planks, the giant dream catcher hanging from the overhead beam swinging from side to side. It wasn't long before he could hear the lock on the door opening. Then the woman appeared.

"I am back," Delroy announced.

At first glance the Medicine Woman wanted to shut the door and forget about that lost cause she had devoted so much of her hopes on. With a second glance though, she could see that something was different. Very different. Around the young man was a powerful glow, an aura usually accompanying a Chieftain, or a medicine man. His eyes, were no longer the eyes of a begging dog, now they were the eyes of a wolf. Feeling moved, she stood up straight, adjust her clothes and smiled.

"Delroy, I think you have finally found that Devil Grass I sent you out looking for."

Delroy had never heard he speak so softly and kindly before. He watched her as she fidgeted, realizing that she was actually nervous in his presence. He could see her aura, turning to warm hues as she stepped to the side and offered him entry into her home! Stepping through that portal for the first time, the young man was assailed with the smell of herbs, earth, and something else he couldn't quite put his finger on.

"I see you have shaken those negative vibes," the Medicine Woman said as she went into the kitchen. Moments later, she came back out with a cup of tea.

Looking around at all the plants that filled the room, he could not see any television, or radio, or any modern device. Even the chairs were made from intertwined saplings, the cushions matted straw. A couple of small song birds flew around freely, no cages in sight.

"Yes, thankfully they are gone," Delroy told her. "I met my spirit guide and he took me to a place where I could shed them." She offered him a seat and passed him the tea, and then allowed Delroy to tell his tale. Her smile was enough for him to know that she was pleased. He also realized that she was only older then him by perhaps five to ten years. Suddenly, he saw her as a woman, and not some dreaded disciplinarian, who haunted his freedom.

"The wheel is broken, but I think I have seen a way to fix it," he declared.

Her eyes opened profoundly.

"We must modernize our thinking and reach out to those who can help," Delroy said. "The people who you sent me to meet is a good place to start. They are good people and have a network that is growing. They embody a lot of the things we believe in and I feel that with their help we can help our people turn the corner once and for all. It will require great effort, and great determination, but the warrior spirit knows not all battles are fought with weapons."

Chapter 22

'Don't fall victim to your own indecision. Consult with your inner elder.'

    The unlikeliness of ever finding the true meaning of life will forever haunt the human psyche. The reaching out into the unknown looking for purpose and reason has been a hot topic since people decided to drink coffee together during midday work breaks. This whole idea that we were meant for something only complicates matters, creating this sense of self-importance, turning what should have been a leisurely walk into a race.
    With this God syndrome forever hanging over the heads of those who seek to control, change, and rebuild the world around them, things never change that much. As fortunes grow, and these ideals of living a productive life continue to influence the cattle from having thoughts of straying, the angst is held in for long periods of time. Like the tectonic plates slowly pushing against each other, creating enormous amount of friction and pent up energy. It is only a matter of time before the cattle stray, as they learn how to navigate around the pitfalls set out in front of them.
    Internet forums were the perfect breeding grounds for these philosophies of discontent to find and attract people who are fed up with the status-quo. No longer needing to go out for that coffee, one could divert much more attention to specific causes with like-minded people. Here people can transform their God complex into virtual beings, becoming their ideals online and then retreat back to their flock-following ways in the real world, until the time was right to reinvent themselves. As America convulsed in upheaval, the internet chat lines were busier than ever. Everyone wanted in. Everyone was for or against something. Political correctness took over and abolished history. Conservative views clashed with liberal. The streets

became dangerous places as people wanted to know where you stood. Clashes against corporations, clashes against the policing, and a general disdain for government in general had washed over and drowned out patience, and due diligence. For too long people had toiled in hopelessness, never knowing if the future would ever be brighter. For many, economic struggles had made life even worse.

These bastions of Capitalistic ideals—GM, Proctor Gamble, Boeing, Lockheed, Chevron, and not to mention the financial institutions that rigged the system to help them win—fell under the eye of scrutiny. Not even in Lenin's most hopeful dreams would he have imagined the American people turning on them with such hate. Riots, looting, and civil unrest. Transportation services were being disrupted and even the failing schooling system was set back even further, as families feared to leave their homes. Times grew desperate in the heartland of freedom. People were no longer willing to take it on the chin.

"You will not understand Thor, until it is too late. That is why we must not set our goals on the future; we must look to the now while we can." Odin had his head cranked around to look at the two passengers in the back seat. They were nearing Atlanta with van full of weekend warrior Vikings in tow and a plan had started to formulate in the mind of the father of the gods.

"I do not understand father," Thor said. "Once the mortals see that we have set them free from this tyranny, they will return to us. Their faith will be renewed, and we will be free once again to return to Asgard."

For a father, it would be difficult to tell his child that all along they had followed the wrong path. They had sought glory, dominion over others, and in fact had created a means to their own end. Eventually people were going to stop feeding their egos as they gathered around coffee shops and spent too much money on a relatively cheap brew. They would stray, as they always do. Away from the power to the path of ultimate freedom.

"Our path has long diverged from the humans," Odin said. "We will not find past glories here, my son. This push towards violence has led them down some very dark paths which we must never lead them down again. Ragnarok was never meant to be a battle, I can see now. My vision had been clouded by my ego back then, so long ago. Our final stand was but a mere shadow of glory. The truth is that no god can bring salvation. The only salvation these mortals will find is by turning towards each other and accepting their enemy as their friend. They must discover that love is the binding force which will eventually prevail. It will not be on a battlefield soaked in blood."

Something very terrible had happened to his father, Thor concluded. The way he was talking made him think that perhaps all those centuries trapped in Limbo had broken what was thought to be unbreakable.

"Then what the hell are we doing, Odin? If our destiny lie elsewhere, then let us find a way off of this world and be free to live as we once had."

It was the driver of the car who turned to look at the angry god. He smiled, and then returned his attention to road ahead. The Russian suddenly wished he was anywhere else than here, as the car raced through the night traffic.

"We have one wrong to right, before we leave," Odin said. "I have found a way for us to return to Asgard, but first we must destroy a machine that these particular evil men possess. No one else knows of its existence but it allows them to see into the future, and this has been their key to manipulating the world to their needs."

"So the future is set in stone?" the Russian spoke up.

"Oh, no. No. The future is flexible, yielding, and forgiving," Odin said. "If one has seen a probability, though, one can aim the ship towards that shore. My visions of the future were anything but certain, for look where it landed us. It may give you the upper hand, but it cannot guarantee. Knowledge of a possible future tends to be destructive, and corrupts the mind quickly. We must destroy this machine, and allow the boat to sail free again."

"Nothing will really change though, will it?" the Russian said. "I mean, these men who hold the reins of power won't just quit. They will still have the money. They will still have the power and the resources to keep their commodities."

"They will," Odin acknowledged. "The rest will be up to you humans. You will have to make the changes necessary. Already the cities of America are burning with anger. The horns of war are being blown, as beliefs over power and reason destroy good judgment. This fire is set to burn out of control soon, as brother turns on brother. The only thing that will change because of our actions will be an unforeseeable future. That will give you a fighting chance at salvaging a better future."

"So Father, what are the humans following us for?" Thor asked, referring to the van load of weekend Vikings behind them.

"A diversion of course. There will be heightened security at the place we must infiltrate, and we will need only the smallest disturbance to give us the time we necessary to gain entry. I have been saving all of my strength for this one act." Odin looked to Loki and nodded as the car pulled up to the large skyscraper that loomed ominously against the night skyline. Where many other buildings had most of their floors lit up, this one was only lit up on the ground floor and the top.

The black car stopped just short of entering the parking lot, and Loki lowered his window, waving for the van to pull up alongside. The window of the blue Caravan slid down to the hum of its own motor, and the Viking enthusiast sitting in the passenger seat looked at the building, then at the driver.

"This doesn't look like a place where they have LARP conventions." the passenger noted.

Bending low and looking across Loki, Odin smiled and waved his hand.

"This is not the place where the convention is being held. We first must complete a quest and we require the brave services of those who seek passage to Valhalla," Odin answered.

"Well we are Thor's men, and we will follow him

anywhere he commands," the Viking responded, playing along faithfully. For these weekend warriors, this was what dreams were made of.

Loki used the button on the door panel to lower Thor's window. Still unsure of the plan, the goal, and his father's sanity, he looked out at the van and spoke.

"The words you hear now are those of Odin, my father and King of the Asgard. To disobey him will mean that your suffering will never end, and you shall never drink in the halls of my ancestors."

The Viking looked stunned by such a proclamation. He was used to really getting into his role, but this Thor impersonator was something else, so much so that he almost actually believed that the man might possibly be the god, if not for reason and sanity hindering such a notion.

"We will do whatever the Father of the Gods commands! We are the faithful."

Loki almost laughed out loud if not for Odin laying a hand on his shoulder. He then instructed the Vikings in what to do as his plan formulated, where to go when done, and praised them for their bravery.

Chapter 23

'In time, we have found the ultimate enslavement trap.'

Carl emerged from the mirror world on the outskirts of Montreal, and took three different buses to get home. Hen had left him with a clearer understanding of what his role in the world could be, and he was chomping at the bit to get back online and start blogging again. The adventure, though it had ended prematurely, had opened his eyes to the possibilities that his talents could offer the world. There were already so many others out there proclaiming the righteousness of pot, so he could focus his attentions more on making the world a better place as a whole.

The mirror world allows one's mind to open doors they never knew existed before. The energy of an undisturbed natural habitat would awaken primal powers that had lain dormant in humans for so long. He remembered listening to the wind and understand what it said. He could feel the rain coming hours before the first cloud breached the horizon. In his own mind he thought he could almost understand what the birds were singing.

In the early morning light he turned on his computer and immediately began working on his latest blog. He made a pot of coffee, watched the sun rise in the east and listened to the morning traffic speed by.

One Grain
by Carl Carlson

"The world is not 'our' home in the singular sense." Carl typed. "It is our home in the sense of the multitude. Inside this hour glass, we are bonded together until that inevitable time in which we have let go, and fall free, through to the other side. Into the unknown, falling with no assurances that we have a purpose or made any impact on the world we leave behind. This home we inhabit is also the home of many other creatures who know their place in the grand scheme of things, better than we ever will. They go about their business with basic needs fueling their drive to survive. We on the other hand, in the wealthier countries, have decided to take certain things for granted. We have created entitlements in our minds and cry out injustice, when they are held back from us.

"The world turns without our consent, provides us the necessary tools to survive without our consent, and forgets about us long after we are gone, burying us deep beneath the surface, one grain at a time. Is our time here pre-determined? Is our future set in stone? How will we survive if we do not understand and abide by the forces that are at work all around us, keeping the balance, finding the harmony?

"We have become masters of our own destiny, in our minds that is, looking no further than the few grains that surround us, wondering how we can keep ourselves on top of the pile, until there are no more grains to fall through. We fight what cannot be fought, and ignore the battles that can be won. In the end, we all pass through. In the end, we are all part of the whole.

"Watching our greed and our needs destroy our home has become a spectator sport. The only combatants fighting the battles that can be won, are fought by those with the most to lose. We have no harmony, we have no sense of peace, and we have no real chance of survival when our voices are second to bottom line economics. This fantasy world that we have created, where equality is driven down on the list of importance, by things like war, consumption, and imaginary borders. We have flags to represent our nations, but what does it really represent when we just stand aside and allow our world to become a hostile environment for all that live upon it.

"Our world is not unique. To believe so is to be blind to the possibilities that the vast universe offers. It is the only one we are capable of living on at the present time, and as such it is the most precious thing we can claim to be our own. How can we push aside such a bold, basic and undeniable truth and call ourselves intelligent. How can we prance around the dance floor proclaiming to be the most intelligent creatures to roam the surface, when we have no respect for the surface, and the comforts it can provide? We are all in the belief that someone else will fix this situation before it becomes too late, and as that happens, another grain falls through.

"On the shore the rock sits quietly. Its fate determined as wave after wave, day after day, month after month and so on, slowly wearing away the hardened facade. Its strength is in its unity, a collection of grains bonded together in survival mode. It abides the laws of nature, though, allowing itself to be transformed, knowing that this is the way of all things. Transformation, through natural progression, allowing the world to adapt around you, slowly, as you slowly adapt to it.

"This is meant to be a symbiotic relationship. We have become parasitic, and yet we still do not look at ourselves in shame! As we throw away the power we have to help preserve, we mock the intelligence we have, and all of the developments we have made as a species.

"Surely we must care for future generations. Even those that make the decisions that continue to poison and destroy our natural habitats will surely want what is best for their children? It is unimaginable to believe that there is a great evil behind it all, driving us slowly towards destruction, but what else can we call it? It is not for the better good. If it was for the better good, then we would make sure that our home is safe, before we leave our families behind. It's our lack of cohesion that has allowed this continue on, as we buy into the invisible lines dividing us. The flags that wave over our heads. The color of our skin making us different, the faiths in to which we hold.

"We fall through. One grain at a time. We come together again on the other side, before passing through once again, endlessly in a natural cycle. The hour glass empties, then it turns. Let us bond long enough this time around to get it right. Let us stop pointing fingers, calling names, and behaving like overgrown children. We must turn our attention to our world, and see that is it more precious to us than anything else we can possess."

Carl posted on his forums, and quickly one after another, the replies came in. There was a nerve struck, a nerve that was already tender and sore. People began to share, and soon the word spread. Like any good movement it would take time. It would slowly build up with persistence, like the wave against the rock. One grain at a time.

Carl spent the remainder of the morning catching up on the developing events in America. Day by day, things worsened as the country skid into a hate filled fit. Flags were being burned, actors were coming out for this, and for that. Even the Pope had warned that if the U.S. were to slip any farther into chaos, the rest of the world would plunge too. Hated or loved, America was a beacon, and if the light was extinguished for any length of time, others who would see this as an opportunity to gain a foothold on the world stage, would not hesitate to do so.

Europe held its breath, praying that stability would return soon as the people of the poorer nations like Greece, Spain, and Ireland began questioning the purpose of a union. The spotlight was being shed on those who really held the power in the world, and the banks became the targets with the bulls eye on their backs. Visiting all of his favorite sites and groups, the feeling was the same everywhere. People were fed up. They were sharing their frustration, and being very public about it.

On the Dudeist websites a different tune was being played. Many voices were calling out for calm, and urging everyone to just take it easy. Instead of turning their anger outwards, most of the dudes felt it necessary, more than ever, to spread positive vibes out into the virtual world. The High Priest of York was organizing a Relaxorcism for the third Sunday of the month, where all dudes could gather online, and only post examples the good things this life has to offer. The Dudely Lama himself was to make an appearance, via Skype, and was prepared to read passages from his new book on finding the Dude within. Even a small squad of Superdudes, were booking their tickets from North America in order to participate in the congregation being held in England.

Lastly before calling it a day, Carl messaged Nuna to see how things were progressing on the Hermit front. He was glad to hear that Hawk and Willow had arrived only hours earlier and that soon work on translating the scrolls would begin. Sounding as hopeful as ever, the monk was glad to see that Carl had found some peace in his travels and applauded his blog. Nuna shared the link with his vast network, doing his part to help spread the words of wisdom.

As the city mobilized for another business day as usual, sleep came quickly. He drifted off, returning in spirit to the mirror world where he found Hen smoking a big reefer. Both exchanged smiles, sitting quietly, enjoying the sounds of nature. Time disappeared again, and he awoke in another dream, where he felt the weight of the world's negativity crushing down. He had a hard time breathing, as people looked at him sitting on a street corner, begging for reason. They laughed, they cursed him, and some just plainly ignored him. He wanted to cry out, but found that he could not speak here. His words dissipating long before they left his lips. People wore shades of black, and gray. Color had abandoned this place, and Carl cried.

Chapter 24

'We are but reflections, harnessing the past to create a present self.'

Beneath the only apple tree in the glade, lie one half of the stone of truth. It was nestled in a small nook, between two of the lower branches where it enjoyed the early morning sun, afternoon shade, and sunset on the Rockies. Three branches above, was a robin's nest with three screaming chicks in it, who were never quite sure if their mother was coming back or not.

Small green crab apples were two weeks away from being ripe enough to pick, and the sheep that grazed around the bottom of the tree looked forward to those that fell prematurely, some of those sheep smart enough to allow the fallen apples to ferment before scooping them up. With the sun at its highest point, Willow, Hawk, The Mad Hermit, and Nuna carefully arranged a rug on the ground beneath the shaded area. Bottles of wine brewed at the monastery were set down beside a platter of goat cheese, fresh bread and some chorizo sausage sliced into thin rounds.

"This might all be for nothing, you know, Nuna," The Mad Hermit voiced. He looked at the box that held the scrolls and suddenly regretted coming. Confronting the future was the one thing not on his bucket list.

"Maybe so, Gerald," the Monk agreed. "This is all really just crazy bumbling in the dark but some of the things that I have translated over the past year have come true. The rioting in Seattle, down to the exact date. There was another one that predicted the plummeting of oil barrel prices, down to under forty dollars per. Even Taylor Swift getting declassified from country music to mainstream pop! I just started to believe after a while, finding too many coincidences, that these were in fact no coincidences at all. The problem is that all the answers to these problems are hidden, if there are any at all."

A warm wind carried the smell of forest fires from far to the north, down along the vast mountain range, and with it a slight haze that ringed the horizon. To top off all of the chaos that had erupted in the past month, temperatures were at their highest point in recorded history in North America, causing a wildfire season that was drawing international attention. Mexico had even sent a thousand of its finest to help contain the biggest fires.

Hawk was beginning to get itchy feet. He paced around the tree, feeling that his job was done here, and that a future of rock and roll was eagerly awaiting. He had grown tired of the Hermit constantly flirting with Willow, and he grew tired of Willow pretending not to be interested. Even as he had tried to sleep on the drive to the monastery, he found it difficult. Perhaps he was jealous; a little, he thought. Then he realized that he was definitely jealous, for even though she was as cold as a mountain lake at times, there was a raw sexuality in her beauty that would make men do stupid things. Things like drive into a city that was rioting to retrieve a man who had forsaken society.

"Well, I say we get to it," Hawk said. "I mean, the inter-dimensional Yeti did kind of clear me of any obligation to this quest, and I would really like to get back on the road sooner than later." Hawk knew he sounded a little childish, like a bored teenager, but he didn't really care at the moment. His exhaustion had reached the point of silent lucidity, and he wasn't really feeling like himself.

"Why don't you open some wine, brother, and relax," Nuna replied. "I know it's been a long journey and you have an even longer way to go. I'm sure this will happen quickly and you will then be set free." He understood what it was like to be the third wheel. Who hadn't been in that position at least once in their life?

"You don't need to wait for me," Willow added. "I don't even know if I'm going back or not." She said as calmly as placid water accepts a rain drop.

"Oh, I'm not waiting for you, sister. I just want to see if this was all worth it. That's all. I know when a fish has been caught, and I'm not baiting anymore hooks," Hawk replied smugly.

"What the hell does that mean?" she said with sudden fury.

"It means, that he knows when he has been fishing in the wrong pond," the Mad Hermit answered.

"And what the hell does that mean?" she replied, turning her anger towards Gerald. He just smiled though, laughed, picked up a bottle of wine, and uncorked it.

"He has a thing for you. What man wouldn't?" Gerald said, pouring some wine into a cup. "He's pissed because you're attracted to a homeless ruffian with no prospects of a solid future. I'm sure in the beginning, before he picked you up in Winnipeg, the excitement of going on a quest was enough to keep him interested, but then once you entered the picture, a whole new level of devotion appeared. He's not the type to come out and make advances; no, he's too introverted in that way, but one look at him now and you can see that I speak the truth. Hen could sense it, I'm sure, and that is why he made sure to let the poor bastard know that at some point his path was going to diverge from yours. He might be a dude, a super one at that, but I don't think he's righteous in that way. His music is his love." Gerald concluded with a big gulp of the sweet wine.

Imagine hitting every nail on a board with one swing of the hammer. Well, that is exactly what the Mad Hermit had done, and it created an uncomfortable silence around the tree. Hawk couldn't deny anything the man said, and in fact, he wanted to commend him on such a good read, but the little bit of pride that he purposely kept in his life wouldn't allow him to. Instead, he grabbed a bottle of wine, uncorked it and walked down by the bubbling brook to sit by himself.

"Was that really necessary?" Willow asked. She hadn't noticed any of the signs from Hawk. Carl was definitely a horny bastard, but the man from Halifax had never even insinuated anything sexual during the journey.

"The truth is the most dangerous weapon one can

wield. He wants to be set free, but didn't know how to do it. I just helped him." Gerald replied. "Now let's get down to it before I lose my nerve. There are things in here I have blocked out completely and have no desire in rediscovering."

Nuna pulled the carefully attached roll of zigzag papers out, doing his best not to damage them. Over time rolling papers tend to degenerate, especially when they have been licked together into one long roll. Even the ink had begun to fade over time. He had thought about scanning them and making a couple of copies, but it just never made it to the top of the list of things to do.

"So these ones here are the ones used for the Daily Dudeisms. It was very easy to decipher your metaphors and hidden meanings, but these others labeled foretelling, are just too confusing." Nuna said, setting aside the roll that would have no bearing on current events.

"Yeah, I used a code," the Herald said. "I was hoping it would be easy enough for someone else to figure it out, but then again I was trying my best to make it hard if not impossible for me to read it once I came off the mushrooms. I stuck some of the predictions in with the daily wisdom's in case it became necessary to go over this stuff at some point. The trouble is remembering what kind of code I used." He closed one eye and tried looking at the letters to see if that made in any sense, but it was just a bunch of random letters apparently. He then tried removing some of the letters and writing out the remainder on a scrap piece of paper that they had brought along, but that got him nowhere. He even tried replacing each letter with the next in the alphabet to see if that was his code. That wasn't it either. An hour and a bottle of wine passed before he threw his hands up in the air in frustration.

"Shit, maybe there is nothing in here," he said, irritated. "I can't remember even writing this stuff down. The metaphor package for the dailies was simple and basic. If you want to say apple, you would mention Adam or Eve. Kid's stuff, that you know all too well, Nuna. This, though, doesn't seem to have any pattern. What the hell was I thinking?"

Willow passed the Hermit some wine and placed a hand on his.

"You weren't thinking, you were tripping and just letting it go," she replied.

"Yeah," he agreed, disappointed. His head drooped for a moment, then sprung up like a Jack in the box. "Shit. Nuna! I've got it. Do you have any shrooms?"

Laughing, the monk sprang up, ran back down to monastery, and returned moments later with a handful of dried mushrooms that another dude had mailed to him from British Columbia several months back. He had been saving them for the upcoming Folk Fest in Edmonton, but realized that this was what they were really intended for.

Gerald managed to swallow down half of a large cap, much to his disgust. The taste was as bad as he remembered, and nothing could take it away until the effects kicked in. An hour later he was laughing hysterically as he pondered the whole idea that there was a stone of truth, and somehow it ended up in the back waters of Alberta.

Willow and Nuna had abstained from taking any with Gerald, and it was difficult to get on his level, but this wasn't a pleasure cruise. They had to discover what it was he had written, and in place they smoked a joint, and drank a little more wine.

Two hours into the trip, Gerald returned from his walk, that he 'had' to have to alleviate the churning in his belly created by the mushrooms. He was a little more coherent now, but still rocking pretty hard, back and forth on his rocker.

"Shit, let's do this." He conceded that he was now able to read. Bending over the scroll he studied it for a long time, mumbling nonsense, bobbing back and forth. At one point he had to duck suddenly, as a raven, over two hundred yards away swooped across the sky.

"Fuck me! This is completely fucked, dudes! What the hell is this mumbo jumbo?" He started laughing again, then he began crying, his laughing fit became so intense. In the middle of his fit, he turned to Nuna, became deathly serious, and spoke. "The code is this: first word, first letter. Second word, second letter, up to seven, like the days of the week. That's it." He started laughing again, jumped up and grabbed his things. "They are coming and I gotta go, baby."

Without hesitation he took off down the meadow towards Hawk, spoke quickly to him and then ran off into the forest. Hawk staggered back across the field to find the other two staring in bewilderment. Mushrooms could bring about some strange behavior, but the way he said he had to leave, one could almost believe he was as straight as an arrow.

"Should we go after him?" Willow asked, feeling very confused.

"I don't think so," Nuna replied, hesitantly. He could see that the sudden departure had upset the girl, but he knew the Hermit as well as anyone could. One way or another he was bound to drift off at some point, mushrooms or no mushrooms.

"Hey guys, what did he mean when he said they are coming?" Hawk asked reaching the tree. He had a wine stain on the front of his shirt, his lips had once again failed to provide a solid seal.

"I dunno," Willow almost whispered staring off into the trees.

"I think I do, but I never told him about it," Nuna replied. The other two turned and stared at the monk, waiting for the other shoe to drop.

"There is a gathering of dudes, happening here. Serious folk who are hoping that we can find something to make sense of all the negativity brewing in the world. I don't expect the first to arrive for a couple of days though. Maybe he had another vision?"

"Oh," Hawk replied then looked down at the rug. "Hey, are those mushrooms, man?"

Chapter 25

'Finally, unadjusting to society.'

    The battle erupted in the parking lot of the Commerce Tower late in the evening. Wooden swords rang against each other as battle cries were shouted loudly from both sides. Inside the building, the few people still working stood alongside the security guards who watched from behind the safety of the glass. In all of their days working at Commerce Tower, they had never seen anything like this.

    The two Viking clans were so heatedly engaged in the battle that one would almost believe the fight was real. The shouts of Thor over Odin, reverberated against the glass as painted chipped off of the shields. Confused by such a thing, and having to see it to believe it, the battle enough of a distraction for the black car to pull around the back of the building will little attention. The driver of the car carefully parked the vehicle beside a large blue dumpster, and exited the driver seat. Odin and Thor followed suit, jumping out, and when the Russian went to join them, it was Odin who turned on him, and told him to remain behind.

    "We need you to keep the car running," he said. "The driver has a nefarious past that will come in handy here, and so he must come. If at any point it feels like that the window of opportunity allowing for an escape is closing, drive away and we will meet up with you at that restaurant you mentioned around the corner; the one that has the stuffed French toast we just have to try." His blue eyes blazed with intensity of a thousand stars, leaving no room for debate.

    "Sorry, Russian. I will share the glory with you upon my return," Thor commented patting his comrade on the back.

    Moving as quickly as they could with the old man

in tow, Loki led the way around to the one of the service entrances into the building. With a quick wave of his hand the coded lock disengaged, though he made a show of it by using a Visa card to pretend as if he had a pass card, for Thor's sake. He had no intentions of revealing himself to a vengeful brother.

Once inside they moved along the service hallway and out into a lobby where the attention of the guards minding the doors was still on the mock battle. Without hesitating, Loki moved quickly and called down an elevator by pressing the up arrow button. When it arrived, he motioned for the other two to make their way over, where he then accessed the control panel, which would allow them to go up to the top floor. Without a pass card no one could access those levels, but when you have the power of a god at your fingertips, such things were trivial.

"There is nothing I can do to stop the guards at the top from being alerted to the arrival of the elevator," Loki said, "there is no way to bypass the monitoring system. The good news is that they will not be receiving an alert status, so you will have a few brief moments of surprise on your side. I hope that you will be able to overpower them, Thor."

"Have no fears, servant. They will wish they had taken the night off," The god trumpeted proudly.

Odin turned to his son. "These men who rule this tower possess a seer's stone. It enables them to see into the future with a degree of accuracy. We must destroy it at all costs."

Loki snickered. For him this was all just part of the game. Soon his debt to the Fates would be paid, and he would be free to go back about his business. He even considered taking a vacation for the next century down in Brazil, where inhibitions were thrown out the window faster than a politicians promises. He could see setting himself up, comfortably overlooking the Copa Cabana, and just letting the world ruin itself for a while. Hell, the humans deserved a break as well.

Once inside of the elevator, Thor became uncomfortable and very confused by this whole plot.

Subterfuge was like acid on the tongue and it did not sit well with him. To make it worse, Odin, the father who had encouraged him to be brave, honorable, and fierce, was behind this idea. This whole assault was nothing like any he had been asked to do in the past. There was something here that he couldn't put his finger on, but it had to do with the driver. It was the way this driver was able to bypass the security so easily, in a world that obviously made it very difficult to do so. He had not set off any alarms in the building, but he had set off alarms in Thor's mind.

"Forgive me, Father," Thor said as he reached out and grabbed Odin by the arm. He then opened himself up, and drawing in some of the life force from the old man. In an instant his mind blasted open, and looking across the elevator. he was able to see the driver for who he really was.

"Loki!" Thor yelled out with his fist following close behind. His fist met an invisible wall just stopping him short of connecting with his brother's chin. Feebly Odin, was clawing at Thor's back trying to gain his attention; meanwhile, Loki just smiled, which was like dropping a match into the gasoline container of Thor's anger.

"By the cursed Seven Hells," Thor wailed again, this time drawing every ounce of power he had into one last attempt at penetrating the other god's shield. The mighty fist hit the shield with such force that the elevator shook, and though he didn't penetrate the shield, the blow was enough to knock Loki back hard into the wall where his head snapped against the metal surface and knocked him out cold.

"You idiot!" Odin cursed, looking at the crumpled body. Thor, seeing red, tried to grab at the traitor but the shield remained intact. "We still needed him, you fool."

Thor whirled. "It was that giant's bastard that brought this all down upon us, Father, in the first place. It was he who helped convert our people to this lunacy of a one god, casting us out into limbo." Seething, Thor was barely able to contain himself.

"I know, son," Odin said, "but he was trying to

atone for that. We needed him for this quest where you and I are not as strong as we once were. I knew that I had to keep his identity a secret from you to prevent such foolishness as this. We may have needed him to get us beyond what lies ahead, and now you have jeopardized that." Odin bent over to touch Loki but had no better luck then Thor with the protective barrier surrounding him. It was at this moment that a bell rang to announce their arrival at the top floor of the Commerce Tower.

A security guard wearing a black suit was waiting when the door opened. Even with the unusual hours that the business council kept, there were generally no unscheduled visitors without a prior phone call. As the door to the elevator slid open, the only thing the guard got to see before a wall of bone hit his face, was a man in a very fashionable suit crumpled on the floor, next to an old man who looked as if he had just left a hospital. Thor leveled him with one blow. His partner, who had remained behind the security kiosk, saw the glowing giant appear from the elevator, dressed in medieval garb. One hand went for the alarm and the other went for his gun.

Thor wasted little time knowing that the strength he had drained from Odin was leaving his body quickly. In a blink he covered the distance and managed to leap up and over the kiosk as the guard got one shot off. Thor felt a sting in his side, nothing more, as his fist came smashing down crumpling the guard into an unconscious heap.

Odin was pointing at the double black doors as he shuffled along as quickly as he could. The sudden return of his body's true age was making each step more and more difficult, as his legs threatened to give out.

"Hurry, those doors. Smash them open!"

Thor lowered his shoulder and charged the door. He made contact with all the strength he could muster, bursting through the aged wood. As he crashed through, several large splinters pierced him in various places. The ground came up to meet him as he stumbled on the other side, crashing into a high back chair, then falling down. Odin was entering the Star Chamber just as Thor turned over, bleeding from several places.

"Are you hurt?" Odin asked.

"Mere flesh wounds, though his dart gun appears to have put a hole completely through me." Thor pointed to the wound in his lower abdomen. Blood was seeping out, and he did his best to ignore it.

"Good work, son, but now I need my strength back." Before he could protest, Odin grabbed a hold of Thor and began to drain his strength. There was so little left, but once again he could feel his body come alive as he took in as much as he dared. By the time he was done, Thor was no longer glowing, no longer looking like Thor. He had reverted to looking like the Irishman's body he possessed.

Chapter 26

'Resorting to insults only proves the doubt.'

The wind stirred the trees as it came down from the north. It carried with it the smell of fire, yet the smoke was still miles behind, creeping along one kilometer after the other. The birds floating on the wind were all heading away from the direction of the forest fires, to their back-up summer retreats. For them, this was not unusual. Summer fires were common, they were part of the cycle of life, and they trusted that the Great Spirit would extinguish them when enough land had been prepared for the next new growth.

For weeks now the fires had raged in British Columbia, North West Territories, Alberta and Saskatchewan. If one was watching the news often, they would be fearing the worst, but Delroy knew that it was all part of the wheel. It turned, it burned, and it brought back life. The only people that had a hard time understanding this, were the people in danger of losing their homes. They could not understand the need of a good forest fire. To them it was unnatural, the government's fault for allowing climate change to go too far.

"The rains are coming," the Medicine Woman stated, standing beside him, her hand in his.

"Yes, great clouds gather. In a couple of days they will move over the mountains and not stop for a week," Delroy added looking to the sky again. The Medicine Woman smiled. The change in the young man had been remarkable. She had always seen potential in him, pushing him to the limits to see if he would finally come around. When he returned from his quest he had shaken off the shackles of youth. His warrior spirit had manifested into a chief, and now he stood prepared to challenge his people.

"We must bury the past with an offering of peace,"

he said. "We must take our campaign to those who will listen, and we must above all else break the hopelessness that prevails over our people. It is time to accept what cannot be changed, and regain the dignity we have lost from our lack of commitment."

Of course, she had heard Delroy say the same thing many times over the last few days in her bed, but she would never tire of such words. Too few men were willing to make the commitment, most would walk away from the path.

"We have set out the fires, and we have called together the women of wisdom. I think you will find there, the strength to mend that which is broken." She patted his back as she spoke.

"Enlisting the help of the right politicians will be the hardest part," Delroy admitted. "We have to appeal to their base first. Get their people to speak to their representatives. Create a dialogue addressing, and press it to the wall. Let us now reach out to our internet savvy friends, and have them commit to our campaign. The wave of the future is not through the beating of drums; no, it is through social networking. Technology is our savior in this instance, and we better get down with it. And yes, we must look to the women."

It is difficult to get people behind a subject that was popular, then fades from the spotlight, replaced by something else more terrible, more vile. Global warming and pollution are not new topics, but for some reason that defies logic, the protecting of one's world could not compete with stories like which celebrity had a sex change or if more guns were the answer to solving violence. The world was hurting, just hanging in there, waiting for a concerted effort on the part of the people who created the problems to rectify the situation. Some leaders spoke of it, but very little made the drastic changes that were necessary to reverse the downward spiral. It had once dominated the headlines, but unless the devastation was immediate, it became second rate, back filler.

For the indigenous people of North America, the

topic was central to their well-being. As the mother slowly died, so did the people. Reaching out to them, and trying to convince them that the future was bright, was no easy task. Delroy began on his reservation, speaking to the youth, trying to inspire them, knowing full well that they would have the tech savvy to help build a new awareness. He traveled further out, to other places where his people lived, shaking his head at the lack of pride they had in their communities. Looking at paint flaking off the siding, the cars up on blocks in the front yard rusting away. He saw a great many of the people turn away from him when he began to speak, but many others stayed. It was these people who still held some hope, whom he needed now. The others would have to be a project for later on down the road. A slow-building movement. These were the kind that had the power to last. Finding those with the commitment to see it through to the end.

    The medicine women from all over central Canada were the first to come out and to support the young chief. They had packed up in vans and followed along in his procession, as it wound its way through Alberta, from High Level all the way to Medicine Hat. Then they crossed into Saskatchewan, hitting every reservation along the way, with the intentions of going to Ottawa to have the government listen. This had been tried before, and promises had been made, but many of those promises disappeared as soon as the demands did. The follow up never came. The dreams died once again.

    Delroy soon acted on part two of his plan: unleashing his social media campaign. He enlisted the help of the dudes, for they found it easy to get behind a good cause such as this, as predicted. Soon, the gatherings were filling up with more than just Native folk, many of the European descendants and others from around the world who had moved to Canada in search of better life, were out to hear this charismatic man speak.

    "Sisters and brothers," Delroy began with a voice as true as the wind, as strong as thunder. "I come from where the mountains meet the sky, the trees meet the Great Plains, and the sky never ends. I come to you humbled, by the greatness of the Mother who gives us all that we need to live, and watches over us with the love only a mother can know. For too long we have drawn lines, lived in the past and in fantasies, and have failed to find forgiveness. Our path as walkers of the earth has become filled with those who no longer travel the great journey, but instead sit on the side of the path and watch those passing by. They have become complacent in their sorrow, in their fears, and in their hopelessness.

"We need to once again stand, this time not alone. Our color, or our heritage, should not be what divides us. It should be what draws us together, as we share beneath the gaze of the Great Spirit and sing in the bosom of the Mother. Those who have come before us, invoked the spirits of fear and hate. They were lost in their desire, no longer respecting the gift of life. It is now more than ever that we should let the past be a lesson, not a log to cling to, as we float away with the current.

"Our sorrow has consumed us and alienated us from the power of unity. The great warrior spirit became bitter and resentful. We must use our fierceness to become stronger than our hopelessness. Stronger than our fears. Stronger than the excuses we create to remain with our heads bowed and our pride defeated. No one is going to make it better for us. It is up to the people to do so for themselves, by committing to the high road. By becoming the strength in the arch of the bow. By throwing away the chains that hold us in place.

"Grab your neighbor's hand, and shake it. Stopping looking at them as the reason for all the suffering that has befallen us. We must take responsibility for the now! We must look at ourselves and see that we have the answers. We have the determination, and we have the backing of the Great Spirit. Love, love, love. The other creatures of this world are watching us, hoping that we regain the love soon. So please, for all of the creature's sake, let us find unity.

"It was always intended that we be the caretakers of this magnificent creation. We were given the power to abide the natural flow, and to harvest it. In our haste, we have lost our sensibility towards responsibility, allowing the continuous progress of the modern world to push too far. We can grow, responsibly. We can adapt the land, responsibly. We find the solutions to our problems by taking the high road to ensure no more damage is done to our world. Where else are we going to find such a place? Where else will we feel so comfortable? We must use our vision and our strength to teach. There is another way. There is another way."

Chapter 27

'You can only do what you do.'

"One day, general strike. Shut down the entire economy for one day and you will get the ear of the politicians," Nuna concluded.

"That's it? All of this, for that?" Willow waved her hands around. Ever since the Mad Hermit had taken to the forest she had been very irritable.

"It makes sense to me," Hawk admitted as he nursed his midday hangover. The homemade wine really packed a punch on both ends.

"Yeah, that is what it says," Nuna said. "There is more stuff here, but it seems to go off on a tangent and doesn't really pertain to our current crisis. A general strike across the board should bring the politicians to the table. The beauty of it is, there is no need for anyone to leave their homes, this can all be organized online, and there is no violence. The problem with all of the protests up to this point in time has been that they tend to attract anarchists and undercover provocateurs who just want to create chaos. That never does a movement any good. If we can do this without a single act of violence, it might really have a chance of working."

Nuna got up and started walking back towards the monastery. He had to get online right away and start sending out his feelers. Soon some serious dudes would be arriving, and if he worked quickly he could have everything organized by the time arrived. Willow and Hawk followed closely behind voicing their uncertainty, but Nuna barely slowed.

"You can't even get people to stop idling their cars even though they know it's killing the air," Hawk pointed out.

"Listen, I know you have your doubts, but after

everything you've been through, don't you see that there is something to this?" Nuna said. "I mean, you met a Yeti, an inter-dimensional being, for god's sake! I would think at this point there has to be some faith involved with what we are doing. As with any predictions, nothing is assured or precise, but this a logical road that has opened up in front of us. I really believe that there is merit to this idea, as it sings out to my reasoning.

"I know this is all crazy, but isn't that just indicative of life. Sometimes things are so farfetched, so impossibly unconnected, that they connect, breaking the rules and allowing for the right thing to happen, even when it seems that shouldn't be the case. Throughout history, stories have been written of miraculous events transpiring in order to preserve the goodness that life holds. Cowards become brave, hero's rise from out of nowhere, and just when it seems like the bad guys are going to win, something happens. Well, in this instance, something is happening. We have a chance to help the people out there who feel that the only way to fight against the injustice in the world is to turn to violence, to put themselves in harm's way. This simple solution might just help us avoid an even greater disaster. America is in trouble, and with it the rest of the world follows. Like it or not, they are our cousins and we, more than anyone else out there, have an obligation to help them out. Sure, as Canadians we might not always agree with their politics, their foreign policies, and their war-like behavior, but they are still our family. Much of what is done in the name of America, has absolutely nothing to do with the people who live there. They are a proud people, with good hearts deep down, and their corporate machine has subverted their freedom into a raging bull. Thankfully, we know something about rustling cattle up here."

They entered the computer room and Nuna signed on to the Dudeist network. He began by sending private messages to the people he knew would take this seriously. His first message went to the Lady Beside Lake who above all else was the best to test an ideas sound reasoning. Next was Bear, of course, then Synod of the Dude, and so forth.

Two hours later Willow and Hawk were sleeping in the main room by the fireplace, the monk was setting up a timetable on a large piece of paper with a black sharpie marker. Something this big was going to take time and a lot of commitment from people. It was easy to say that one would just not go to work one day, but the fear that work held over people would be a tough nut to crack. For most people, their job was the only thing keeping them out of the poorhouse, and unless there was real proof that this wouldn't cost them their jobs, most would just say they were in and would bail at the last minute.

The next morning saw the arrival of many Canadian dudes who had traveled far in the call to find peace in our time. The Duder, donning his magnificent cape. Watson, the creator of Canadiandudeism.ceh!, Moses, the TV personality. The Duddha drove up from Calgary, and even Majman had hitched a ride all the way from Ontario. These were the Dudes that really worked hard at promoting Dudeism in Canada, and these were the dudes that felt it in their best interest to help their brothers and sisters down south.

This was a first for all that gathered. Up until this point they were all just icons on a screen, sharing common ideas and stories. Now, though they were meeting face to face, dudes without the internet and social media, this sort of thing would probably never have happened. Again, the argument that technology was destroying social interaction, was quietly dispelled.

After the warm greetings, and with everyone settled in, they got down to work, discussing how best to organize a general strike. The idea expanded, encompassing as many countries as possible to get the message out that people really did care about the way they were being treated, their environment was being treated, and what kind of world they were going to leave behind for Keith Richards. It was going to be a long slow, process, and they would have to recruit as many organizations as they could to join in the cause. The great thing about the Dude network was that it had people from all walks of life, which meant on many roads. A Campaign to Reclaim was the catchy title they came up with, and soon after the appropriate sites were set up, and domain names purchased to secure a virtual base from which to work from. From this point, it would be elbow grease lubing the gears, as members would have to start writing and emailing, writing and emailing, over and over, to get the word out, and get the ball moving.

 Willow left the meeting feeling out of place within the all-guy group. She walked out to the edge of the forest where she watched the sheep eat grass, break wind, and butt each other occasionally. For no good reason she felt lost. Her quest had ended, The Hermit had run off, and once again the future was uncertain. She had used this journey to run from her problems, and she was well aware of it. Somehow, that raggedy, half-crazed man had made her feel alive. Perhaps it was the way he expressed his freedom. It wasn't love that she felt for him; it was envy.

 "Your true love is still out there," Hen said appearing out of thin air.

 She looked up and smiled. Normally one would not react so calmly when a creature magically appeared out of thin air, Willow, though, had enough weed and wine coursing through her veins to keep her mellow.

 "I was just thinking about that, you know."

 "Yes, the Hermit. He is incapable of reciprocating love in the same way. For him freedom is the only thing he desires," Hen said sitting down, patting the ground beside him.

 "Yeah, I know you are right," Willow admitted, sitting beside the Yeti. "I wasn't necessarily attracted to him in the sexual sense, I was envious of his complete lack of caring about the way life should be lived. I've struggled with it for so long that it seeing him be so free was a slap in the face."

 "The strength that lies in the female does not necessarily have to be so closely guarded," Hen said. "It has been a long road for women in finding equality in this world. Even this modern society that exists here in North America still lacks in basic recognition. Men have been playing in the sandbox for too long without realizing that women deserve just as much time in the box as well. Your struggles continue even when men believe they are over, and until the time when men realize that there is no middle ground, that equality is straight across the board on all levels, you will have to persist in your fight."

"How can it be that men can be so stupid and so ignorant of the facts?" Willow wondered in frustration.

"You see, until it is fully presented to them in a unified stand, such as they are proposing right now on other issues down there in the monastery, they will just keep assuming that all is well in your world. Men do not empathize well, so sometimes you have to beat them over the head with your thoughts until they realize that you are really passionate about what you are saying, and that you expect respect for your input. Like right now, they are down there coming up with this great plan, but it will fail because it lacks something," Hen concluded.

"A woman's touch?" Willow asked.

"Exactly. Try to accept yourself before you go down there, though. Your envy of the Hermit's freedom should be the trigger you need to pull. You have carried this weight for so long, this feeling of being on the outside. We are all part of the whole. We each have our purpose, and you have to learn to love yourself before love will find you. I know these cliches get old, but they stand the test of time because they are true. Once you accept yourself for who you are, you will become unstoppable. You will no longer fend off interested advances, seeing them as a threat to your freedom. You will see them for what they really are. An attraction, a pull, a natural process which the entire universe runs on. I have seen countless lives pass where people have never let their guard down for fear of being hurt. What they fear only prevents them from experiencing the good and the bad. For a young, powerful woman like yourself, the world will be yours to enjoy and roam, if you can only just let go of yourself long enough to see that you will not fall far, in being free."

Willow hugged the big hairy beast, and kissed him

on the cheek. She asked him if he would like to come down and say hello to the rest of the gang, but he politely declined and slipped away into the forest. Feeling alive, Willow turned towards the monastery and marched down there with determination riding the wind behind her.

Chapter 28

'Fear not what you have yet to encounter.'

Thor slumped against the door to the Star Chamber, blood leaking out of his mortal body. Odin helped him in and settled into the chair that was normally reserved for the most secretive banker in the world. The Elder God could sense that the device which enabled the mortals to see into the future was somewhere nearby; he moved as quickly as his aged joints would allow him. Phones had been ringing and buzzers buzzing, which meant that soon more guards would be on their way. With little time to spare, Odin closed his eyes and reached out with the last of his god-like strength. There, in the middle of the star-shaped table, was panel and under the panel was the device he sought out.

"Odin, I don't think this body is going to hold out much longer." Thor was coughing, his head drooping.

"We will be done soon, son. Then we will be free of this place." Odin climbed up on the solid table and began to pry at the panel with his fingers. The sealed lid would not budge as put all of his strength in to his efforts.

"You'll never open it like that," Loki announced as he strolled in rubbing his head. He looked at Thor and smirked, then sat in Rupert's seat.

"Well how in the Seven Hells do we open it then?" Thor managed to yell in a crackling voice.

Odin looked to Loki, knowing that his trust in him was not well founded, but something of necessity.

"If you can help just this one more time, Loki, you will be rid of us forever. We will return to Asgard and never step foot on this world again," Odin pleaded. His fingers were bleeding from his efforts to open the lid. His back was screaming in pain from the exertion, and his heart was thumping erratically in his chest.

"You may not want to destroy it, Odin," Loki

advised. "You can remove it, but I think you will be surprised at the source of its power. Also, for the record, I have to inform you that every time these men of power have activated the device, some other poor soul has been the recipient of visions from the future. Since its inception, people have been gifted with the sight at one point in time or another, and it wasn't until the dawn of this last industrial age that its power has finally been understood. These men, whose families have had it, stored in this very room for the past seventy-five years, have used it subtly to subvert, to change the course of the natural tide, yet remained fully unaware of what they were giving people out there," Loki pointed to a spot on the wall. "The answers to all the problems. People of this world rarely listen to simple solutions though, so they discard them as easily they discard their burger wrapper as they are flying down the highway on their way to a keg party. People you never knew, Gandhi, Lennon, Martin Luther King, Jr., just to mention a few, were given a glimpse of the sight, while the forces at work in here conspired to keep humanity under their thumbs. Since the gift of this sight has generally got the people who received it killed, I think that there are probably a lot of other people out there that never came forward."

"Thanks for the lesson, Loki, but can you open the damned thing or not?" Thor asked. He now sat in a pool of blood that was dripping onto the carpet below.

"Of course I can," Loki admitted. He snapped his fingers and the table cracked into two pieces. Odin went tumbling with one half and Thor just barely managed to roll out of the way of being impaled by one of the stars spikes.

In the center of the room was the 4-d hologram projector. Loki walked over to it, lifted a glass panel and removed a spherical object. He held it in his hand and then held it up to the light. After inspecting it he threw it at Odin who just managed to catch it before it hit the floor. As he turned his hand over he was surprised to see that it was an eyeball, encased in amber. He instantly recognized it.

"There you go! Mystery solved," Loki exclaimed.

"It's your own eye, Odin. The one plucked from you on the tree to give you visions of the future. The Raven who took it thought it only fair that the humans have the chance to define their own future and so it was given to a man in the Middle East, and with it he tried to change the course of mankind, only to be killed for speaking the truth. Ever since then the thing has been cursed, crossing oceans with armies, hiding in monasteries, and even spent some time changing the sound of music. All thanks to you. So, yes, I may be of some blame for helping with the downfall of my own brothers and sisters, but it was this very eye that actually showed the people a way to do it. After that, of course, they really muddled the whole thing up. So take it, feel free to blame yourself, and have fun trying to get out of here."

Loki disappeared. Odin looked at the eye and could see visions of the future trying to fill his mind. He warded them off, knowing that his own arrogance had started this whole tragedy. A bell rang once in the hallway, and he knew that more guards had arrived. He stood up, quickly placed the eye underneath the base of one of the heavy wooden chairs and turned to face the guards as they came in with guns drawn. Without hesitating they fired on the old man, shooting him six times before he fell backwards onto the chair. With a loud crunch, the flat bottomed base crushed the amber coating surrounding the eye, and squished its contents.

Thor feebly cried out and received three more bullets into his chest.

Loki appeared beside the Russian. He smiled and looked at the mortal who was looking back at him in complete bafflement.

"Look, just start the car, and let's get out of here, okay?" he said. "Your friend has made the ultimate sacrifice for your people and you would be disgracing such a sacrifice by getting arrested."

The Russian pondered this for a brief moment, wondering how an actual Russian would react to this situation. He nodded his head, turned the ignition on and drove away. As they passed by the front of the building, the Vikings, who had started to file back into their van after being threatened by security, nodded as the black car passed by.

"Were they successful?" the Russian asked.

"They were." Loki replied.

"They are dead now?"

"They are immortal, fool. They cannot be killed. Gone maybe from this world, but not killed."

"Well, this is good, no?"

"This is good, yes. Now shut the hell up and drive. We've got some mischief to get up too."

Chapter 29

'Slander is the tool of the incompetent'

  Nothing happens when you want it to happen, it always happens when it should. The natural order of things, the flow. When we take on this attitude that we are in control, then we really open ourselves up to disappointment as the universe continues to follow the path it always intended on following. Some have called this karmic law: what goes around comes around, and justifiably so. For the most part if it was going to come around; it was going to come around anyways.
  The tide comes in and the tide goes out, and with it, the transfer of energy maintains a very specific balance. Cycles on top of cycles that help regulate and provide a hospitable environment. When one loses touch with the natural rhythms of the world, one loses the ability to see the simplicity in which everything is held in check. Without being held in check, the system falls apart, and the world no longer exists as it once did.
  As people conquer the lands and the seas, they soon begin to develop this idea of mastery, and soon begin down the walk down the road to that fabled land of control. They start believing that they are the ones in charge, making the rules and are essential to the well-being of the whole. They develop the God complex, masters of all that they survey, and in some respects they are, though they fail to realize that all masters have masters above them.
  The power to create, the power to destroy. The ability to harvest, the ability to recycle. All of these things grant people an edge over the other species that inhabit the planet Earth, and such gifts should never be taken for granted. Without the other forms of life on the planet, this home will cease to exist, as it does in its present state. The environment will become hostile, trying to kill off the very

life it was designed to protect, in the same way that people have helped kill off other species that once called this home.

The three little dots bounced inside the conversation bubble. One after the other, then they would wait approximately three seconds before they would start again. Serendipity was waiting for this dude, Carl Carlson, to reply to her question. She had been reading his blogs as of late, intrigued by his "One Grain" composition. Ever since the disappearance of Mr. Olsen, she had a lot of questions crossing the neural network of her brain.

"Do you think that gods exists?" she had written, and now she waited. With the videos that had surfaced on the Church of the Latter-Day Dude's page, of what appeared to be a Norse god fighting a Roman god, she was in the entertaining notions mood.

"Let me tell you, that this is definitely not the only world with life on it in this universe," Carl responded. "In addition to this, the universe is attached to other mirror universes, with worlds just like ours but different. So, yeah, the possibility of super powerful beings does seem plausible."

Carl had a new icon now, one that he had photoshopped of an earth with another earth over top of it, yet slightly transparent.

"You sound pretty sure," Serendipity responded. For her, the idea seemed a little farfetched. She was logical, critical in her thinking. That was what had drawn her to the medical field. Five more years of study and she'd be done with nursing, studying in a lab as a doctor.

"I've been to one, and I have been assured that there are many more."

"By who?"

"By an inter-dimensional being who will remain anonymous."

Skepticism is a powerful wall to scale, especially during an internet conversation with a stranger. True, he was a fellow Reverend of the church, but that didn't mean he was completely sane.

"I don't suppose you could prove it?" she asked. Like any good scientist, the proof was in the proof.

The three dots bounced up and down for a while, Serendipity started to think that perhaps this pothead had just nodded off.

She was about to leave the conversation believing it was just some ploy by a guy trying to get attention, when finally a picture appeared. It was a path in a forest, dead straight with trees as tall the great red woods in California, except these were pines and spruce. She didn't think much about it until she read the comment.

"I dare you to find me a picture of trees this big from anywhere on this Earth!"

She laughed. Of course this guy was a semi-professional blogger and probably a Photo-shop expert, yet as hard as she looked she could not find any sort of sign of doctoring. The man standing at the base of the tree was so small she almost mistook him for a squirrel.

"Is that you?"

"You bet," Carl responded quickly.

"Who took the picture?"

"A native dude named Delroy. He is currently on a speaking tour with the intention of going to Ottawa. He's pretty dude! I've been linking his stuff with my pages. You should check out what he has to say. He isn't talking about the mirror worlds, but he's been there, and if you asked him he would confirm it."

Serendipity checked out Carl's page and the links to Delroy's. She scanned it quickly, realizing that he was saying a lot of things that she believed in. Suddenly this Carl character seemed a little more credible.

"So what do you think about the video of the gods fighting at the medieval feast. Apparently, and I'm only quoting this from a really unreliable source, this wasn't a staged event there. That what you see wasn't doctored after the fact, no makeup, or lighting crews were present. That instant where one guy suddenly transforms is supposed to be real."

"Let me tell you something, Maude," that was her

online name. She didn't use her real name because many employers now did background checks on potential employees and Facebook was a great source for finding out what a person is truly like. "Anything is possible. We didn't just head down this path without some intervention at some point. If you ask me, we were the children of some ideal at one point, but that ideal faded when we discovered the potential each and every one of us has. Yeah, maybe we were ruled by gods at one point, but I think somewhere along the line we decided we would be fine without them."

"We had a guy around here who claimed to be a god. In particular, he claimed to be Odin, and when he saw that video he swore that the person he was seeing was his son, and he kept calling him Thor. Now I know just how crazy that sounds, because I really thought it was just a ploy, a way for an old, lonely man to reach out for attention. I even checked his past records and there was no mention ever, of this level of delusion until two weeks before this video popped up."

"So what do you believe now?"

"Honestly Carl, I have no idea. He's disappeared, and the police are involved now, but without any clues it just seems to be a complete mystery."

"I've had a thought on the subject and it doesn't really hold much water at this point but after seeing what I have, I think that as a species, here on this planet, we are really limiting ourselves in our current role as consumers. Take for instance the fact that we have developed schools of study which allow us to define, understand, and manipulate the world we live in. If you couple that with the fact that we haven't discovered the full potential of our brain, it really opens up the possibilities. Perhaps this man, claiming to be a god, is able to manipulate the forces governing our world because he has unlocked the full potential of his brain. What if these unlocked areas of our brains are control centers for forces that exist all around us? Will we be able to travel with a thought, lift things with our minds? Create an electric static charge out of the air around us, and so forth. Tales of super humans and super beings have been around as long as man has recorded time, and perhaps there is some truth to it. What if these beings, who we've labeled as gods, were here to teach us, and once we have been pointed in the right direction, they move on to other worlds. If super beings do exist they would grow tired of us, I imagine, and all of our petty whining. They would either be interested in exterminating us, controlling us, or guiding us, and I would have to say that I am leaning towards the latter. It would be far too easy to accomplish the other two results. I mean, it really opens up a lot of doors if you think about it.

"Now stay with me here for a moment, and let's just say our 'growth' is based off of evolution to keep everything within the natural realm; would it then depend upon our passing and the births of new generations over and over to reach the ultimate goal? A death count so to speak. Say, for example, once our species hits a trillion deaths, perhaps our energy patterns will reach the transformation stage? I know it sounds crazy, but for life to evolve it usually requires environmental changes. It requires new birth, altering slightly to adapt to the new surroundings. DNA is a true marvel that just knows to how make slight adjustments! How would it know if it wasn't being guided by past memory? Crazy, right. So here you have this species that has all the potential, but still has to pay the dues. We've gone from the stage where we believed in many gods, to fewer gods, to where we are at the point where we are not even sure if such a thing exists because we have started to solve mysteries that never would have made sense to us back when our brains were more focused on surviving attacks from predators and our fellow man. Since the world has started to settle down in the violence department, and it has, trust me. There is less killing today then there was a hundred years ago, even though it doesn't seem like it. It has given us more time to delve deeper into the workings of our world, and now we can explain all kinds of phenomena that seemed like magic just a hundred years past.

"I know I am rambling, but just hold on one more

minute.

"So we have the know how, what is next? Of course we will start finding solutions to more of the problems that nag at our understanding, and as we do, our minds will evolve, opening those closed doors. The DNA will remember what the last life had learned, make a few minor adjustments and bang! The door will open and inside of your mind another connection is made. Our physical bodies will require less and less adaptation as we master our world, but that fundamental drive the energy devoted towards evolution will never cease to push us in other ways.

"The gods may have been here to protect us from the things we could not control, or foresee, because we had not the experience to do so. Perhaps the fear they could invoke was nothing more than a way of keeping us safe long enough for our minds to catch up with our physical bodies. The real shame is that we have left behind our connection to nature in doing so, for the most part, but perhaps that is all part the process? When we finally awaken, with our minds fully charged and ready to go, we will reconnect with our world, and perhaps be considered gods by our standards today."

Serendipity took a minute to read the whole rant. Obviously, the idea hadn't just dawned on him.

"Are you high by any chance?" she asked.

Carl responded with an lol first. "Hey, it could be possible, right? I mean you are the one asking if gods exist, and I am trying to give you plausible theories to how and why they might."

"I know. You just remind of that guy on television. You know the Ancient Alien dude who always claims that it was aliens who did everything that can't be explained."

"Oh shit yeah! I love that show."

The night descended into the deep. The glow of the computer screen, the only light in her little apartment, the questions in her head of her missing patient were ghosts echoing their thoughts in the room. It would be easy to chop it up to age, or mental sickness, though it just didn't feel right in her gut. Learning to trust your gut instinct was something one should never forget, for it was an ancient wisdom. Perhaps some kind of DNA-released message. Perhaps if he had performed some miracle, it would be easier to outright accept, but everything that she had witnessed was easily explained. She continued to research the subject on gods long into the night, coming to the conclusion that it was always going to come down to faith. If it took faith, did that faith have an energy of its own and could it infuse itself into the being, perhaps opening parts of the mind that allowed for great deeds, and miracles?

    Well, dudes, some say we just don't know.
    Others insist we do.

Book III

Well, That About Wraps Her all Up… Parts, Anyway

Chapter 1

'One man's trash is another man's second glance.'

    Somethings cannot be prepared for. Even the best measures to ensure the success of plan A are subject to the forces of the universe, which have plans of their own. The most advanced security system in the world, with some of the most highly trained security guards was still not enough to prevent the disaster that occurred on the top floor of the Commerce Building in the Star Chamber. Of course, this was a story that would never make the news. It would never leave the room now occupied by the five members of the council. It was a tale that would just kind of disappear like the remains of Adolph Hitler.
    The two intruders were still lying on the floor, side by side and as dead as two people could be. One was well into his seventies and the other perhaps early thirties. The table had been pushed to the side, cracked perfectly in half, and the four-dimensional viewer was now a worthless piece of junk. The security guards injured in the attack were being detained in another room by several of their colleagues, answering the same questions over and over again. A lot of things just weren't adding up and even the video footage of the attack had been scrambled somehow, preventing anyone from seeing the events that transpired.
    Rupert Van Klaussen scratched his head in disbelief. Robert Klein was on his cell phone yelling in Yiddish at someone. Sir Richard Evenmore was actually touching the dead, younger man, looking for some kind of markings or tattoo that could possibly link him to one of the criminal organizations that were always looking to make a step into the big leagues. Francisco Vocelli was fuming mad, and Manuel Juarez Ricardo Lupe Fernandez was smoking a Cuban cigar and instructing the security supervisor on how to remove the bodies.

"Does any of this make sense to you?" Francisco asked the group. His anger was hanging on the end of every word he spoke.

"From my understanding, no one outside this room knew of the existence of Odin's Eye. Perhaps we have a disgruntled member?" Rupert replied calmly. His eyes scanned the other four, skipping over the security chief. It didn't matter if he heard this conversation, the entire crew would be sanitized after this.

"Well, that would not serve in anyone's best interest, unless they thought they could bring some new players along, starting some side action, but we all know that there is no one else can afford the ante at our table," Sir Richard pointed out. It was true, to be part of this group you had to have access to money in the trillions. As far as the world knew, there was no one that fit that bill, and as far as the Star Chamber knew, only the five present had that kind of pull.

"They are nobodies! Complete, utter nobodies!" Robert announced, getting off the phone with his man in Mossad. "The old fellow was a resident at a retirement home in Toronto up until four days ago, with no connections what so ever to anything we, or anybody else is involved in. The brute was just some thug from Boston who had a few prior convictions for intimidation, drug possession, and possession of an illegal firearm. Other than that, he was just a nobody."

"Well, this makes even less sense," Francisco raged. "The guards say that they were able to bypass all the security systems including, silencing the automatic door alerts." He was beginning to see a pattern that was very disturbing.

"So someone who knows all the security protocols can bypass fail safe systems, and can even edit the video footage if responsible, and if only the five of us know of the Eye's existence, then I am going to go out on a limb here and say it as a certainty that someone here is not telling the truth and is making a play to end our partnership," Francisco concluded.

This accusation was enough to create an uncomfortable silence. The five men looked at each other, watching each others wheels turning. Eventually it was Manuel who spoke.

"Jumping to conclusions is like chasing an angry burro with a broom. He is not going to care what you are swinging at him, he is just going to focus on his anger with you."

"Well this is very disturbing. Very disturbing indeed," Robert grimaced. "We've been relying on that tool as of late with our side investments. We all stand to lose a lot of money if we don't play it careful."

"Well, it's not like we don't have other aces up our sleeves," Sir Richard added." Perhaps being reliant on the Eye has made us weak. This has shown us our vulnerability and it time to shore up our defenses."

"Only a man involved in deception would look at this great mishap as a lesson to be learned from. This is not something that you just simply replace. Ever since you began asking for compensation, sneaking behind my back and purchasing land in my country, I have had my suspicions about you, gringo." Manuel confessed. His voice was stern, hardened by mistrust.

Sir Richard laughed. Of course the Mexican would blame the white man. That slimy piece of…Well, that man had built his empire on blood and misery. He was the upstart, the least trustworthy, and the most likely to gain from this. The silence in the room was unbearable.

"Of course, if one had been bred in a house of honor, one would never make such an accusation without proof," Sir Richard said. "Since there is no honor here amongst this gelded group, you may accept this as my official resignation from your little club, since none of you are jumping to my defense, I assume you all figure that it is I who committed this act, and so to you all I bid a farewell." Sir Richard turned, signaling the security chief to call the elevator for him. With that bold move he left, breaking the biggest monopoly on resources the world had ever seen up to this point in time.

"And the rest of you? Are you all okay with this?" Francisco said pointing the Englishman's back.

It was Rupert who spoke up this time. He was the best with words, and he knew that he had to act quickly before the other parties decided that without the Eye they were better off on their own.

"We will crush him, as it becomes plain that he is now our enemy," he said. "Piece by piece will erode the castle from under him, filling his moat with the curses of his ancestors who had devoted their entire lineage to amassing such a fortune. The four of us will continue on, with the might of the industrialized world behind us. Soon the name Sir Richard Evenmore will be a name mothers use to teach their kids a lesson."

"And what about our little war?" Robert asked. The banker always wanted war. It was his breakfast, lunch, dinner, midnight snack, and night cap.

"Oh, we will still destroy this country," Rupert assured him. "Sir Richard has no way of stopping that, and I feel that he will have no interest in doing so either, for he still has vast sums tied up in it. No, our friend will wait this out, and we will pretend to ignore him for now until we have actual troops on the ground. Agreed?"

There was a round of agreement.

On the elevator ride down, Sir Richard received an incoming call from an unknown number. His first instinct was to ignore it, but it had turned out to be a very interesting day, and so he felt adventurous.

"Hello, Sir Richard Evenmore?" the man on the other end asked with a Russian accent.

"How did you get this number?" Everyone asks this question thinking that the person on the other side was obligated to tell you, and in this case the Englishman would not get the satisfaction either.

"Never mind. My boss would like you to know that you have a powerful ally, if you are in the market."

Sir Richard could only assume that these were the people that had destroyed the Eye. Who else would know that such an action would create a void that may need to be filled?

"You know that if I was to find out who you are, you would not be alive long enough to beg for mercy?" he replied.

"Of course not, but as I say, my boss could be a powerful ally," the voice retorted. "He knew of your machine, he was able to get into the building, and he was able to help destroy it. As you know, no one was supposed to know of its existence it, but he did."

"Okay, chap. I am intrigued. What is your boss's offer?" Sir Richard asked.

"Equaling out the playing field, Englishman," the man responded.

Going to bed with the Russians was never considered an option before. They drank too much, loved the limelight, and could turn on you without a moment's notice if the feeling to do so came upon them. Sir Richard had no worries about that, though; he just didn't like working with loose cannons. His family had kept their fortune and power secret for over two hundred years. Tying up loose ends was no great feat on his part. Interested by such a bold move, he decided.

"Okay, let's meet."

Chapter 2

'The nugget of truth is surrounded by processed meat.'

It was only when the Mad Hermit had stopped long enough to drink from a stream that he realized he had taken the staff of the Wandering Abider with him. In his hands, it felt so natural, an extension of his arm. A long time had passed since the two had traveled together. They roamed through the forests, skirting forestry roads and only making contact with humans when hunger overrode all other matters. He had come across a drilling rig camp, looking pathetically desperate and hungry, and the catering staff that worked there filled up a t-shirt bag full of sandwiches, fruit, and baked goodies. He wished him well and took off, back into the forest. At night he hunkered down under the bows of spruce trees which kept the weather from reaching him. His layered clothing kept him warm, for which he was grateful, but then again he did have a lot of practice at this, being a homeless man and all.

Guided by luck and intuition, he navigated along the base of the mighty mountains, and headed into a narrow valley that had no roads or trails leading through it. This was the deep wilderness. The place where man rarely went. Here the great-sized grizzlies roamed, and he made sure to take a wide berth of them whenever he sensed one near. Not showering for as long as he could remember worked to his advantage out here, for nothing screamed human more than the odor of soap and cologne.

Three days out of the monastery and back into British Colombia territory, Gerald discovered a cave that was in plain view of the valley below, about a hundred feet up the side of a mountain. His first instinct was to avoid it like the plague for a bear or, even worse, a mountain lion might inhabit it, but his curiosity was almost too much to bare. Instead he decided to watch from a safe distance, just above the tree line a thousand yards away and see if anything came or went. It was a steep climb to the entrance which wouldn't deter a lion, but might deter a bear. Hours passed and nothing moved. With the sun making its way behind the great peaks, Gerald took hold of his staff and climbed up to the entrance confident that it was uninhabited. Inside was very dark, and he decided to announce his presence and get any surprises out of the way.

"Okay, supper is here! Come and get it!" He yelled into the opening. Nothing stirred. He moved in closer, picked up a rock and threw it. It traveled for two seconds before it hit a wall telling him that he wasn't missing much in the darkness. He threw another just to make sure, and again two seconds, and no disturbances.

"Well, hell yeah," Gerald pumped his fist to the sky. A cave was exactly the kind of place where he could chill for a while, at least until he decided what he intended on doing.

Fearing that an inhabitant of the cave may still return at some point in the night, Gerald began urinating all around the front of the cave. He had been living off of roast beef sandwiches and hoped that the smell of meat would linger in his pee. Next he rolled some of the larger boulders in the back of the cave by the fading light, close to the entrance where he made a small wall in which he could lie behind and defend himself if need be. Against a bear or a lion, it probably wouldn't do him much good, but there was some small piece of mind that came with the fortifications. Tired, sore, and happy to have such a great view, Gerald drifted off to sleep gripping his staff tightly.

The sound of sniffing woke him. Clouds had moved in sometime during the night and the result was a pitch blackness that could not be penetrated. A shuffling of rocks nearby accompanied the next round of loud sniffing and Gerald knew that whatever it was, it was close and getting closer. Normally fear would force a man to seize, but not in this case. The Mad Hermit had long ago thrown away his fear of death, and figured that if now was the time, at least it was happening in the dark where he wouldn't see a thing.

Still, he wouldn't go without a fight, and so doing what only came natural to him he jumped up with his staff and roared as loud as he possibly could. When he finished there wasn't a sound to be heard.

"Gerald?" A voice called out.

Surprised by the turn of events, Gerald didn't know what to say. The last thing he expected was to meet anybody here.

"Gerald, I know it's you. This is Hen. I came to see how you were faring?" The Yeti called again.

The Mad Hermit relaxed instantly. Of course, no human would be wandering around in this darkness. "What the hell are you doing, Hen?"

"Have you been eating roast beef?"

"Look, do you have any way of shedding some light on this situation?" Gerald asked.

Hen laughed. "Oh, yeah I forget sometimes that you humans really don't take advantage of all the gifts you have." The Yeti produced a pack of matches, and lit one. The pack cover had a picture of 69 El Camino, red and chrome, with a white stripe down the side.

"Like that car do you?" Gerald asked as he looked around for something to burn. Fortunately, there was a small pile of wood stacked neatly in the corner. The match went out, and he felt his way over. Picking up a couple of the logs he brought them to the middle of the cave and dropped them.

"Huh, oh yeah, dude, I dig it," Hen said. "If I were in to such things this would be my choice." He lit another match and passed the pack over to Gerald. The wood was very dry and the bark on the outside lit up instantly. With some persistence, and a lot of lung fuel, soon there was a good fire burning.

"The natives used to use this cave on hunting expeditions," Hen commented. "They would keep cougars away by hanging a bear skin over the opening. They would keep bears away by hanging a wolverine skin over the bear skin. In the wild, no one messes with the wolverine."

"Great. What would I hang if I wanted to keep the

Yeti out?"

"Well, you did the right thing by pissing around the front of the cave. That is usually enough." The large creature stretched out on the ground and propped his head up on a flat piece of slate.

"Next time I'll have to remember to leave a number two behind as well," Gerald snarled.

The Yeti laughed. It was a loud booming laughter that one could easily mistake as a cry of pain by some wounded animal.

"To put your mind at ease, Hermit, I am not here to convince you to turn around," Hen explained. "Quite the contrary, actually. I wanted to just make sure that you were adjusting to the wild comfortably, and so far you seem to be doing okay. Normally I would recommend bringing an ax instead of a staff, but any way you slice it you have done pretty well so far. The big test will come when you run out of goodies that you got from that oil rig camp."

Another of the dry logs was added to the fire; they must have been there for a long time to burn so quickly. Gerald studied the fire, then the Yeti again. His frown slowly turned upside down and he waved his hands in the air.

"This is a true home for a Hermit! I am where I am, and that is where I am meant to be." He concluded, laughing. "So, it is my good fortune to have a nature expert around to help me get my bearings."

"Well, dude, we are all in this together, are we not? You may go your own separate way but that doesn't mean we'll abandon you. If its privacy you want. Have it. If it's total freedom you want, here you go. Tomorrow I'll show you where to find food, what to look for in the way of danger and how to make friends with the others that live in this valley. I think you will find that even the bears can be approachable if you just know how to do it properly. As for the tale that you got drawn into, well, your part is done my friend. As a reward I want to make sure that you are safe, that's all."

"Thanks Hen," The Hermit replied.

"There is no thanks needed. Although your part may have been small, solving that one little riddle has set the group on a path that may succeed. It is still hard to tell at this stage, but it is much more promising than any of the other ideas thrown around out there. Enough of that though. How about some nice quite time staring at the fire. After that, get some sleep. You will be safe tonight. Tomorrow we will turn you into a real hermit."

Chapter 3

'I don't always vote, but when I do it is to get rid of some rat bastard.'

  The path of righteousness is never the easiest path to take. Sometimes it means going against the flow. Fighting the head waters and developing a thick skin. Those easy to anger or those easy to be insulted can never really follow through to the end when it seems like the world is against them. This focus on the self is the first obstacle that needs to be overcome. You have to become your cause and rise above the pettiness that will be thrown your way. Sometimes the more pettiness thrown your way indicates the more righteous your cause.
  Taking that step on the golden path will single you out. It will place you under the scrutiny of others as they try to comprehend something that had not occurred to them. Many great people throughout history have rose to the importance of their cause, like Gandhi, John Lennon, Martin Luther King Jr. Unfortunately for them it didn't end well. Their cause brought too much resistance to the establishment, and in the end meant their demise. The righteousness of what they stood for lives on for eternity, though. It is the modern age of heroism. We no longer need the warrior with the sword, or the woman inspiring a nation to war. Now we need people who look to peace as the only option, and who live the life they represent.
  As the riots increased throughout the American cities, fueled by hate and anger, another force rose to meet it. A force filled and backed by love. People who were caught in the middle decided to stand up for themselves, valiantly protecting others as the violence grew. It was this pulse that had to be tapped in this time of darkness. This vibe had to be reinforced and fed with more love and support. As the country teetered on the verge of civil war, a

single cry came out across the virtual world.

Equality!

The rallying cry of those oppressed. It was the back bone of liberty in the true sense, not the consumer adopted liberty that had been sold on eBay to the highest bidder. People could understand this. This was something that a vast majority of the populace wanted. How do we achieve this, was the question. Fighting wasn't going to help. Feeding a negative vibe as large as this one with more negativity only created a beast infinitely bigger and angrier then the one already looming over the country. It was going to take a large, concerted effort with as many diverse parties being brought into the throng. The Buddhists for peace, the Liberals for freedom, the dudes and their Church of the Latter-Day Dude. Moms Against Drunk Drivers, the Sunday fishing clubs, the Curlers of Nebraska Association, Hands Across America, Doctors Without Borders, even the Marxists of New York. Equality could only come about under a unified, and unshakeable front. One by one groups were recruited to help start the revolution in America.

The message was simple.

Equality.

One year, three months, and two days to the day that the Mad Hermit remembered the code that enabled the dudes to decipher the scrolls, a general strike, nationwide, including Canada, occurred in which thirty-two percent of the population called into work sick. Both countries were effectively shut down, even with the larger percentage of people still showing up to work. For a large majority who did show up to work that day, fear had driven them in the car in the morning. For a small percentage, they went to work happily, change being the last thing they wanted.

Righteousness was the hammer that drove the nail. When a country is stopped in its tracks the first thing the engineers do is find out how to get the motor running again. This is where the dialogue begins. This is where true convictions are tested. This is where we see if the people have the back bone to carry out their beliefs, or if they will take the lazy way out and just accept a small victory.

It all boils down to choice. What kind of world do you want to live in? What kind of world do others around you deserve?

And what kind of world will be left for our children?

The quest for answers to these questions still abides.

The End

I'm tired
I dont want to work
Yay! lost 2lbs
Wish this app had a repeat.
I like this toast.
Dont want to work.
Swollen leg... die?
Busy day. 12' Tree, Expectations.
Work Bitch.
So thirsty. So busy. So alone.
Home Time.
So Tired. x/o Energy to cook.
Order Subs? Lin Home!
Bed time. New phone.
Noom.